Can't Get Enough

A NOVEL

CONNIE BRISCOE

Harlem Moon   Broadway Books   New York

Published by Harlem Moon, an imprint of Broadway Books, a division of Random House, Inc.

A hardcover edition of this book was originally published in 2005 by Doubleday, a division of Random House, Inc. It is here reprinted by arrangement with Doubleday.

PRINTED IN THE UNITED STATES OF AMERICA

HARLEM MOON, BROADWAY BOOKS, and the HARLEM MOON logo, depicting a moon and a woman, are trademarks of Random House, Inc. The figure in the Harlem Moon logo is inspired by a graphic design by Aaron Douglas (1899–1979).

Visit our website at www.harlemmoon.com

First Harlem Moon trade paperback edition published 2006.

The Library of Congress has cataloged the hardcover as:

Briscoe, Connie.
Can't get enough : a novel / Connie Briscoe.— 1st ed.
p. cm.
Sequel to: P.G. County.
1. Prince George's County (Md.)—Fiction.   2. African American families—Fiction.   I. Title.

PS3552.R4894C36 2005
813'.54—dc22

ISBN 0-7679-2129-1

10 9 8 7 6 5 4 3 2 1

Can't Get Enough

THE DOORBELL RANG and Barbara Bentley moaned, lifted her black silk eyeshade, and glanced at the clock on her nightstand. 8:00 a.m. She frowned with frustration. Who on earth would be rude enough to ring the doorbell at this ungodly hour on a Friday morning, a full hour before her usual wake-up time unless she was going to work out at the country club?

She shut her eyes and listened. Maybe, just this once, the temporary housekeeper would do something right and answer the damn door. Her husband was at work, and Phyllis, their regular housekeeper, was on her annual two-week vacation visiting her family in Bermuda. The new woman was never where she should be or doing what she should be doing. She was lazy and worse, she blasted that horrid hip-hop music when she worked. Barbara didn't understand how the agency could send out such shiftless help.

The chime rang again. Barbara hissed between clenched teeth and tossed the silk sheets aside. "Trifling woman," she muttered. She slipped her toes into a pair of sensible black velvet Stubbs & Wootton slippers and grabbed her bathrobe from the foot of the bed.

The floor-length robe flowed behind her as she strode briskly down the hallway and glanced in each bedroom, looking frantically for the help. Barbara worried that she was not presentable, with her hair in rollers and cream on her face. She *had* to find the help. What was that woman's name again? Aleesha or something. The new ones all had such odd names.

Aleesha was not in any of the seven bedrooms or the kitchen or the family room below. Nor was she in the great room. Barbara walked quickly back toward the kitchen, and as she entered, she heard a thump behind the closed door of the laundry room. Could Aleesha be doing the laundry? Miracles did happen, Barbara thought wryly.

She walked past the granite kitchen countertops, opened the door to the laundry room, and jumped back a foot. Aleesha was spread out on the floor with her legs wrapped tightly around a young man. The two tan bodies were so absorbed in each other that they didn't even notice Barbara standing there. Then Barbara saw something totally appalling. They were having sex atop her precious $1,500 Pratesi sheets! Barbara gasped.

"What the devil is going on here?!"

Aleesha and her guest scrambled to stand up. Barbara clenched her fists and glared in fury as Aleesha tugged her denim skirt down and the young man zipped his blue jeans. Barbara had been reluctant to keep the woman when the agency first sent her. She'd had a bad feeling about her. Aleesha had the exotic sensual look that often came from mixed Hispanic and African-American ancestry and she was no more than twenty-five. The last thing Barbara needed around her wayward husband's roving eye was some pretty young thing like this. Attractive younger women never went unnoticed by

Bradford, and they generally found her husband—a dashing, wealthy black business owner—hard to resist when he laid on the charms.

But she had learned that Aleesha was married so Barbara thought it was safe. Aleesha's young Hispanic husband picked her up and dropped her off for work every day, but this young man, with a short Afro and goatee, was *not* Aleesha's husband. The saddest part was that Barbara didn't dare fire the woman, even now, even after this. Who would do the laundry, make the beds, and cook the meals? She couldn't possibly keep a seven-bedroom, eight-bath home clean herself. She would call and have the agency send a replacement as soon as possible, but for now she wanted Aleesha to get to work.

Barbara turned her attention to the young man. "You!" she exclaimed between clenched teeth. "Get out of my house now. And use the back entrance." Barbara pointed hastily toward the kitchen door, and he ran past her.

"And you, Aleesha," she said as the woman reached for her G-string from atop the washing machine. "Get back to work this minute."

"My name is Ayisha, miss."

"Whatever!" Barbara glared at her with icy eyes. "Just get back to work. And pick my damn Pratesi sheets up off the floor!"

Barbara stormed out and raced to the front door just as the chime rang for the third time. "Slut!" she murmured as she yanked the sponge rollers from her hair. She took a deep breath to calm herself then opened the door only to see a courier heading back down the walkway. He turned when he heard her, ran back, and handed Barbara a letter-size envelope. It was a rich crème-colored linen paper with a gold-embossed script addressed to Mr. and Mrs. Bradford Bentley of Silver Lake, Maryland. Barbara thanked the courier and shut the door against the chilly spring air.

She turned the envelope over. There was no return address. How odd, she thought, as she stuck a perfectly manicured forefinger, courtesy of Pearl's Salon and Spa, beneath the flap and tore the envelope open.

It was an invitation to a formal housewarming party the next Saturday from their new mysterious neighbors down the block, the ones building the mega mansion reminiscent of a French chateau. Construction had begun almost a year ago and now looked near completion.

Everyone in Silver Lake was talking about the mansion. But Barbara had never met the owners, and neither had Bradford or any of her other neighbors as far as she knew. That was strange in itself. Normally when someone was building a new custom house in Silver Lake, they were frequently in and out, keeping a close eye on the construction. But with these new neighbors, all Barbara had seen was an endless stream of trucks and construction workers climbing the hill to the site.

She placed the envelope on the hallway table for Bradford to see when he came in from the office. The invitation looked promising, provided Bradford hadn't made other plans. He was founder of a software and technology firm and one of the most successful black business owners in Prince George's County, Maryland. She and Bradford were always being invited somewhere.

They had spent the previous weekend at the annual spring gala at the Kennedy Center in Washington, D.C. Bradford's firm, Digitech, was a key sponsor of the gala and the Bentleys always attended. This year the event was a tribute to Duke Ellington, and it was a splendid weekend filled with receptions, performances, cocktails, and dancing. The highlight for Barbara was when the gala chairman introduced her to singer Nancy Wilson.

Barbara hoped they were free for the housewarming party. The new mansion was shaping up to be the largest home in Silver Lake, and she was dying to see it. If it was half as fabulous inside as out, this party should be a real treat.

She took a deep breath and glanced toward the kitchen. Now to deal with the horny help. But first, she picked up the pack of Benson

& Hedges and her gold cigarette lighter lying on the hallway table and lit up. It was a long-standing on-and-off-again habit. Currently on again. But hell, it was better than her other on-and-off-again vice—a pint of Belvedere vodka daily. Thank goodness she had shed that habit a year ago. Still, she needed something to help her get through the days.

She took a long drag and exhaled as she walked down the hallway. With any luck, her randy housekeeper was laundering the Pratesi sheets now instead of getting into more trouble.

SOMETHING HIT THE office floor with a thud, and Jolene Brown nearly shot straight up into the air.

"Fuck! What the hell was that?" she muttered.

Brian, the office painter, groaned softly and whispered in her ear that it was nothing. For a second, Jolene wanted to shove him off. He had her pinned to her desk, and the skirt to her peacock blue St. John suit was hiked up around her hips. The loud bang had startled her, and anyone just outside the office could have heard it.

But then she realized that the noise was probably the stack of notebooks falling from her desk. Besides, it was Friday after work hours, and her staff had gone home for the day. She closed her eyes and told herself to relax. She and Brian had snuck quickies in her office after hours many times without getting caught. Everything was fine.

Still, she moved her hips faster. He always took so long to climax, way longer than she did. And the smell of latex paint on his fingers was stinging her nostrils something awful.

He shuddered, relaxed, then stood and pulled up his white painters trousers. A satisfied grin played around his lips as Jolene wriggled her tight skirt down over her hips, and she wanted to smack him upside the head. It was annoying as hell to have this lowly laborer staring at her like that. After all, she was Jolene Brown, a GS-15, the highest level one could reach in the federal government without going through a special selection process or getting a presidential appointment, and he was just some lousy-ass painter.

She avoided his eyes as she fastened her black bra and slipped back into her suit jacket. She hated the smirk that always spread across his face after they had sex. It served as a constant and annoying reminder of the dreary situation she'd gotten herself into over the past several months—lowly painter regularly bangs the boss at work.

Disgusting, she knew. But the painter sure could screw, and as a divorced black mother with no decent prospects on the horizon, this was one of the few things in her humdrum life that she could look forward to. She worked hard and by the end of the day, she sometimes needed to let go.

Nothing was better for that than some quick sex. It made her feel alive and powerful, almost as good as the high she got from the two grams of coke she and Brian usually snorted just before doing it. Unfortunately, the feeling of euphoria from both lasted only a few minutes.

Brian made a move to kiss her on the lips, but she jerked her head away and flipped her dyed-blond weave off her shoulders. She wanted a kiss from him about as much as she wanted a snake wrapped around her neck. She held her hand up to his face.

"Please. Don't get mushy on me here."

Brian chuckled and stepped back. "Fine. Whatever suits you, my fine chocolate diva sistah."

She rolled her eyes, slipped her feet into her tobacco-colored Jimmy Choo slingbacks, and walked around to sit at her desk. She picked up a pencil and pretended to be hard at work as Brian reached for his undershirt. Their little tryst was over, done, and she wanted him out of her office as quickly as possible. She could barely stand to look at the man unless she was high and horny.

Not that Brian was bad-looking. His honey-colored face was quite handsome. She just had to overlook the uncombed hair and the thick love handles around his waistline that were a common feature among men approaching forty. At thirty-eight, she was about to round that corner herself, so she understood. But Brian was the frigging office painter, a laborer with a criminal record to boot—not at all what she was used to, especially after her fling with Bradford Bentley last summer. Now there was a guy with class—successful, rich, and drop-dead handsome.

Unfortunately, Bradford had dumped her, and her husband, Patrick, had walked out when he found out about the affair. That had been, without a doubt, the worst time of her life. She was sitting on top of the world, or at least on top of Silver Lake, when she was married to Patrick and screwing Bradford on the side.

Now she was at an all-time low when it came to men, and it showed in the extra pounds she couldn't keep off her hips. For the first time in her life, she had to squeeze herself into a size 10. She had once worked out at the country club five days a week, but ever since word got around about her affair with Bradford Bentley and her husband walked out, she had found it hard to go to the gym at the country club.

The one thing she had thought she could always count on was that Patrick would be there for her. He had once loved her so much, she thought he would never leave no matter what she did. But he had and now he was spending all his time with that fat bitch Pearl Jackson. Even worse, he'd taken in Lee, his teenage daughter from an affair he'd had early in their marriage. Jolene still found it unfathomable that Patrick had left her and their beautiful daughter, Juliette, and was now spending all his time with a hairdresser and a troubled teenager.

Pearl was so working-class; she lived in a cheesy little town house for God's sake. And Lee was bad news if ever there was any. The girl had shot her mother's boyfriend, supposedly because he was abusing her. But still, she had shot him. Then she'd run away and lived on the streets of Baltimore for weeks doing God knows what. Now the little thug was living with Patrick, and when Juliette went to visit her father she was around that horrible girl. What the hell was Patrick thinking? At fifteen, Juliette was very impressionable, and Jolene didn't want her exposed to trash.

She tapped the eraser end of her pencil on her desk and admired Brian's rear end as he bent over to gather the notebooks that had fallen off her desk. *That* view reminded her of just what she saw in him—he was muscular and fit enough to take her just about anywhere, whether on top of her desk, up against the wall, or flat on the floor.

Hell, she was in her prime and still not bad-looking. And she worked her ass off every day. Her unit at HUD was so productive they were letting her expand the office suite—new paint, new furniture, the works. A busy woman like her didn't have time to search to fulfill her needs. Brian was always there, always willing.

Still, if anyone ever found out about this hanky-panky going on in the office she would be in big trouble and she couldn't have that. She wasn't a filthy rich housewife like Barbara Bentley and some of her other neighbors in Silver Lake. She had bills coming out her ass with the big new six-bedroom house she had built last summer, not to mention a fifteen-year-old daughter only two years away from college. She didn't need problems on the job.

"Let me remind you, Brian, that this stays between us," she said in her best supervisor voice as he dropped the notebooks on the edge of her desk. "And another thing, I don't like you calling me 'your diva sistah' or '*your* anything' for that matter. I don't care if we fuck till the sky turns brown, I'm still your boss around here. Got it?"

His eyes flashed with raw anger, and suddenly he was looking more like the ex-con that he was. Jolene's breath quickened. Maybe she had been a little too harsh. They were alone in her office, and this asshole was making her feel uneasy with that mad glint in his eyes. He had done time for murder no less—something to do with a gang war in D.C. in his youth. Naturally, Brian claimed it was self-defense, and the way Jolene saw it, the dude Brian wasted was probably a worthless thug. Besides, Brian had paid his debt to society with a lengthy prison sentence.

Still, once a murderer, always a murderer. She picked up a housing report from her desk and pretended to read it. She couldn't let on that her knees were shaking beneath her desk. "I have work to do now, Brian. Shouldn't you be somewhere painting a wall or something?"

He slipped into his shoes and shoved his Washington Wizards cap on his head, all the while staring down at her silently. She couldn't read his face, as was often the case with Brian, and that unnerved her. So she pretended to be busy at her desk, determined not to look up and let him see the fear she felt. She heard his feet back away and she held her breath until the door shut behind him.

She dropped the pencil and leaned back in her chair to look out the window. How had she reached this point? She once had a full life with parties, shopping, and men. The only excitement in her life these days was screwing a convicted murderer. That, and buying lottery tickets twice a week. Since the affair with Bradford and the breakup with Patrick, she was on the Silver Lake social blacklist. People rarely invited her anywhere anymore, either because they didn't want to offend Barbara Bentley or they were afraid she would try to steal their husbands.

Jolene swung back around toward her desk and her eyes fell on the invitation to a party at the mansion being built across the street from her house. The towering new home on the hillside dwarfed her house, and Jolene would love to see the inside of it. One of the reasons she had moved to Silver Lake was for the social life, but the thought of mingling with her snobby neighbors was downright depressing. She picked the invitation up, ripped it in two, and tossed it into the wastebasket.

She stood, slipped her mink jacket off the hanger on the back of her door, and picked up her Coach briefcase. Juliette was staying with her father as she usually did on weekends, so Jolene would be eating alone again tonight. She switched the lights off and shut the door to her office.

As she walked down the long dimly lit hallway, she reminded herself to stop and pick up a Maryland Lotto ticket for Saturday night's drawing. She always got a tingle in her breast at the thought of winning millions of dollars. She could do so much with that kind of money. She could add an extension to her house so it wouldn't look so tiny in comparison to the one being built across the street. She could pay off her mountain of bills. She could buy more cars, jewelry, and furs and thumb her nose at her neighbors.

First she had to win the damn thing. She knew it was next to impossible, but what else did she have to look forward to?

PEARL JACKSON SET three Safeway grocery bags down on the passenger seat of her Dodge Caravan, hopped in, and pulled out of the parking lot. The minivan was nearly twelve years old and had almost 100,000 miles on it. The engine sometimes rattled so badly that Pearl was afraid to turn the thing off, fearing it would never start back up.

She had bought the minivan when her son Kenyatta was fifteen years old so she could shuffle him and his friends to school and basketball practice. Then when Kenyatta went off to college at Morehouse, as a single mother she couldn't afford to replace the minivan and pay his tuition plus the mortgage on their town house in Silver Lake.

But Kenyatta had graduated, and she had recently made the final payment on his tuition loan. Patrick was always reminding her that it was time for a new set of wheels. She knew he was right, but it was hard to let this one go. It held so many fond memories of the times she spent carpooling her son around Prince George's County during those last couple of years before he went off to college. Now that he was all grown up and had recently moved out to live with a woman, the minivan was one of the few reminders Pearl had left.

She was no longer a divorced mom raising a son alone, a label she had carried since Kenyatta was a toddler and she and her ex-husband divorced, but it was going to take some time to get used to that. Her new life living alone and dating again was tough, especially because she was in her forties and the man she was dating had two teenage daughters from previous relationships who resented her presence.

The girls couldn't be more unalike. Lee was a seventeen-year-old, smart-mouthed, streetwise brat. Juliette was a fifteen-year-old snob. They had different mamas and they hated each other's guts. When both were at Patrick's house on weekends, they were usually either arguing or not speaking to each other.

Pearl sighed and braked at a stoplight. Patrick was such a sweet guy that he was well worth the agony, and she couldn't really blame the girls. Lee had been through so much in her seventeen years. She had grown up with her mama in a rat-infested apartment in Seat Pleasant, Maryland, and had learned that Patrick was her daddy only about a year ago. That wasn't Patrick's fault, since Lee's mama had taken off when she got pregnant and never told Patrick about the baby.

Patrick found out about Lee when she ran away from home after shooting her mama's boyfriend, a wily dog of a man named Clive who had sexually abused her. Lee thought she'd killed him and she went searching for the daddy she had never met. She had lived on the streets of Baltimore for weeks until she found him, and only Lee and the Lord knew how she had managed to survive out there all alone since she refused to talk about it. Thankfully, Clive had survived and Lee was exonerated.

Juliette was just a spoiled child who still hadn't gotten used to the fact that her daddy had left her mama almost a year ago. That had to be tough on a fifteen-year-old kid.

Pearl turned left at the entrance to Silver Lake and nodded at the male attendant stomping his feet to stay warm in the chilly spring evening. She passed through the gates and turned the van toward Patrick's town house. As she approached the hill at the construction project across the street from Jolene Brown's, she slowed the minivan. The home being built on the hill was bigger than all the others in the neighborhood. In fact, Pearl thought she'd never seen anything so grand in all of P.G. County.

She stared and shook her head as she drove by. It reminded her of the European palaces she'd seen on television and in magazines. Who on earth could be building such a house here in Silver Lake? Pearl had heard many rumors in her beauty salon but she'd been around long enough to know they were just that. Rumors. Nothing more. No one seemed to really know what was going on up there on the hillside.

She rounded a corner and turned down a narrow street leading toward the town houses on the southern side of Silver Lake, where both she and Patrick owned homes.

Patrick was always telling her to hang in there. Juliette and Lee were both decent girls and he hoped they would both come around to accepting her sooner or later. Pearl had done absolutely nothing to hurt either of them.

Lee was angry at the world about what she thought was a rotten, unfair life. Pearl had no doubt that Lee's mama was well meaning, but raising a kid on your own was tough, and Pearl knew that from experience. But Lee was a strong kid. She had managed to survive on some of the toughest streets of Baltimore all alone with her will intact. Some kids had a spirit that couldn't be crushed no matter what happened to them. With some good old-fashioned parenting and a lot of loving, she and Lee would learn to get along.

Juliette was going to take a little more work. She wasn't angry at the world. She was angry at Pearl. Juliette had been given everything on a silver platter by her parents, and she could be a selfish brat, just like her mama, Jolene. Not long after Patrick left Jolene, he began dating Pearl, and to a kid who didn't know any better it looked like Pearl had stolen her daddy from her mama. Juliette's sheltered, little-rich-girl life had shattered, and she needed someone to blame.

Pearl pulled up in front of Patrick's town house and reached for the grocery bags on the passenger seat of the van. She had promised Patrick she would fix them all a special dinner that Friday evening to try and help break the ice. And if there was one thing Pearl always felt up to it was cooking. She had a feast planned—a good old pot roast, collard greens, and macaroni and cheese, with a homemade sweet potato pie for dessert. She believed that good food soothed the soul.

And her belief showed in the ample size of her hips, unfortunately, as she was reminded when she climbed out of the car, always a bit of a struggle. She wouldn't be able to eat much of the meal she was fixing, not if she wanted to keep losing some of this weight sitting on her rear end. Since she began dating Patrick, Pearl was determined to get down to a healthy size 12, maybe even a 10.

It was going to be tough. She hadn't been that tiny since her son had gone away to college. After she divorced her husband, Kenyatta had become her whole life. No boyfriends, no partying, no traveling, no nothing. It was all about Kenyatta. And when he left for Morehouse College it seemed the only friend she had left in the world was food. She worked in her beauty salon, drove home, cooked, ate in front of the TV, and went to bed. It was a wonder she wasn't bigger than a size 14.

She had tried every diet ever dreamed up, but nothing worked for more than a few months at most. Now she had a man in her life for the first time in more than twenty years and she was going to lose the extra pounds even if she had to starve herself doing it. Patrick was always sweet about her weight, saying he liked her just fine as she was. But look at that skinny woman he went and married. Jolene couldn't weigh more than 130 pounds, even though she had put on some weight recently. Sheesh. Pearl knew she would never be that small; she was such a slave to good food. But she could do better than this. She *would* do better.

Pearl walked up to the house, rang the bell, and put on her biggest smile.

Juliette swung the door open, wearing her usual skintight blue jeans and holding a bottle of red nail polish. She greeted Pearl with a grimace. Still, Pearl kept on smiling.

"How you doing, baby?" Pearl asked.

Juliette flipped her brown hair weave and shrugged. "I was fine until the bell rang."

Pearl ignored the comment. The girl looked just like her mama whenever she threw that fake hair around. She had the same pretty brown complexion as her mama, and they both had weaves. From what she had learned of Juliette since dating Patrick, the child acted like her smart-ass, diva-acting mama, too.

Pearl shoved one of the grocery bags into a startled Juliette's arms and headed toward the kitchen just as Lee bounded down the stairs wearing a bathrobe and tennis shoes and bobbing her head to music she was listening to through the headphones of her portable MP3 player. As soon as Lee saw that it was Pearl, she rolled her eyes, turned her caramel-colored face, and ran back up the stairs.

So much for warm greetings, Pearl thought wryly. "Is your dad here, Juliette?" she asked over her shoulder as she entered the kitchen.

Juliette dumped the bag on the kitchen table and grabbed an apple from a bowl on the countertop. "No, he's not," she said tartly. "I think he went to see my mother."

Pearl placed her bags on the counter, removed her black wool coat, and slung it over a chair. "Oh?" She turned to see Juliette smiling smugly.

"He'll probably be gone for a while," Juliette said, one hand on her hip.

Pearl smiled back at Juliette, determined not to let the little vixen think she was getting the better of her. Pearl had total trust in Patrick. Jolene lived less than half a mile away, and it was only natural that she and Patrick would have to see each other from time to time. They were still raising a child together, and what a handful that child was.

"Hmm," Pearl said as she turned to the sink to wash her hands. "I guess I'll get started on dinner then. Would you like to help?"

Juliette coughed. "I can't. I have to do my nails and I've got homework."

"On a Friday night?" Pearl asked doubtfully.

Juliette shrugged. "Whatever."

"Well, what about Lee?" Pearl asked. "What's she up to?"

"She's in the tub by now. Drowning I hope." And with that Juliette turned up her nose and dashed off.

Pearl shook her head as she unpacked the groceries. Welcome to *The Brady Bunch*, P.G. County–style.

4

BARBARA BENTLEY WHEELED her new black Mercedes-Benz S500 sedan onto the grounds of the Silver Lake Country Club on Monday morning. The new Benz was supposedly an early gift from her husband, Bradford, for her upcoming fifty-first birthday in June. But Barbara knew the score: it was really a gift to pacify his wife for his latest slipup in the fidelity department. She didn't know exactly what he'd done or who he had done it with. It could have been the wife of one of his business associates or a neighbor. But the fancy new cars and furs and expensive jewelry always meant that he had been up to *something*.

The car *was* nice, with slick leather upholstery and a burl walnut finish on the dashboard and door panels. And it drove like a dream, but she would much rather have a faithful husband, one who would love and cherish her as she aged. Nevertheless, it seemed the older she got, the younger Bradford's mistresses became. Some of them looked like they were barely twenty. Barbara had pretty much learned to look the other way when it came to his women. It wasn't easy, but it was preferable to leaving him and giving up her lifestyle as Mrs. Bradford Bentley.

She smashed her cigarette out in the ashtray. God, how she hated getting older. She was still a size 8 thanks to regular workouts at the club and gardening with the help of her longtime gardener Emilio, and people were always telling her that she looked ten years younger than her age. But she was starting to get a few gray strands in her hair and enough cellulite around the thighs to stay away from skirts that fell more than an inch or two above her knees.

She knew the cigarettes certainly didn't help her complexion when she was trying to compete with twenty-year-olds, but a woman who elected to stay married to a philanderer like Bradford Bentley was entitled to a vice. She hadn't touched a bottle of vodka in a year. She was damned if she would give up nicotine, too.

Barbara glided the Benz up to the valet stand, checked her lipstick in the rearview mirror, and grabbed her sports bag off the passenger seat. The young parking attendant opened her car door and she stepped out.

"Good morning, Mrs. Bentley," he said as he helped her out of car. John was her favorite of the club's three attendants. All of them were nice young black men in their late teens and early twenties, but John was the most courteous and friendly.

"Good morning, John," Barbara said. "Beautiful spring day, isn't it?"

John nodded politely. "It is, ma'am. Supposed to get up to seventy degrees. How long will you be today?"

"Oh, a couple of hours probably. Has Marilyn arrived?"

"No, not yet."

"When she gets here, tell her I'm in the weight room, will you, please?"

John bowed his head in response, and Barbara skipped quickly up the stairs to the club. She was wearing only her workout clothes and there was still a chill in the early morning air.

No doubt, Marilyn had worked late yesterday evening showing a house to a client, and she'd probably overslept. Marilyn had been selling real estate for as long as Barbara could remember, and she was one of Prince George's County's top real estate agents. Barbara worked in real estate, too, or rather dabbled in it, as Marilyn would say, and she always looked forward to the advice she got from Marilyn during their weekly meetings at the club.

Barbara walked across the plush carpet in the lobby and back to the women's locker room. She dropped her bag in one of the lockers. She hated working out, but she had no choice. Gardening didn't interest her the way it once had, and she left most of the work to Emilio these days. Now that she was working part-time as a Realtor, she needed a more strenuous form of exercise to stay in shape. Many of her coworkers were young and energetic, and she had to be able to keep up, particularly with Noah Walker, a thirty-eight-year-old schoolteacher by day who sold real estate in the evenings and on weekends. They were both part-time Realtors and often helped each other out.

Noah had been divorced for several years and was saving to buy a house of his own. Barbara was surprised that no young woman had snatched him up yet, since he was hardworking and very attractive, with shoulder-length dreadlocks and a smooth chestnut complexion. He was also a top tennis player and in great shape.

Just as she removed her gold bracelets and placed them in the locker, she thought she heard Jolene Brown's voice. She quickly looked around. She certainly hoped she was mistaken. Barbara couldn't stand the sight of that woman since learning of her affair with Bradford last summer. Out of all of Bradford's mistresses, Jolene was the one she despised most. Bradford's mistresses were usually silly little bimbos far removed from her life in Silver Lake and they could easily be dismissed. Jolene had been the exception. She was a successful woman who

Barbara had considered a casual friend. She lived right in Silver Lake, North, only a few blocks away, and her ex-husband Patrick had once worked for Bradford. They often attended the same parties and had even visited each other's homes for dinner.

Barbara didn't see Jolene and relaxed a bit. Fortunately, Jolene had a nine-to-five job in Washington, D.C., and she rarely showed up at the club on weekday mornings. In fact, Barbara reminded herself as she slammed her locker shut, she hadn't seen Jolene at the club much at all recently. She hoped it would stay that way.

P EARL SHUT THE door to her town house, tossed her Adidas
sports bag, newly acquired online from eBay, on the passenger seat of her Dodge minivan, and hopped behind the steering wheel. She loved shopping online, and the sports bag was her
latest purchase. Her salon was open Tuesday through Saturday, and
some days she didn't get done until nine p.m. That didn't leave her a
lot of time to run around malls searching for what she needed.

She always looked forward to Monday mornings, when her salon
was closed and she could wait until midmorning to hit the gym at
the country club. Normally she had to rise at six a.m. to squeeze in
an hour of exercise before coming home to shower and grab a quick
breakfast of cold cereal. Then she dashed out again to open the salon
by nine a.m.

Barbara Bentley, Pearl's long-standing and dearest customer, had been generous enough to give Pearl a membership to the club on the tenth anniversary of the salon's opening. Barbara had also paid Pearl's membership fee each January as a Christmas bonus. Pearl was eternally grateful for Barbara's generosity. Lord knows she couldn't have afforded the $30,000 initiation fee herself, let alone the $3,000 annual membership fee. The salon did well, but not *that* well.

Her earnings had allowed Pearl to raise her son as a divorced single mom, to send him to Morehouse College, and to buy a house in Silver Lake. It might be only a town house on the southern side of the community, rather than the more prestigious north side where Barbara Bentley and Jolene Brown lived and where that new humongous mansion was being built. But it was still Silver Lake, the most exclusive community in Prince George's County, and that was what counted.

Pearl and Jolene hardly spoke to each other since Pearl had started dating Patrick. Not that they had ever been all that friendly. Jolene was a snob as far as Pearl was concerned. She hated everyone who lived in the town houses, except maybe Patrick. After the divorce, he had wanted to stay near his daughter, and a town house was all he could afford in Silver Lake since he had to pay child support.

The town houses were a good half mile from Jolene's precious mini-mansion, yet Jolene still thought they degraded the upscale neighborhood and she was never shy about saying so to anyone who would listen. Before the town houses were built, Jolene had organized some of the other families to try and stop the builder from constructing them, and she and her followers had continued to protest even after construction began and Pearl and some others had made deposits.

Fortunately, Barbara Bentley eventually stepped in and supported the town houses. Barbara had initially been against them herself, but as she later explained to Pearl, she began to see the value in supporting economic diversity in Silver Lake. There was so much racism in the world, and she hated to see black people discriminating against one another for any reason. Once Barbara came around, Jolene's objections meant little, given all the clout that Barbara wielded as the wife of one of the most successful businessmen in the county.

Pearl parked her minivan and walked across the parking lot to the main entrance of the club. She smiled and nodded at John as he held the door open for her. The country club had valet parking, but she used it only in bad weather. She was perfectly capable of parking her own car and walking to the door of the club, especially since it saved her a few bucks in tips.

She entered the locker room and quickly changed into a black T-shirt and baggy workout shorts, then checked her rear end in the full-length mirror to make sure her panty line wasn't showing, and patted her short natural hairstyle in place. She couldn't afford the designer workout clothes that most of the women here like Barbara Bentley wore, but she always tried to look halfway decent. She was just thankful that she no longer had to shop at Lane Bryant as she did when she was a size 16.

She pushed the door open to the weight room and the first person she ran into was Barbara Bentley. They hugged and exchanged air kisses.

"How are you?" Barbara asked.

"Oh, hanging in there. Working hard at the salon as always, you know."

Barbara touched Pearl's arm. "I've been meaning to ask, you know the house that's being built across from Jolene Brown's?"

Pearl's eyes grew wide. "It's unbelievable, isn't it? It gets bigger and fancier every time I drive by."

Barbara nodded. "Have you heard anything more about the owners? I thought maybe someone at the salon . . ."

Pearl nodded eagerly. "I've heard plenty more."

Barbara leaned in closer. "Yes?"

Pearl lowered her voice. "Well, I can't be sure, but Diane Hamilton—you know her? She lives two doors down from Jolene."

Barbara nodded.

"She claims the couple moving into that house is royalty and . . ."

Barbara's head snapped back. Royalty? Silver Lake had dozens of illustrious families living inside its gates, from professional ball players to prominent businessmen and local politicians. But royalty? She was impressed. "Really? I had no idea."

Pearl nodded vigorously. "A count and countess from some small country in Europe, is what they're saying. Some place called Chateau de something or other."

Barbara's heart picked up a beat. "You're kidding. Sounds like they must be white then."

"From what I understand, he's European and she's African American. She met him over there and they got married."

Barbara blinked. A count and countess in Silver Lake! And the countess was black. This would lend a lot of cachet to the neighborhood. Not that Silver Lake needed it, being one of the wealthiest communities in America. But it was a predominantly black community, and some people tended to write off anything mostly black no matter how much money was involved. "This is so exciting. I can't wait for the party this weekend so we . . ."

Pearl narrowed her eyes. Party? What party? She hadn't received an invitation to any party. She tightened her lips. No doubt because she lived on the wrong side of Silver Lake.

Barbara paused at the expression on Pearl's face. Oh, dear, she thought. How rude of her to blurt out about the party like that. But she had assumed that everyone in Silver Lake received an invitation. "I'm so sorry, Pearl. I thought . . ."

Pearl tried to smile. "Don't worry about it," she said curtly. "You can fill me in when you come and get your hair done."

"Nonsense. I'm sure it was a simple mistake. The new owners probably got our names and addresses from the Silver Lake Neighborhood Association and somehow you were missed. I'll look into it for you."

Pearl wasn't so sure it was a mistake, since Patrick hadn't gotten an invitation either. It sounded more like another anti-town-house thing to her. Even the Europeans were in on it.

JOLENE GRABBED HER sports bag and climbed out of her Lexus. She held her keys out to John and dropped them into his extended palm. There was a time when she would have smiled at John as she handed him the keys, but then he started trying to make a lot of small talk with her and that was getting a little too damn familiar. He was the help, not her buddy. She had quickly put a stop to all the chatter by avoiding his eyes. It was good to see that he remembered his place, even though it had been almost a year since she was last at the club.

She entered the locker room and changed into her workout clothes—a sexy pink Lycra bra top and black short-shorts. She had stopped coming to the club after word got out about her affair with Bradford Bentley. But she was tired of hiding, she thought as she studied herself in the floor-length mirror. She paid a lot of money to belong to this country club—had even taken out a home equity loan to pay the hefty initiation fee—and she had as much right as anyone else to be here. She pushed the door to the locker room open and walked out.

"Don't go to a lot of trouble, Barbara," Pearl said.

"It's no trouble," Barbara insisted. "I'm on the Silver Lake Neighborhood Association board and I'll call . . ." Barbara paused and nearly gasped as she caught a glimpse of Jolene Brown entering the weight room. Barbara was shocked that the woman had the nerve to show her face here. And as usual Jolene looked like a tramp, with her boobs popping up out of that pink workout bra like two brown balloons.

Pearl noticed a change in Barbara's demeanor and turned to see what had caused it. She spotted Jolene walking in their direction and quickly looked away. This was the first time she'd seen Jolene up close in ages. She occasionally saw Jolene driving by in her car or from a distance at the supermarket and that was close enough for her.

"Whoa," Pearl whispered. "Wonder what made her decide to show up here." She knew that if anyone disliked Jolene more than she did, it was Barbara Bentley.

"I'm the last person to ask," Barbara said. She abruptly stopped speaking as Jolene approached.

Jolene noticed Barbara and Pearl whispering to each other and she suspected that they were gossiping about her, judging from the cold expressions on their faces. So what. She wasn't going to let their pettiness bother her. The affair between her and Bradford had ended almost a year ago, and it was time for that anal bitch Barbara Bentley to let it go.

"Good morning," Jolene said, smiling brightly as she nodded in the direction of Barbara and Pearl. To her astonishment not only did they both ignore her but Barbara had the gall to turn her body away, and Pearl studied her fingernails as if she had just discovered them. Jolene was furious. Who the hell did they think they were?

She clenched her fists, whirled around, and stomped all the way back to the locker room. "Fuck," she muttered as she flopped down on a bench, arms folded. They had no right to keep treating her this way. Especially that salon frump Pearl Jackson. Come to think of it, how the devil could she even afford a membership here? Did Patrick get it for her? He better not have. They were deep in debt and barely making ends meet, with two mortgages, a home equity loan, and saving for college for Juliette. Not to mention the annual fee for her own country club membership.

Jolene jumped up and opened her locker. She yanked her gym bag out and threw it on the floor. She was so pissed off, she didn't even feel like working out anymore. Being snubbed by Barbara Bentley was bad enough, but being snubbed by Patrick's town house trash was intolerable. She never should have come here.

She slammed the locker door shut with a loud bang, and a woman a few lockers down turned and stared at her. Jolene couldn't remember the woman's name but she recognized her as Barbara's snobby next-door neighbor. She turned pointedly toward the woman and fixed her with a long, icy glare. The woman quickly turned away as Jolene snatched her gym bag off the floor and marched out of the locker room.

She was halfway to the exit when she changed her mind about leaving right away. She stopped and whirled around. She wasn't going to take this shit one more minute. She burst through the weight room door and found Barbara and Pearl still talking near the entrance. They both froze the minute they saw her.

Jolene stomped up and inserted herself between them. Pearl stumbled and had to catch herself to keep from falling as Jolene turned toward Barbara. "I'm tired of being dissed by you all the damn time," Jolene yelled.

Barbara coolly looked away. "I have no idea what you're talking about."

Two women walking by with tennis rackets slowed down and stared in their direction. Jolene ignored them and leaned in closer until her nose was within inches of Barbara's face. "You know *exactly* what I'm talking about. It's been almost a year since I screwed Bradford. Get over it. You don't have to keep being so fucking rude to me."

This was too much, Barbara thought. She pointedly looked Jolene up and down with disapproval. "You're the last one to talk to me about rudeness," she said, her voice dripping with sarcasm.

Jolene put her hands on her hips. "God, you're such an uptight snob. I . . ."

"You can call me whatever you want," Barbara said coolly through a sly smile. "At least my husband didn't walk out on me."

Pearl blinked hard. Oh, lordy. What did Barbara have to go and bring *that* up for? The last thing she wanted was for Miss Barbara Wannabe to turn her attention to her.

Jolene backed away. "Fine, Barbara," she said calmly. "If that's how you want to be." Jolene whirled around. "Bitch," she muttered as she stormed off. She was going to get her annual fee refunded and she was never coming back to this snooty club again. Hell, she might even move out of Silver Lake. She didn't need this.

"Whew!" Pearl said, fanning herself with her hand as soon as Jolene was out of sight.

"God, I can't stand that woman," Barbara hissed under her breath.

"Take it easy, Barbara."

"Did you see how she just ignored you?" Barbara asked, still fuming. "And she calls *me* rude."

"It doesn't matter," Pearl said. "I'd rather be ignored by Jolene anyway. 'Cause she scares the heck out of me."

O N WEDNESDAY, BARBARA returned home from the country club as usual and tossed her sports bag on the bed. Thank goodness Jolene had not showed her face again. Jolene's showing up at the club on Monday had practically ruined Barbara's entire day. This morning, Barbara felt refreshed and ready to get out and sell some real estate.

She sat in an armchair near the bedroom fireplace and bent down to untie her tennis shoes as she pushed that unpleasant encounter with Jolene to the back of her mind. The woman was an insane, greedy, immoral social climber. That's all she was. Barbara had run across more than her share of that kind of woman in dealing with Bradford's mistresses, and she had become a pro at shoving all thoughts of them aside.

She noticed that the bed still had not been made up even though she had called the agency and gotten a new temporary cleaning woman after that sordid incident with Ayisha. Were any of them capable of doing anything right? Thank goodness Phyllis would return that afternoon.

Barbara pulled the top to her workout clothes over her head as she entered her walk-in closet and strolled down the suit section. She picked out a midnight blue, chalk-stripe pantsuit and a wine-colored jacquard suit and held them up at arm's length. The pantsuit was classic Armani, sophisticated but understated. The jacquard by Albert Nipon was more feminine. Neither was what she really wanted, she thought as her eyes roamed the closet. She had a closing that afternoon, and then she and Noah were meeting with a client for dinner that evening. She wanted to feel young, fresh, hip.

How ridiculous, she thought, as she rifled through one cedar hanger after another. She had a closet that was bigger than the average person's bedroom and it was full of designer clothes, yet she couldn't find anything suitable to wear to the office. She supposed the size of one's closet had little to do with that, since she could distinctly remember having this very same problem before Bradford had started making millions, back when she could count the number of suits she owned on one hand.

She finally settled on the Armani, and after a quick shower she applied her makeup, then selected the Mikimoto pearl earrings from her jewelry box and skipped down the stairs. That was when she noticed the scent of tobacco coming from Bradford's study.

Her pumps clacked on the marble floor as she crossed the foyer and entered the wood-paneled library. Bradford was sitting at his mahogany desk puffing on a cigar and reading several newspapers all at once—the *Wall Street Journal*, the *Washington Post*, the *New York Times*, and one or two others.

"Working at home today?" she asked as she inserted her earrings.

"Just for a while," he said without looking up from his newspapers. "I have a meeting with a client late this afternoon."

"And I have that closing today," she said. "Then I'm having dinner with Noah and another client. So I'll be late getting home."

He glanced up, and she knew what he was about to ask before he opened his mouth. "Phyllis will be here by noon," she said. "I left instructions for her to get your dinner before she goes home for the day."

"That sounds fine." He went back to his papers.

"Bradford, did you hear what I just said? I'm closing on a house today. I may not run a multimillion-dollar technology firm, but this *is* my first sale and it's important to me. The least you could do is pretend to show some interest."

Bradford looked up again. "Sorry, Barb. It's just that I have a long day and I was trying to get through the financial pages." He put his cigar in the ashtray then stood, walked around his desk, and kissed her lightly on the cheek. "Congratulations. Sounds like you done good."

"Thank you," she said, smiling with pride.

"Is the house nearby?"

Barbara shook her head. "No, it's a town house on the southern side of Silver Lake, over there near where Pearl lives."

Bradford sat down, leaned back in his black leather chair, and puffed on his cigar. "Who's the buyer?"

"A young black woman named Sharon. She's single, in her late thirties. She's an up-and-coming lawyer but she couldn't afford to move to this side of Silver Lake. At least not yet."

Bradford nodded. "What was the sale price?"

"Two-sixty."

Bradford made a clucking sound. "Is that all those town houses are going for? I don't see why you bother with a two-bit deal like that, Barb. Your commission will be what? Around fifteen thousand?"

She shrugged. "Less since I have to split it with the buyer's agent."

He shook his head. "You should be going after clients like the

Wrights. They were in the market for something just over a million, weren't they? Did you ever clean up that mess with them?"

Barbara winced. She thought about telling him that Bernice Wright was the client she was having dinner with that evening, but Bradford blamed her for a recent real estate fiasco with the Wrights and she was reluctant.

Bernard Wright was one of Bradford's business subcontractors, and Bradford had introduced her to the Wrights when he learned that they were hunting for a new house. Barbara preferred clients who had not been referred by her husband, because she wanted to make it as a Realtor on her own. But the real estate business was tough, and she could only afford to work part-time with all the committees and boards she sat on. So she had learned to swallow her pride every once in a while and take any help she could get.

After weeks of house hunting with Bernice Wright, the couple had finally settled on a gorgeous contemporary-style $1.2-million-dollar house just up the block. They were three days away from closing when Bernice Wright called Barbara late on a Sunday night to say that the deal was off. Barbara was half asleep when she picked up the phone and heard Bernice screaming that she and Bernard were getting a divorce and wouldn't need a new house.

Barbara was appalled. She tried to get Bernice to calm down and not act so rashly. Couldn't she move into the house alone with alimony? Or could they live in separate wings? It was a big house and it was going to be difficult to back out when they were this far along. But Bernice had just caught Bernard in bed with his secretary a few hours earlier, and she had kicked him out. She wanted nothing to do with him.

A few weeks later, Barbara heard that the Wrights were back together. Then she heard that they were separated again.

Barbara put her hands on Bradford's desk and leaned forward. "Honestly, Bradford. There wasn't anything I could do about that."

"Not about them separating, but it seems to me that . . ." His voice trailed off as he puffed on his cigar.

"That what?"

"Forget it," Bradford said with a wave of his hand. "It's not important. I'll see you when you get back this evening." He flipped a page of the *Wall Street Journal*.

"Dammit, Bradford." She banged on his desk. "Those silly papers can wait. Look at *me*." She snatched one of the newspapers and threw it on the floor.

He stood up so quickly that his leather chair smashed into the wall behind him. He glared at her. "That wasn't necessary."

"Then how would you suggest I get you to pay attention to me?"

"Not like that," he blurted as he picked up his newspaper.

"I can't control it if my clients decide to get a divorce and they change their minds about buying a house together."

"No, you can't," Bradford said tersely as he sat down and put his newspaper back together. "But you could persuade one of them to start looking for something on their own. If they're getting a divorce, someone has to move out."

"Oh, please, Bradford. Don't you think I'm trying that?"

"Maybe you need to try harder. I can only judge by the results."

She couldn't take his condescending attitude a minute more. "Well, for your information, Bernice is the client I'm having dinner with tonight."

Bradford cocked his head to the side in question.

"They've separated again," Barbara continued. "She's looking for something for herself, but she wants to be in Northern Virginia to get away from Bernard. I'm not licensed in Virginia, but Noah is, and he's going to show her around. If she finds something, we'll split the commission. I'm going to introduce them to each other tonight."

"Excellent. Why didn't you tell me that before?"

She shrugged. "Bernice just called me last night. And you gave me such a hard time when the deal fell through before. I was going to wait until I was sure I could work something out."

"I don't mean to be hard on you, Barb, you know that."

"Hmm," she said doubtfully.

"And who is Noah? You two share an office or something?"

She shook her head. "I share an office with Marilyn. But since Noah and I are both part-time, we look out for each other. He teaches elementary school during the day."

Bradford nodded with understanding. "Well, good luck with Bernice."

"Thank you."

"Now do you mind if I get back to my papers? I have to make a phone call in about thirty minutes and . . ."

Barbara smiled thinly and waved her hand. "Yes, Bradford, go back to your papers. Oh, there is one other thing. Don't forget the party at our new mystery neighbor's house this Saturday night."

"How could I? You've been reminding me every day since we got the invitation."

"I just want to make sure you don't make other plans. I'm really excited about it."

Bradford nodded. "You and everyone else around here."

Barbara closed the door softly behind her and paused. Somehow, much of the excitement she had felt just moments ago about closing on the house and meeting with Bernice had all but vanished. It was tough getting Bradford to pay attention to her, and when he did he was so patronizing.

He had an uncanny knack for deflating any moment of joy or pride for her unless he had contributed to it, as when he lavished gifts on her. No doubt, if she closed the deal with Bernice, Bradford would be genuinely happy for her because he could claim she owed it to him in some small way. But the deal with Sharon had been all her own doing, and he had barely reacted to the news.

That was why working with Noah was so refreshing. He never belittled her accomplishments. When she got the news that Sharon had been approved for the mortgage loan, Noah seemed more excited than she was. In contrast, her husband had forgotten all about the deal even though she had been talking about it for weeks. Barbara shook her head. Bradford was one in a million.

She looked down at her chalk-stripe suit. She hated this thing. It looked like something Bradford would have picked out for her. Dark and dull. She needed something fresh and bold, splashy even.

She skipped up the staircase and strolled briskly down the hallway toward her eldest daughter Robin's bedroom. The house was so quiet these days, in contrast to when she had two teenage daughters living here, she thought as her Burberry tweed pumps glided along the oriental runner. Robin had moved into a condo a few weeks earlier, after finishing graduate school and landing a new job as a policy analyst, and her youngest daughter, Rebecca, had gotten married almost two years ago. This big house with no children around sometimes made Barbara feel lonely, and it was going to take some time getting used to it.

At least Robin had left some of her things behind until she could find the time to get back with a moving van. Barbara searched through dresser drawers until she found a silk Hermès scarf filled with soft shades of pink, coral, and blue. She pulled the scarf out and looked in Robin's full-length mirror as she draped it around her suit jacket.

She smiled. It was just the accessory to liven up her look for her dinner meeting with Bernice and Noah.

P EARL GLANCED AROUND at all the solemn faces at the dinner table. These meals with Patrick and his daughters were always either quiet or boisterous, depending on whether the girls got into one of their frequent arguments. Juliette sat on her side of the table looking glum as she picked at her mashed potatoes and gravy. And Lee, seated on the other side, was shoving her pot roast down so fast that Pearl was afraid she would choke.

"Not hungry, baby?" Pearl asked Juliette.

Juliette twisted her lips. "The stuff you fix is always so fattening," she said, her nose wrinkled with disgust as she picked at her food. "It's full of carbohydrates. My mother said all they do is put pounds on your hips. I don't want to get big as a pig and not even be able to get into my designer jeans." She gave Pearl a sly, pointed look.

Pearl glanced away and kept her mouth shut. If she said what she was thinking to the smart-mouthed little tart, Patrick would probably throw her out of his house. The child was getting more like her materialistic, trash-talking mama every day.

Pearl glanced across the table at Patrick. He smiled reassuringly at her, then turned to Juliette. "I don't think you have to worry about gaining too much weight, sweetheart. Pearl went to a lot of trouble to fix this meal. Try to eat some of it."

"I didn't put any fat in the greens," Pearl said. "I haven't cooked with fat in years. The greens just have a little olive oil and chicken bouillon cubes in them."

"The greens are delicious," Patrick said. "Try some."

Juliette frowned. "I've had greens before," she said, pouting as she shoved her food around on her plate.

"Well, have them again," Patrick said firmly.

Juliette put a tiny forkful of greens into her mouth.

"Aren't they good?" Patrick said.

Juliette rolled her eyes to the ceiling.

"You don't have to eat all of your food," Patrick said. "Try to eat at least half."

Pearl picked up her glass and tapped her foot. Patrick should insist that Juliette eat every morsel of food on her plate. Look at the child. She was no bigger than a bean pole. Shoot, he needed to make her eat seconds. So what if she had to buy her designer jeans in a junior size 5 instead of a 3.

Pearl turned her attention to Lee. "And what's the rush with you?"

Lee paused, put her fork on her plate, and licked her fingers. "Phillip is coming over. We're going to check out a movie."

"It's Wednesday night," Patrick said. "Don't you have homework?"

"I already finished it."

"Well, who is this Phillip?" Patrick asked.

"A dude in my class. A friend."

"As in *boy*friend?" Juliette stared at Lee from across the table with obvious surprise. "Don't tell me *you* have a boyfriend."

"I won't tell you," Lee said curtly. " 'Cause it ain't none of your damn business, no how."

"Watch that mouth, Lee," Patrick said.

"He's probably her pimp from the hood," Juliette said, her voice dripping with sarcasm.

Lee jumped up out of her seat and jabbed her finger at Juliette. "Why don't you just shut your fat mouth, bitch? 'Fore I shut it up for you."

Juliette cut her eyes at Lee. "Maybe if you kept *your* mouth shut, people wouldn't know how dumb you are."

"Girls," Patrick said, holding up a hand.

"At least I don't sound like some lame-ass white bitch," Lee retorted, interrupting her father.

Pearl blinked. She couldn't believe these two girls. Patrick was a dear man, but he didn't have a clue when it came to raising his daughters. He was much too lenient with both of them as far as Pearl was concerned. Maybe it was out of guilt for leaving Juliette's mom and for not being around during Lee's early years.

Whatever the reason, Pearl wished he would crack the whip more often. If her son had talked like this around her when he was a teenager, she would have served him his head on a plate and he knew it. She wanted to step in and give both of them a firm talking-to, but she didn't feel it was her place with Patrick sitting right there at the table.

"Whoa," Patrick said, holding up his arms. "That's enough, both of you. We don't curse like that in this house, Lee. You know that."

"She started it," Lee protested, folding her arms defiantly. "People always messin' with me."

"What do you expect," Juliette said. "Look at you. Look at your hair. Cornrows are so ghetto."

"My hair looks better than that rag sitting on top your head."

Juliette tossed her hair off her shoulders. "I wear my hair long like this, 'cause my mother says we have European ancestors not that far back. Isn't that right, Daddy?"

Lee fake-coughed. "Please, girl. You got that rag at the salon, and a cheap one at that."

"At least I don't walk around wearing funky sneakers and those baggy jeans. I have taste and . . ."

Lee lunged at Juliette from across the table and knocked her glass of water over. Patrick jumped up and held Lee back. "Sit down," he said firmly as he picked up Lee's glass. "You're acting like this is the Jerry Springer show."

Lee sat down and stubbornly turned to face away from Juliette.

"Now, I don't care who started it," Patrick said. "I want you both to stop."

Juliette shot Lee a vile look and turned her body away from the table. Pearl thought it was way past time for the belt to come out. They could both use a good licking, and she didn't care how old they were. But she kept silent.

"Can I be excused?" Lee asked bitterly.

Patrick nodded, and Lee stood up and stormed off.

"May I be excused, too?" Juliette asked. "I promised Monica I would text her when I was done eating."

Patrick frowned. "You promised her you would do *what?*"

"Text her. Send her a message on her cell."

"No," Patrick said firmly. "You haven't finished eating."

Juliette reluctantly turned to face the table. "I can't believe you let Lee go like that," she complained as she took a bite.

"She finished most of her food," Patrick said, beginning to sound weary from all of this. "Unlike you."

"But I don't like this stuff."

Patrick sighed, "You can go after you eat your greens." He turned to Pearl. "Excuse me. I'm going up to talk to Lee, try to calm her down."

Pearl nodded as he stood and walked to the stairs. Juliette shoved her greens down her throat, jumped up, and pushed her chair back.

"Put your plate in the sink," Pearl said as she stood and gathered her own plate and Patrick's. "And take Lee's, too."

"Excuse me?" Juliette said, jerking her head back with indignation. She put one hand on her hip. "No way." She wagged a finger in Pearl's face. "I'm not cleaning up that girl's mess."

Pearl glared at her. She couldn't take any more of this insolent behavior. "I don't remember asking you to comment, young lady. Just do as you were told, and do it now."

Juliette stared as if she couldn't believe that Pearl was talking to her like that. She turned to look for her daddy, but he was gone. She looked back at Pearl, who by now had a vicious scowl on her face. Juliette blinked, picked up both plates, and dragged her feet into the kitchen.

The doorbell rang, and Juliette placed her dishes on the sink and ran out of the kitchen. It was funny how ringing doorbells and telephones seemed to light a blaze under a teenage girl's rear end, Pearl thought.

By the time Pearl entered the small foyer, Juliette had opened the door for a handsome young man with a mocha complexion who looked to be about sixteen or seventeen years old. He was fairly tall, with curly brown hair in a short Afro and was dressed in baggy blue jeans, a letterman jacket, and a new pair of K-Swiss tennis shoes.

At least the jeans weren't hanging off his butt, and he wasn't wearing a do-rag on his head, Pearl thought. He looked like the kind of boy a mother would want her daughter to bring home—a little hip-hop but not too.

Juliette obviously agreed, given the way she was hanging all over the poor guy. Pearl thought this must be Phillip, Lee's date for the evening, but judging from the way Juliette was touching his arm as she whispered into his ear, Pearl considered she might be wrong about that.

Or maybe not. Lee suddenly flew down the stairs, taking them two at a time, and raced across the foyer. She nearly knocked Juliette over as she planted herself firmly between Juliette and the young man.

"You can go now," Lee said, fixing Juliette with a hard glare.

Juliette flipped her weave, batted her eyelashes coyly, and stepped away. "I was only trying to be nice to your date while he waited for you. Don't you have to get dressed?"

"I *am* dressed," Lee responded curtly.

"Oh," Juliette said, looking at Lee's baggy jeans and tennis shoes with disapproval. "You're wearing *that*?"

Lee cut her eyes at Juliette and shoved her hands into her pockets. Pearl noticed that Lee had changed but only into a fresh pair of jeans.

Phillip gave Lee a sideways glance. He was obviously uncomfortable being wedged between the two warriors, and Pearl felt sorry for the guy. What an introduction to the household, she thought.

Pearl extended her hand and smiled in an attempt to break the ice. "Hi. I'm Pearl, a friend of Lee's father. You must be Phillip."

He smiled and nodded as he shook Pearl's hand.

"Lee obviously has good taste," Pearl said, winking at Lee. "You seem like a very pleasant young man."

Lee glanced down, looking so embarrassed that Pearl thought she would melt into the floor. "Well, he is, girl," Pearl said. "No harm in saying it."

"Thanks, ma'am," Phillip said.

"Got manners, too," Pearl said, smiling. "I like that." She nudged Lee playfully, and Lee smiled reluctantly.

As Patrick came down the stairs and greeted Phillip with a hearty handshake, Pearl noticed that Juliette was still lurking at the bottom of the stairs.

"So what movie are you going to see?" Patrick asked.

Phillip shoved his hands into his jeans pockets and glanced at Lee. "I don't know. What would you like to see?"

Juliette moved closer. "If you like comedies, I heard that . . ."

"Later, y'all," Lee said as she steered Phillip toward the door. Pearl didn't blame Lee. She would have gotten her man out of there quickly, too. The way Juliette was carrying on, in no time she would have been inviting herself on the date. Pearl supposed she shouldn't be surprised at Juliette's behavior. Her mama was the biggest flirt in Silver Lake.

"I want you to help me with the dishes," Pearl said to Juliette as soon as Lee had taken off with her date.

"Not now. I gotta go text Monica."

"She can wait a few minutes," Pearl said.

"No, *you* can wait," Juliette said smartly.

Pearl was so stunned to hear a child speaking to her like that, she lost her voice for a second.

"Don't be so rude," Patrick said. "Apologize."

"But Monica's my best friend," Juliette protested. "And Lee didn't have to wash the dishes."

"Apologize," Patrick said firmly.

"Sorry." Juliette muttered the word so softly that Pearl could barely hear her. Pearl expected Patrick to tell the girl to speak up, but he dismissed her with a wave of his hand and Juliette flew up the stairs.

"I can't believe you let her go," Pearl said. "I wanted her to help me with the dishes."

"I'll help you with the dishes."

"That's not the point, Patrick. That's what's wrong with her. You and her mama let her get away with murder."

"She's been dying to call Monica or text her or whatever all evening."

"Pfft. I don't care if she's been dying to call Monica all her life. She can't talk to me like that when I ask her to do something."

"She gets that from her mother. They both like to have their way."

Pearl shook her head. "That's no excuse," she said as she walked toward the kitchen.

"I know, Pearl, and I'll talk to her later. But I don't want to get into a big argument with her now. I rented a video and I want us to enjoy a nice quiet evening together."

He danced around her to try and cheer her up as he followed her into the kitchen. He looked so cute dancing like that, Pearl thought, and she was tempted to smile. Sometimes when she looked at him, she felt so lucky that a kind, attractive man like Patrick was interested in her. But she was still upset that he had let his daughter get away with being disrespectful to her. She tightened her lips.

"C'mon, baby," he said, doing a little Latin step. "We can make some margaritas, pop some popcorn, and go downstairs and watch the movie on the big-screen TV."

She began stacking dishes in the sink, and when she still didn't smile, he stopped dancing and stood close to her. "Well, say *something*."

Pearl could feel herself calming down as she picked up the dishrag and a handful of utensils. Watching a video and cuddling with Patrick certainly sounded a lot more appealing to her than steaming about that ornery child. She smiled a little. "Hmm. If you put it like that, how can I resist?"

He gave her a peck on the cheek. "Good. I'll make the margaritas. You do the popcorn."

"Sounds like a plan to me. And Patrick, all that dancing reminds me. I've been meaning to tell you that Barbara Bentley got us an invite to a big party at the mansion on the hill this Saturday night."

Patrick raised an eyebrow. "Now *that* should be interesting. Place looks like a damn museum."

"I know. It's black tie. Should be *very* interesting."

Patrick frowned. "Does that mean I need a tuxedo? I've always rented 'em when I needed one. But maybe I should go ahead and take the plunge and buy one, since my baby hangs around people like Barbara Bentley.

"Pffft. I just do her hair. But I guess you and me got some shopping to do." Pearl sighed. "Not exactly my favorite thing since I never have enough money. But I don't have a thing to wear."

"I thought all women loved to shop."

"Not when they're a size fourteen and broke half the time."

"You'll look fine in whatever you wear," he said. "I like a little extra sugar on my brownie."

He smacked her playfully on the rear end, ducked, and scooted out of the kitchen, just avoiding the slap of the dishrag upside his head.

JOLENE KICKED OFF her red stilettos, strolled to the bar in the family room, and fixed herself a big stiff vodka martini. Although it was Wednesday, Juliette had stayed at her dad's past the weekend as she sometimes did so that Jolene could work late, and Patrick should be bringing her home any minute. Jolene sank down into one of two black-and-white cow-print chairs in front of the fireplace and leaned back. She was so tired. She had worked late every day this week, her only relief a quickie on the office floor with Brian just before she left that evening, and stopping to buy a lottery ticket on the way home.

That sordid episode at the club with Barbara Bentley on Monday morning had left a bad taste in Jolene's mouth. The woman was such a damn snob. But it wasn't just Barbara. Everyone in Silver Lake treated her like dirt.

Even when she got pregnant at seventeen and the baby's father wouldn't marry her, she hadn't felt as alone as this. Her snooty family had practically abandoned her back then. They lived on upper Sixteenth Street in Washington, D.C., a black neighborhood so prominent that it was called the "Gold Coast," and back in those days a pregnant daughter was a huge embarrassment.

Patrick had come along and married her, and even though she eventually lost that baby, together they had built a life worth envying. They had climbed from the depths, with not much more than some clothes and a beat-up Ford, to living in a mini-mansion in Silver Lake, North.

Now she lived alone and Patrick was screwing Pearl Jackson, of all people. Lately, Jolene had been thinking more and more about moving. Why the hell should she stay here when everyone treated her so shabbily? She could make a fresh start somewhere else, maybe Atlanta or even New York City.

The only thing holding her back was that she would have to take Juliette away from her father. Juliette adored her dad, and Jolene really didn't want to do that to her. The divorce had been hard enough on Juliette. To this day, even almost a year since the separation, Juliette wanted her parents to get back together more than anything. What kid wouldn't?

But people were so nasty around here. She needed to start thinking about her own needs before she went mad.

She took a sip from her martini glass, closed her eyes, and thought about Brian ravishing her on the floor of her office earlier that evening. She was so conflicted about that man. One minute she couldn't stand the sight of him and the next she was ready to have an orgasm just looking at him.

She had to stop this behavior. If they ever got caught, she would be ruined at work. And what would Juliette think about her mom screwing the office painter if she ever found out? That would be a terrible example to set for her daughter.

Jolene had always prided herself on being a good mother. No matter how much she screwed up the other parts of her life, she wasn't going to mess that up. Juliette was her only child, and Jolene wanted her to have the best of everything.

She had become the black sheep in the family when she got pregnant as a teenager. And even though she had eventually married and she and Patrick had a beautiful daughter together, she still wasn't good enough for her uppity family. Her father the judge, her mom the society maven, and her sister the snobby Spelman College graduate all looked down on her. She had disgraced the family, and even living in the most exclusive black neighborhood in Maryland now didn't make up for that. Sure, there was a lot of black money in Prince George's County, but it was *new* money, as her father had made clear. If people didn't have the right pedigree, all the money in the world didn't matter.

When Juliette was born, Jolene swore her daughter would never be exposed to that kind of snobbishness. Money was money, and Jolene didn't give a damn where it came from.

The one thing she felt she had failed at with Juliette was giving her a stable family life with both her mother and her father living together under the same roof. That was hurting Juliette more than anything. Jolene had noticed that Juliette was developing a hard edge, probably out of bitterness over the divorce, not to mention spending so much time around Lee. Juliette used to be such a sweet child but now she had quite the mouth on her.

Recently Jolene had toyed with the idea of asking Patrick if he wanted to give the marriage another try for Juliette's sake. Getting back together with Patrick would also help her in the image department. She didn't give a damn what Pearl thought of her. Who the hell was she? But Barbara Bentley was another matter. She was the doyenne of Silver Lake, and Jolene knew that she *had* to get back into Barbara's good graces or she was never going to be accepted around here. Barbara and Patrick had always gotten along well when the four of them got together for dinner. If she and Patrick remarried, Barbara's bad feelings toward her might change.

The problem was that she didn't know how Patrick would feel about getting back together now that he had taken up with Pearl. She had no doubt that this thing between them was temporary. Pearl was an overweight hairdresser, and Jolene couldn't imagine Patrick ever marrying someone like that. Jolene knew that she might have put on a few pounds, but she was thirty-eight years old, not forty-eight, like Pearl. And she had style. Pearl dressed like a shabby matron.

Jolene downed her drink just as the doorbell rang. That would be Patrick bringing Juliette home, she thought. She stood up, placed her glass on the bar, and slipped back into her heels. She walked into the foyer and at the last minute decided to undo the top button of her berry-colored Moschino cardigan. Hell, yeah. Let Patrick see what he was missing. She put on a big smile and opened the door.

Juliette and Patrick stood there talking and laughing. Jolene knew that Juliette blamed her mother for her dad leaving, and at times, Jolene felt a twinge of jealousy at the way Juliette looked at Patrick with such open adoration.

Jolene kissed Juliette on the forehead as she entered. "Hello, darling."

"Hello, Mother," Juliette said coolly, barely glancing in Jolene's direction. It hurt like hell when Juliette treated her this way but she tried to brush it off.

"How was your visit?" Jolene asked.

Juliette shrugged. "It was fine," she said. She kissed Patrick goodbye on the cheek and brushed past Jolene with her overnight bag.

Juliette was headed to her bedroom and the telephone no doubt, Jolene thought. Jolene wondered if Juliette was giving Pearl as difficult a time as she was giving her own mom. She sure hoped so.

"Pearl fixed us a nice pot roast dinner," Patrick said from the other side of the threshold.

"Your favorite, how nice." If he caught the sarcasm in her voice he didn't show it.

"Lee went to a movie with a friend, and Juliette ran her mouth on the phone while Pearl and I watched a video."

"Patrick, you spoil Juliette rotten," Jolene teased. "I hope she finished her homework."

"They both finished their homework before dinner. Well, I guess I'd better run. If Lee's back, she's at the house alone since I just dropped Pearl off at her place. And if she's not alone 'cause she invited that boy in, I want to be there."

Jolene waved her hand. "Oh, I'm sure Lee is fine. Why don't you come in for a minute?"

Patrick hesitated and glanced at his watch. "I really should get back."

Jolene pulled him in. "For goodness' sakes, Lee is seventeen years old. Juliette's only fifteen and I've left her here alone for brief periods. I want to talk to you about something important."

That was a lie. Jolene just wanted to get him into the house. It had been ages since they'd really talked in person, and she missed his presence. Brian was great for sex but he could barely put two intelligent sentences together. And she wanted a chance to feel Patrick out about getting back together.

"I guess I can stay for a quick minute," he said and followed her into the family room.

Jolene walked to the bar. "Can I get you a drink?" She sensed that he was about to decline as he sat on the black couch across from her cow-print chairs without removing his leather jacket. He looked so uncomfortable. It was hard to believe that he had once lived here.

"C'mon, Patrick. Don't be a spoilsport. Just a little?" She held her thumb and forefinger an inch apart and put on her sweetest smile. She wanted him to relax, and when they had been a couple her smiles used to always win him over.

He smiled back at her. "OK, what are you drinking?"

She lifted her glass. "Martini."

He nodded. "I'll have the same. But just a little. I'm driving."

"For God's sake, Patrick, you only live ten damn blocks away. And take off your jacket."

He accepted the drink from Jolene and removed his jacket. Jolene was reminded that he was in great shape for a forty-year-old man, as she noted his firm, muscular arms and shoulders. She poured a fresh drink for herself and settled on the couch next to him.

"Looks like you've been busy decorating around here," he said, indicating the chairs.

She smiled. "Do you like it?"

"It's nice. But what was wrong with the old family room furniture?"

"Just that, it was old."

He stared at her incredulously. "You just bought it when the house was finished last summer."

"I know, but I decided it was all wrong for this room. I wanted something more modern."

Patrick shook his head. "Can we afford it with two mortgages? Yours and mine? Not to mention . . ."

She waved a hand. "We're fine, Patrick. We always manage to pull through one way or another. Stop worrying about money."

"Someone's got to do the worrying, the way you spend it."

"I'm better than I used to be. I haven't bought many new clothes in ages."

"Uh-huh," he said doubtfully, eyeing her designer outfit. "So, what was so urgent?"

"It's not exactly urgent. Does it have to be urgent to get you to sit and talk to me for a minute?"

"Nooo. I just thought . . . well . . ." He shrugged and sipped his martini.

"We're divorced but that doesn't mean we can't get along," she said. "I mean, we're still raising a daughter together."

"You're absolutely right. I actually think we get along better now than we did when we were married. At least when it comes to the last few years of our marriage."

She smiled and turned toward him so he could get a good look at her legs below her short pink skirt. "I've noticed that, too. It's almost like when we first met and we were just getting to know each other. Remember?"

"How could I forget? You were only seventeen, pregnant by some dude and frightened out of your wits."

"Until you came along." She gently brushed the tip of her shoe against his pant leg. "It felt like I had suddenly found someone who understood me and could protect me. I still sometimes feel like you're the only person who really understands me."

He shrugged. "We were married for twenty years, Jo. I probably do know you better than anyone else."

"But it's more than that. I feel, you know, like I can be myself around you and you won't judge me. I never felt that way with my folks or anyone else. And I thank you for giving me that."

He smiled. "My pleasure."

She took a sip of her drink and he glanced at his watch.

"I know. I know," Jolene said. "You have to run. I really wish we had more time to talk about what's been going on with you. How do you like working as a director in county government since your promotion?"

He put his glass down on the coffee table, stood, and put on his leather jacket. "So far, so good. Better than working for Bradford Bentley."

Jolene cleared her throat and rose with her glass in hand. He *would* have to bring that up. Was he rubbing Bradford in her face because she'd had an affair with him while they were married? Patrick and Bradford even got to exchanging blows at the housewarming party she had thrown shortly after they moved into this house. But all that happened almost a year ago, and she didn't want to get into it now. That was the quickest way to an argument.

"Good. I'm glad you're happy in your new job."

"Yeah, I am. So how about you, Jo? How's your job?"

"Oh, you know. Same old, same old."

"Still kicking butt, huh?"

She laughed. "You know me."

"Don't I, though? But let me get going. We'll talk again soon."

She touched the lapel on his jacket. "Better yet, Patrick. Why don't you stay for dinner when you pick Juliette up on Friday for the weekend? She would love that."

He shook his head. "I promised Pearl I'd go shopping with her Friday after work. She wants to get a dress for the party Saturday night at that new house up on the hill."

Jolene rolled her eyes. Pearl, Pearl, Pearl. She was sick of hearing that name. "Oh, *that*."

"You're not going?" Patrick asked with surprise.

"I was invited but, no, I don't think so."

"Any particular reason? There was a time when you would never have passed up a big party like that."

Yeah, plenty of reasons, she thought. Starting with the fact that everyone in Silver Lake now despised her. "It's only a party. It's not that big a deal. No one even knows who lives there, and I have other plans."

"Uh-huh."

She was lying and Patrick knew it. The only plans she ever had on a Saturday night were to check her lottery tickets. He didn't know why she was lying, but she could see him trying to figure out why she wasn't going to a big party. Time to change the subject.

"So how about next Friday, then?" she asked.

"You mean for dinner here? I'll have to think about that. I want to see what Pearl has planned."

Dammit. She was going to have to slap him if he uttered that name again. "Oh, just this once. Juliette still blames me for our divorce, and if she saw us getting along better it would go a long way toward helping me patch things up with her."

"I'll have to let you know."

He said it with such finality that Jolene decided to drop it. Fine, she thought. Forget the party, forget Patrick, forget every fucking thing. She didn't need any of it.

She shut the door behind him and drained her glass. That had been a total failure, just like her life. She walked back into the family room and reached for the martini shaker. She was planning to pour herself another drink, but she stopped suddenly and stared at her glass. Not only was she turning into a fat pig, she was also becoming a lush. No wonder Patrick preferred Pearl to her.

What a fucking rotten life. "God!" She lifted the glass up high over her head and hurled it into the fireplace.

BARBARA WATCHED NOAH from across the table at Georgia Brown's, a trendy restaurant in the heart of downtown Washington, D.C., as he explained the housing market in northern Virginia to Bernice. They were eating crab cake and roasted chicken, and Noah had turned his smile on full blast for Bernice. That adorable brown face could be awfully hard to resist, and he was obviously having an effect on Bernice given how she kept leaning forward in her low-cut animal-print blouse and exposing her double-D breast implants.

She had never seen Noah work the charm quite like this, Barbara thought as she watched Noah flirt with Bernice. He had never flirted with *her*, and for a moment Barbara found herself wondering why not. She and Bernice were about the same age, but Noah was always all business with her.

"From what Barbara has told me about you," Noah said, "I think Northern Virginia is ideal. It has some really nice neighborhoods and it's not all that far from D.C. I see you somewhere with a lot of class. Maybe Great Falls."

Barbara smiled. By the time Noah was finished with Bernice she would be ready to buy ten houses.

"Yes, well, as long as it's far away from Prince George's County and my ex," Bernice said. "Did Barbara tell you I was getting a divorce, Noah?" She leaned so close to Noah that Barbara worried she would topple into his khaki-clad lap.

Noah smiled at the obvious come-on. "Yes, she did. Sorry to hear that."

"Sorry? Don't be sorry, baby," Bernice cooed. "I'm single again and loving it."

Barbara had been surprised by the change in Bernice's style of dress. When she was with Bernard, conservative suits were her signature attire. Now she wore short tight skirts and low-cut tops. Talk about being liberated.

"You look fantastic," Barbara said, in an attempt to change the subject. Bernice was getting a bit too brazen. Not to mention that the two of them were acting like she wasn't even sitting at the table.

"And I *feel* good," Bernice added. "How old do you think I am, Noah?"

Noah cleared his throat and laughed. "Oh, no. You're not getting me to go there."

Bernice beckoned with her finger. "Come on, baby. Guess how old I am."

Barbara twisted her napkin in her lap. Noah was obviously on the spot. Bernice was well put together but she looked every bit her fifty-something years. If Noah said anything to offend her, they could lose a client.

"He knows how old you are," Barbara interrupted. "He saw the papers I had you fill out." Noah hadn't seen a thing and even if he had, Barbara suspected that he would hardly remember Bernice's age. But she didn't want this discussion of age to move one inch further. Noah managed to slip a thank-you wink to Barbara during the split second when Bernice wasn't looking at him.

"Uh, yes," Noah said. "Now that I think about it I do remember seeing something. You definitely don't look your age."

Bernice smiled brightly at him, and Barbara sighed with relief. "So, um, you're looking for something just for yourself, then," Barbara said. "Three to four bedrooms, fireplace . . ."

"Fireplace in the bedroom," Bernice added, her eyes glued to Noah.

"Fireplace in the bedroom," Barbara repeated as she took notes. She looked back up to see Bernice's eyes boring down into Noah. Barbara was really getting annoyed. She was tempted to remind Bernice that Noah was a Realtor, not a gigolo.

"Two- or three-car garage, Bernice?" she asked, trying to hold back the edge in her voice.

"Hmm?" Bernice asked absentmindedly. "Oh yes, definitely a three-car garage." She looked at Barbara. "And a pool and solarium. Spare nothing, since it's that bastard's money I'm spending."

Barbara cleared her throat. "Certainly."

"And all high-end appliances," Noah said. "Viking range, built-in Sub-Zero refrigerator and wine cooler. I'm sure we'll be able to find you just what you want."

Bernice smiled. "I like this guy. Where have you been hiding him, Barbara?"

Barbara laughed. "Noah is a gem. I'm sure he'll look out for you."

"No question," he said. "I'm looking forward to working with you, Bernice. Any friend of Barbara's is a friend of mine. Now if you ladies will excuse me for a minute. I need to call a client about something." He stood in his khakis and navy sports jacket and smiled at them as he removed his cell phone from his jacket pocket. He leaned down and whispered to Barbara: "I won't be long. I need to check on another client, OK?"

Barbara nodded.

"You be sure to hurry back, baby," Bernice cooed.

Barbara rolled her eyes to the ceiling as Noah walked toward the entrance. Bernice removed her compact from her purse and touched up her cocoa-brown nose.

"Are you sure about the swimming pool?" Barbara asked as she flipped through her notes. "Some people don't want the trouble of maintaining one."

"Who the hell said I would be maintaining it? I'll hire someone and send the fucking bill to Bernard."

"Of course," Barbara said, glancing down at her notes. "So pool, solarium . . ."

"Tell me something, Barbara."

She looked up at Bernice.

"Are you screwing him?"

Barbara frowned, not understanding. Then her eyes grew wide as it dawned on her that Bernice was talking about Noah. She nearly dropped her Montblanc fountain pen. "Goodness no, Bernice. He's a coworker. And I'm a married woman."

"Heh! I don't think that would stop me. That chocolate hunk is *too* fine. I love locks on a young man. And I think he has the hots for me, too."

Barbara blinked. "Bernice, please."

"You saw the way he looked at me, didn't you?"

Barbara was tempted to slap some sense into the silly woman. "Noah is like that with everyone. He's very charming and he knows how to make you feel special. That's why he's such a good agent. He's a schoolteacher and only sells real estate in the evenings and on weekends during the school year, yet he's still one of our top agents. If he worked at it full-time he would be unbeatable."

"Listen to you, girl, gushing about him."

Barbara felt her cheeks go hot with embarrassment. "I'm only . . ."

Bernice held her hand up to silence Barbara. "You don't have to explain to me, sister. He's so cute, I don't blame you. Don't worry, he's young enough to handle the both of us."

Barbara bit her bottom lip. The things one had to put up with to keep a client. "I'm sure I don't know what you're talking about, Bernice. There's nothing going on between us. I would never do something like that to Bradford."

"How very honorable of you, Barbara. I have to admit that Bradford is quite the catch. He must be near sixty but he's still looking good. And rich and successful to boot. I bet you have to beat the women off him. Bernard is like that or at least he thinks he is."

Now Bernice had gone too far. Barbara had limits when it came to discussing her personal relationship with Bradford, especially with nosy women she barely knew.

Mercifully, Noah reappeared, and again Bernice practically forgot that Barbara was even sitting there as she flirted shamelessly with him. Bernice turned her legs from under the table, faced him, and hiked up her skirt. At the rate she was going, Barbara half expected her to give him a lap dance at any moment.

Noah just smiled and acted like nothing was out of the ordinary. Why the hell didn't he tell her to back off? Barbara wondered as she cleared her throat. "Can we get back to discussing the features you want in the house?"

Bernice waved her hand irritably. "Oh, Barbara, I'm sure you understand what I want. Nothing all that different from what you and Bradford have, just smaller since it's only me. I'm really all talked out about houses now." She smiled at Noah. "I want to relax and enjoy the company."

"That's fine with me, Barbara," Noah said gently. "I've got a pretty good idea what she likes. And as I show her a few houses and get her likes and dislikes, I'll have an even better idea."

"You got the right approach, baby. Now, tell me, Noah, how do you like to spend your free time?"

Barbara settled back and took a sip of her latte. She glanced around discreetly. The way Bernice was acting was embarrassing. She had seen hookers show more restraint.

Barbara almost felt sorry for Noah. He would have to put up with this outrageous behavior for weeks if not months while Bernice shopped for a house. If a male client had flirted with Barbara like that she would have walked out on him by now. But not Noah. That was probably why he sold so many more houses than she did. He could put up with this kind of nonsense from clients. Maybe he even enjoyed it.

After coffee the three of them stood outside the restaurant in a heavy downpour, Bernice under one umbrella and Barbara under another, as Noah stood at the curb in an all-weather coat and hailed a taxi for Bernice. He walked her to the cab and held the door open as she climbed in, then he rushed back to the sidewalk and stood under the umbrella with Barbara. His coat was dripping wet as he took the umbrella handle and held the umbrella over both of them.

"That was quite an experience," he said, shoving one hand into the pocket of his khakis.

Barbara shook her head. "I had no idea she was like that. But you handled her perfectly."

He shrugged it off. "Don't worry about it, ma'am. I've dealt with her type before. It goes with the territory."

He called her "ma'am," but he flirted with Bernice, she thought wryly. For some reason she felt really old at that moment. She adjusted her Hermès scarf around her neck. "I hope you're wrong about that. I couldn't handle a male client if he acted that way."

"You'd better prepare yourself, Barbara. You meet all types in this business. Sometimes you have to let it wash off your back if you want to make the deal, then move on to the next one."

Barbara looked at him doubtfully. "I couldn't put up with behavior like that."

"Even to sell a million-dollar house?"

"Not even to sell a *five*-million-dollar house."

"You're not as hard up as I am," he said, only half jokingly. "Still, sometimes I think you should lighten up a bit. What do you do for fun? You know, parties, games? Something besides getting manicures and pedicures." He smiled down at her teasingly.

"Very funny."

"I'm just kidding, trying to get you to loosen up. But I'm going to have to give up for now. It's nasty out here, and we need to get out of this rain. Where are you parked?"

"A few blocks that way," she said, pointing north.

"I'll walk you to your car."

"Thanks," Barbara said as they headed in that direction. "You can walk me to my car and then take the umbrella. I'll get it from you next week when I go into the office."

"You're not going back into the office until next week?" he asked as he casually draped his free arm around her and rested his hand on her shoulder. The move surprised Barbara. But she supposed it made sense to walk together this way, to keep from bumping each other as they shared the umbrella.

She shook her head. "I have a meeting tomorrow with the literary committee that I'm on and some other things to take care of on Friday." Like shopping for the party on Saturday at the new mansion in Silver Lake, she thought. She already had a stunning new Bill Blass silk chiffon gown, but it needed accessories. Probably better not to mention that to Noah.

He nodded. "Busy society woman."

Barbara rarely thought of herself that way but she understood why it looked like that to Noah.

"Now that I think about it, that idea of yours won't work because you have to walk from your car to your house. You'll get wet if I keep the umbrella."

"We have a garage."

"Right," he said, smacking his head. "Dumb city dude. What do I know?"

She smiled. At times it felt like she and Noah were worlds apart. Then she remembered that they *were* worlds apart—different ages, different lifestyles. They had an agreeable working relationship and their differences were sometimes easy to forget.

"You look very pretty when your mind wanders off like that."

Barbara blinked and glanced away. She hoped that it was dark enough that he couldn't see that she was blushing. Noah had never said anything like that to her before, and she wondered if being around Bernice had something to do with it. He had obviously loosened up.

They walked the rest of the way in silence. When they reached Barbara's Benz, they stopped and faced each other. She smiled. He was such a cute young man, and for a fleeting moment she wished that she was ten years younger—and single.

"There you go again," he said.

"What?"

"That faraway look you get when your mind wanders."

She glanced down. "Oh, that." She laughed nervously and looked back up at him. "Well, um, thank you for walking me to my car. I'll see you next—"

Suddenly his lips were on hers. She was surprised at how warm and soft they felt, and she was too stunned to move. Noah was kissing her in the moonlight on a crowded street in Washington, D.C., and she was letting him. Had they both lost their minds?

She jerked her head back and shoved him away. "What are you doing, Noah?"

He smiled awkwardly. "Huh. Good question."

"I can't believe you did that." She wanted to smack his hand like she would a naughty schoolboy.

He shook his head as if to clear it. "I don't know what came over me. It's just that for a minute there in the rain and under the moonlight you looked so . . ." He shook his head again. "I don't know. It seemed like the thing to do. Stupid, huh?"

"That's an understatement."

"I'm really sorry, Barbara. Look, can we pretend this never happened? I don't want to ruin our working relationship."

She thought for a moment. What he had done was shocking and completely out of line. But he really looked embarrassed, and she didn't want their relationship harmed either. She needed him. "Fine. Just see that it doesn't happen again."

He nodded and handed the umbrella back to her. Then he pulled a Redskins cap out of his coat pocket and slipped it over his head.

"You sure you won't take the umbrella?" she asked.

"I'll be fine," he said abruptly.

She hated to part with Noah under such strained terms, but there wasn't a lot she could do about that. He obviously felt bad. He *should* feel bad. "OK. So, I'll see you at the office next week."

"It'll probably be a few weeks, since I start vacation next week."

"Oh. Going anyplace special?" she asked.

"Jamaica to visit some relatives."

"I didn't realize you had relatives in Jamaica."

"My father is from there. He moved back after my folks divorced."

She nodded as he lifted the wet collar to his jacket, gave her a weak smile and jogged up the sidewalk. Barbara's heart thumped harder with every step he took away from her, and she watched until he rounded a corner and disappeared. What the hell had just happened? That was so unlike Noah.

Then she realized she was standing in a hard rain. She found her car keys and hastily unlocked and opened her car door. She pressed the button to close the umbrella but it was stuck. She pressed again and again, still no luck. "Dammit," she muttered. "Stupid umbrella." She was getting soaked, and her hair would be a mess.

She dropped her bag on the driver's seat and squeezed the button on the umbrella with both hands. Still, it wouldn't close. She stomped her foot and shook the umbrella, as if that would help. She tried once more to get the button to work and when it didn't, she threw the umbrella on the sidewalk and hopped into the car.

She slammed the door, sat and stared at the rain as it pounded the pavement. Suddenly she found herself giggling. She covered her mouth. What a night. It had been ages since an attractive man had flirted with her, including her own husband. She had forgotten how giddy it made a woman feel.

She also felt a bit guilty. Not that Noah had kissed her but that she had liked it so much.

She shook her head to clear it. She had no reason to feel guilty. She put a stop to it before things got out of hand. Although why she would feel the slightest amount of guilt when she was married to Bradford Bentley was beyond her. He certainly had no reluctance about doing a lot more than kissing other women. Joan, Vickie, Sabrina, Jolene. And those were just the recent ones she knew about. They ranged from sluts to society women, old to young, married to single and everything in between. Sometimes there were long periods where he seemed to be faithful, and then boom. Another bimbo came along.

Early in their marriage, when Barbara realized that Bradford was never going to quit the womanizing, she made the bottle her companion. Good old Mr. Belvedere had kept her company for many lonely nights until finally she understood that all the booze was making her hurt more.

She didn't want to leave Bradford. He was the father of her two lovely daughters and a pillar in their community. She enjoyed her lifestyle with him. A part of her still loved him.

But she didn't want to stoop to Bradford's level either. Just because he cheated, didn't mean she should.

She started the car. She had done the right thing by putting a stop to that kiss. Noah was young, attractive, exciting, and for those reasons alone she had to keep him at a distance.

She was glad it would be a couple of weeks before she saw him again. She hoped that by that time, what had happened tonight would have faded in both of their memories, and their relationship could go back to the way it had been before the kiss.

J OLENE OPENED HER eyes and stared at the ceiling of her bedroom. It was a ten-foot-high ceiling, as were all the other rooms
in her 6,000-square-foot dream house. She had scrimped and
saved to build the house, going against Patrick's wishes. He thought
their first 4,000-square-foot house in Silver Lake had been big
enough. Her determination to build her dream house had nearly
wrecked their marriage.

But it hadn't. Patrick didn't even leave when he discovered that
she was screwing the architect building the house. It wasn't until he
discovered her affair with Bradford Bentley last summer that Patrick
decided he'd had enough. Bradford was his boss and a neighbor.
That was too much, even for passive Patrick. So he had quit his job
and left his wife.

She sat up in bed and sighed so loudly it was nearly a sob. She hated this fucking house. It seemed that all her problems had begun when she'd moved in here. And now it was being dwarfed by a monstrous mansion going up right across the street. Her damn house looked like a hut standing next to that thing. And no one had any idea who was building it. The Osbournes could be moving in across the street from her for all she knew.

Her Bose clock radio blared, piercing the silent air, and she moaned and touched her forehead. She had a splitting headache. She reached over and smacked the button to shut the radio alarm off, and that was when she noticed the empty bottle of Veuve Clicquot champagne and the crystal flute on the nightstand. Now she remembered that last night after Patrick had left she had brought a bottle up to her room and partied by herself. No wonder her fucking head hurt.

She forced herself to sit up. As much as she dreaded going in to work, she had an important business meeting at eleven o'clock. It was at times like this that she despised all the rich ladies in Silver Lake like Barbara Bentley who didn't have to work because their husbands made insane amounts of money. And here she had to work like a damn slave for the government to make ends meet. Never mind that she was a GS-15 with a staff at her command, it was still work.

She slipped into her Stuart Weitzman animal-print mules and pulled a robe around her black lace teddy. The mules were last year's style and long overdue for updating. The sexy lingerie was a sad joke since no one was around to see her in it and no one had been for months. These days she felt about as sexy as a withering old maid.

She walked down the hallway and glanced in Juliette's room as she passed by. Her daughter had been up and out by seven-thirty as usual that Thursday morning to catch the bus to school. Her bedroom looked like a tornado had touched down in the middle of it, with all the outfits she had decided not to wear strewn about and her bed hastily made up. Jolene had learned to do without a lot of new things so she could pay the mortgage and all her other bills, but she tried as much as possible to make sure Juliette had all the clothes and accessories that any teenage girl would want.

Normally she would have rushed in to tidy up after Juliette but she was not in the mood this morning. She needed a quick hit of coffee and a shower. Then she was going to drag herself in to the office.

She opened the front door and walked down the driveway to pick up the morning's *Washington Post*. Two huge moving vans were parked across the street in front of the new house, but still no sign of the neighbors and only two days left before the big party.

She picked up the paper and glanced at the front page of the Metro section. One of the headlines was about the police lieutenant who had been found dead in his garage from a bullet wound and the wife who had been arrested and charged with his murder. Jolene scanned the article quickly. The house where the body had been found was only a few miles from Silver Lake, and Jolene couldn't believe something like that had happened so nearby.

It seemed that the man's wife had admitted that she had hired a hit man to kill her husband for 1 million dollars in life insurance money. The wife was a former stripper turned real estate agent, and her police officer husband made only $75,000 a year. The couple had recently declared bankruptcy and their half-million-dollar house was in foreclosure. The wife had agreed to pay the hit man $200,000 once the trigger was pulled and she had collected on the insurance policy.

A car horn blared and Jolene glanced up to see Ellen Johnson waving as she drove by in a sleek silver Jaguar XJ. Ellen didn't usually bother speaking to Jolene anymore but she was showing off her shiny new car. Jolene smiled thinly and waved. "Bitch," she murmured under her breath. Another one of those rich hussies like Barbara Bentley who scrounged off their successful husbands.

Ellen was probably dashing off to the mall to shop for the party or to the country club to shed a few pounds so she could fit her fat ass into her new ball gown. It seemed that everyone was going to the party Saturday night, even Patrick and Pearl. *Everyone but her.* Sometimes she didn't understand why the hell she stayed in Silver Lake. Living around all these wealthy suburban housewives was too damn depressing.

She walked back in the house, poured herself a cup of coffee, and sat at the kitchen table to finish the article about the murder for hire. Declaring bankruptcy and having the bank foreclose on your house must be awful. Patrick had often worried that something like that would happen to them if she didn't curb her spending habits. They struggled to pay their bills at times Jolene knew, but they were nowhere near as desperate as the cop and ex-stripper had seemed. Still, how could anyone be stupid enough to think that such a drastic step would solve their problems? That greedy cop's wife was in more trouble than ever now.

She remembered her Maryland Lotto ticket from the previous day and dug out the Metro section of the paper. Then she stood and walked up the stairs, taking along her coffee mug. She had been too depressed after Patrick left last night to watch the drawing on television. No doubt the ticket would be a losing ticket just like all the others and just like her sorry life.

She entered the bedroom, set her coffee mug down on the nightstand next to the champagne bottle, and dug the ticket out of her Coach bag. The bag was beginning to look shabby, with frayed threads on the shoulder strap. There was a time when she would have replaced the bag with a new one months earlier but she would probably just have it repaired. She had to be thrifty these days.

She held the ticket in one hand, the newspaper in the other, and moved her eyes back and forth as she compared the six numbers. She noticed almost immediately that the numbers were very close. She rubbed her eyes to clear them and compared each of the numbers again, one by one. When she was done, she stopped and blinked. Her heart was beating so fast, she thought it would sprint right out of her chest. All six numbers matched. Not two or three or four. *All of them!*

She found herself choking. She sat on the bed and took a sip of coffee. Calm down, girl, she told herself as she fanned her face.

She banged the coffee mug down on the nightstand, jumped up, opened all the blinds, turned on all the lights and slowly studied the numbers again. When she finished, she ran to the middle of the bedroom floor and raised her arms to the ceiling.

"Sweet Jesus!" she yelled. She had just won $5 million. She screamed.

T HE LONG DRIVEWAY curved gracefully to the top of the hillside on Peacock Lane and ended at a circle decorated with a
massive lighted fountain.

Bradford pulled up in his silver Jaguar XK, and a uniformed parking attendant opened the door on Barbara's side. The attendant extended a gloved hand as Barbara placed a satin heel down on the
pavement. She was pleasantly surprised to discover a smooth black
carpet beneath her foot. She had attended many glamorous affairs,
large and small, hosted by top government officials and Bradford's
wealthy business clients, but this was her first carpeted walkway.

Bradford walked around the car, and she took his arm as the attendant drove off to park. They smiled at each other but didn't utter
a word. They didn't need to. She knew from the extra sprint in
Bradford's step and the sparkle in his eyes that he was immensely impressed with what he'd seen so far.

As they climbed the wide staircase to the front door, Barbara looked up to see the most elegantly decorated stone and stucco mansion she had ever seen in P.G. County, let alone Silver Lake. It was in the style of a French chateau, with turrets soaring toward the dark evening sky, graceful arches, and windows with diamond-shaped panes. Whoever built this magnificent mansion had elevated Silver Lake to a new lofty status as the premiere black community in America.

The Bentleys reached the landing, and Barbara subtly adjusted her Russian sable stole across her shoulders. The copper-colored wrap had been last year's gift from Bradford for their thirty-first wedding anniversary, and Barbara thought it was perfect for such an occasion at this time of year. It was a chilly spring night, not cold enough for one of her full-length mink coats but too blustery to go out without something. The stole also nicely complemented her black Bill Blass evening gown.

She smiled at Bradford as he lifted his arm and reached for the door chime. He looked extremely handsome in his new Brioni tuxedo. Even after more than thirty years of marriage, raising two daughters and the many highs and lows they had been through, she still found him sexy. She couldn't count the times she had spotted him across a crowded room at a party or charity event and felt proud that the most magnetic man in the room was her husband.

She still had a good figure herself and barely a wrinkle on her face. But as she and Bradford aged, they had to work hard at staying fit and looking youthful. She worked out regularly and routinely used all the latest in creams and lotions. Bradford lifted weights nightly in the exercise room in their house.

In contrast, Noah was still young enough not to have to worry about staying fit. He played a lot of tennis, and . . .

She caught herself. How in the world had Noah crept into her thoughts just now? She was attending a glamorous society event with her successful and much admired husband beside her—and here she was thinking about a young schoolteacher. Ever since that kiss, she found her thoughts drifting to Noah at the oddest moments even though she hadn't seen him since that night. She had to stop this. He was probably in Jamaica now, sunning and partying with beautiful young women. He certainly wasn't thinking about *her*. Barbara shook her head to clear it.

A middle-aged black man with a clean-shaved head opened the front door and stepped aside as they entered a large foyer with inlaid marble floors and a vaulted cathedral ceiling. Hostesses at many of the private parties they attended hired temporary butlers for the evening, herself included, Barbara thought as the man graciously took her stole. But she had a feeling that this butler was a permanent fixture in the household.

He led them across the foyer, under an arch, and down a short flight of stairs where they were met by an elderly white man. They followed this servant down a long corridor lined with paintings, and Barbara recognized the works of Jacob Lawrence, Ossawa Tanner, William H. Johnson, and other prominent African-American artists. She and Bradford owned a few paintings by talented black artists such as Alix Baptiste of Savannah and Lisa Quinn from Bermuda, and even one prized Jacob Lawrence painting. But Barbara had never seen such an extensive collection of art by top black artists outside of a museum. She and Bradford exchanged quick glances of admiration.

Barbara's mind raced as they rounded a corner and walked down yet another corridor. It seemed likely that the owners were African American given their taste in artwork. But who could they be? A celebrity such as an actor or a sports star? Maybe a prominent black businessman like Robert Johnson, founder of Black Entertainment Television based in Washington, D.C.? Or perhaps it was, as Pearl had heard through the rumor mill at her salon, a black woman who had married European royalty.

All the possibilities were thrilling, and Barbara felt butterflies dancing in her stomach as the servant stopped in front of a set of hand-carved wood double doors. He opened them, stepped aside, and bowed as Barbara and Bradford entered a large chandeliered room. It had a towering stone fireplace at one end and a grand wrought-iron stairway with stone detailing at the other. Best of all, the room was filled with many of the residents of Silver Lake and Prince George's County.

Barbara noticed Bradford staring into the room with open fascination. He was not an easy man to impress. It was usually others who stood in awe of Bradford's accomplishments and possessions, and Barbara was dying to know who was responsible for putting this expression on her husband's face. Not to mention her own.

PATRICK PULLED INTO a parking space about a block away from the mansion on the hillside and took Pearl's hand as they walked up the long driveway. Pearl wasn't thrilled about trekking up a long hill in an evening gown and heels, but so many cars were parked along Peacock Lane that there didn't seem to be much choice. It looked like everyone in Silver Lake was attending this affair.

As soon as they reached the end of the driveway, Pearl realized that they had already committed gaffe number one when she saw the parking attendants. Drat. They should have expected attendants at a party like this. She and Patrick looked at each other and rolled their eyes to the sky. It looked like it was going to be a long awkward evening.

She forgot their faux pas as soon as she stepped onto the carpeted walkway leading to the front door and looked up at the mansion. The place looked even bigger and more elegant close up, with all sorts of the kinds of doodads that appear in magazines like *Architectural Digest*. Pearl didn't know the terms for all this fancy stuff, but it was mind-blowing nevertheless, especially the big lighted fountain at the entrance. The whole thing looked beautiful against the clear night sky.

It was nearly enough to make her forget that she might have to face Jolene Brown with Patrick on her arm. Jolene had called Patrick the day before claiming that she had won millions in the Maryland lottery and that she might see him at the party. When Pearl thought about Jolene winning a pile of money, it made her shake her head. Jolene was the last person to deserve something like that.

Patrick had tried to assure Pearl that Jolene had gotten past her ill feelings in the year since he'd left her and started seeing Pearl. But Pearl wasn't convinced, especially after their encounter at the country club earlier that week. Women like Jolene always had long spiteful memories.

Still, she was dying to see inside the mansion that had been going up in Silver Lake all these months. She was thankful to Barbara for calling the president of the Silver Lake Neighborhood Association. He had made several calls and got Pearl an invite within a matter of hours, and now she was finally going to find out who lived here. At one point, she and many others thought it had to be Michael Jordan. Not many African Americans in Maryland had this kind of dough. But Wizards owner Abe Pollin had fired Jordan, and the basketball star split from the city. So much for that theory.

One of her salon clients had insisted that the owners were royalty. Pearl thought that seemed far-fetched. She knew how often the rumors she heard at her salon turned out to be false. The people who built this mansion might not even be black for all she knew. Still, somebody big and important had built this place, and it was exciting to be a part of it.

In the foyer, she eagerly removed her black coat. It was her best lightweight coat, but it looked silly with a long dress. She needed a stole or formal jacket but she certainly wasn't going to spend her hard-earned money on a new fancy coat for this one affair. It would be a lifetime, maybe never, before she got invited to a mansion like this again. Heck, this thing was more like a castle, she thought as she looked up at the vaulted ceiling in the foyer. It dwarfed all the other houses in Silver Lake, even Barbara Bentley's.

She reluctantly handed her coat to the butler, fully expecting him to smirk or something. But he was cool about it, and Pearl realized that he was far too professional to smirk at a guest. She and Patrick followed yet another man past several paintings and sculptures, most by black artists. How impressive, she thought. She took Patrick's hand and squeezed it to keep from pointing and oohing like a fool. He smiled and gave her an "OK, calm down" look.

The servant stopped at a massive set of double doors and opened them with a grand gesture. It was all Pearl could do to keep from giggling. She felt like she was in a movie.

The servant stepped aside and allowed Pearl and Patrick to pass by, and this time Pearl gasped aloud. She couldn't help it. She had never seen so much glitter and glamour. There was a big, sparkling chandelier, a fireplace that seemed to reach to the sky, and a beautiful long staircase. The room was filled with women in elegant ball gowns and fine jewelry and men in designer tuxedoes. She was eager to learn who had put all this together.

J OLENE GLIDED HER Bentley sedan up the long driveway to the fountain in front of the mansion. It was a 2000 Bentley Arnage with only 37,000 miles on it, and she loved everything about it, from the way it looked to the way it handled. She had spent the entire previous day shopping for this baby and had paid a little over a hundred thousand dollars for it—next to nothing when you had millions.

And fucking-A fabulous it was. The exterior was a rich creamy white, and the Wilton carpets had been made by a British company that produced flooring for royal and presidential palaces. Barbara might have the name Bentley, but *she* had the car.

If only she could find a way to get an American Express Centurion Card, known as "The Black Card." Now *that* was the epitome of arriving at the top. But she'd heard that it was an invitation-only card, offered to Platinum Card members who spend over a certain six-figure amount on the card each year. Now that she could charge that kind of money on her Platinum Card, she definitely planned to look into how she might finagle an invitation.

She stepped out of the Bentley in her new white Gucci gown and paused in front of the two young black parking attendants for maximum effect. The gown had a V-neck that plunged to her waistline, and she had carefully placed the golden buckle in the shape of a G at the end of the vee. Her suede Gucci stilettos were covered with gold mink and had sexy ankle straps and four-inch python heels. Topping it all off was the pièce de résistance: a floor-length Blackglama mink coat. Granted, it was a little warm for a full-length fur, but Jolene couldn't resist looking like the legend she knew she was.

Jolene noticed the hungry looks on the faces of the parking attendants and she smiled seductively as she dropped her car key into the palm of the one nearest her. Between the Bentley and the boobs, the poor guy was panting like a dog in heat. Jolene's smile widened with pleasure. It felt good to be back on top.

She lifted her gown as she climbed the stairs to the mansion. It was a pity she had no gentleman to accompany her. She couldn't possibly have invited Brian to such an elegant affair, and Patrick was coming with Pearl. But if she didn't have a man, at least now she had moola.

Jolene looked up at the soaring turrets and knew that she would not be able to live quite like this. People who had homes like this didn't stop at one. They often had other places all over the country or even around the world. Hell, this might not even be this owner's biggest spread. This kind of living took a lot more than a few million in the bank. But with her lottery winnings, she intended to come as close to this style of living as possible.

Inside, the butler asked for her coat, but Jolene shook her head and waved him off. No way was she handing over a brand-new

$20,000 mink coat before anyone had a chance to peep it. Why would she do anything so idiotic?

She followed an older man down a long hallway past beautiful paintings and sculptures. She stopped to check the names of some of the artists as the man stood at the end of hall and waited patiently. She had no idea how much an original piece of art by these artists would set her back but she intended to find out.

Jolene continued on as the man opened the huge double doors. She stepped inside, paused for a moment to take it all in, then discreetly opened and dropped her Gucci bag to the floor. The contents spilled out, and she gasped loudly as the old man scrambled hastily to pick everything up. When the voices died down and all nearby eyes had turned in her direction to see what the commotion was about, Jolene ceremoniously slipped out of her mink coat and held it at arms length to the man.

Nothing like a grand entrance, she thought. She had dreamed of making entrances like this.

Barbara noticed Jolene Brown immediately, even before her little stunt with the dropped evening bag. She had been keeping an eye on the entrance in eager anticipation of the arrival of the host and hostess. But trust Jolene to create a scene as she arrived. And trust the stupid tramp to wear a full-length mink coat on a forty-five-degree spring evening. Jolene Brown always had to overdo everything. What an ostentatious nut.

And if the rumor that Jolene had just won $10 million in the Maryland lottery was true, then Barbara was certain that more ostentatious nuttiness wound be on display for all of Silver Lake in the weeks and months ahead.

Barbara turned back to Bradford and the lieutenant governor and his wife. As boring as politics was, listening to Bradford discuss budgets and deficits was preferable to being distracted by that foolish woman.

Pearl spotted Jolene as she handed her mink coat to the servant and quickly looked away. Jolene told Patrick that she had won $10 million in the Maryland lottery. Patrick later checked and learned the drawing was for only $5 million, but that was still a lot of money. Pearl was sure that Jolene would be gloating. Maybe she and Patrick would be able to avoid Jolene in this massive ballroom. Pearl certainly hoped so.

To Pearl's horror she heard Jolene's voice behind her as soon as she had turned away.

"Hello, Patrick."

"Hi, Jolene," Patrick said, smiling at her. "How's the million-dollar woman?"

Jolene smiled back. "Never better."

Patrick gestured toward Pearl. "You remember Pearl Jackson, I'm sure."

Pearl nodded at her stiffly, but Jolene chose to ignore the reintroduction. As far as Jolene was concerned, Patrick's whore was hardly worth attention, especially when she was wearing a hideously lame little black gown that looked like it had come straight off the rack at Kmart. That is if Kmart even sold formal dresses. She certainly wouldn't know since she never put a foot anywhere near those discount stores.

She wanted to talk to Patrick privately, away from Pearl's prying ears. "Patrick, darling, I really need to speak with you about all this money I just won. Can you step away for a minute, please?"

Patrick frowned. "Fine, but can't you speak to Pearl first? There's no need to be rude."

Pearl shook her head and touched Patrick on the arm. "It's all right. I would expect nothing less from her."

Jolene inhaled deeply. "At least I don't look like a walking mannequin for a damn thrift shop." Fat-ass bitch, she thought.

"That was mean," Patrick said, shaking his head sadly.

"I'm just being . . ." Jolene paused as a hush came over the crowd, and she glanced in the direction everyone was looking.

The room grew silent as all eyes fastened on the top of the grand staircase opposite the main entrance. The guests awaited eagerly for the next scene to unfold in the months-long drama of the mansion on the hillside.

Barbara stretched her neck upward to see above the crowd and noticed a young woman walking down the second-story hallway, her hand gliding gracefully along the wrought-iron railing. The woman paused at the top of the stairway and smiled down at the guests.

"Ladies and gentlemen," boomed the voice of yet another male servant at the foot of the stairs, "may I present Baroness Veronique Odette Valentine de Marjolais."

The woman smiled and descended the stairs slowly in a shimmering strapless red gown that hugged her hourglass figure. She paused when she was about halfway down and stretched out her arms. That's when Barbara noticed that she wasn't as young as she had first appeared. In fact, Barbara thought the woman was probably closer to her age. But she had the body of a thirty-year-old and eyes that sparkled so brightly they could be seen clearly even from a great distance. She reminded Barbara of a youthful Tina Turner.

A black baroness, Barbara thought with excitement. Not quite a countess but still very impressive. She glanced up at Bradford and nearly gasped at the startled expression on his face. Barbara looked back toward the baroness. Yes, she was special. Yes, the house was stunning. But why on earth did Bradford look so upset?

"Good evening, everyone," said Veronique. "And welcome to my home. As your newest neighbor, I'm thrilled to be here in Silver Lake and very anxious to meet you all. Please enjoy yourselves this evening, and let one of my gentlemen know if you need anything at all."

How about a check for a cool $5 million, Jolene thought, as she watched the baroness elegantly make her way down the rest of the stairs. That would go nicely with the five that she had just won. Hot damn! Royalty living across the street from her.

Jolene's eyes stayed glued to the baroness as she made her way around the room and introduced herself. She had a smooth brown complexion that had the look of expensive spa treatments, and big round eyes. As beautiful as the baroness was, Jolene would have bet her Blackglama mink that the woman was at least forty, and probably closer to fifty since these rich women always managed to look younger than their actual years. And they should, given that they could afford to spend a fortune keeping up their appearance.

Jolene walked away from Patrick and Pearl and maneuvered through the crowd to get closer to Veronique. An introduction to the baroness was far more important than fussing with her ex- and his whore.

As Veronique glided about the ballroom greeting her guests and Jolene moved in that direction, Pearl said a silent "Amen." Thank God Jolene was gone, she thought. Now she could focus on the baroness. The first thing she noticed was how rich her honey blond hair color looked. No doubt it was bleached, but the effect with her coppery brown complexion was stunning.

The baroness approached Bradford and Barbara and extended a hand crowned with the biggest emerald-cut diamond ring Barbara had ever seen. Barbara waited for Bradford to offer his hand first, as she always did when they met new people as a couple. But Bradford still had a strange expression on his face, and it seemed that he was going to take an eternity to introduce himself, so Barbara reached out to the baroness.

"Hello. I'm Barbara Bentley," she said as they shook hands. "And this is my husband, Bradford. We're pleased to meet you."

The baroness smiled broadly, exposing a perfect set of pearly white teeth. "Ah, so it is you, Bradford. I thought so. You've aged some, but very gracefully I should add." She turned to Barbara. "And it's lovely to finally meet your wife."

Barbara's jaw nearly dropped to her hemline. She stared at Brad-ford. He already knew the baroness? How could that be? Never once had he mentioned knowing a baroness, and Barbara thought that would be something a spouse would share at some point during a thirty-year marriage. She wanted to kick the man.

Bradford kissed Veronique on her cheek with studied coolness. Apparently, he had regained his composure, Barbara thought as she waited for him to say something.

"It's good to see you again, Veronique." He glanced at Barbara. "And just so you know, dear, Veronique wasn't a baroness when I knew her several years ago."

Then what was she, dear, Barbara was tempted to ask. *One of your mistresses?* She knew her husband's type, and the baroness more than fit the bill. Barbara bit her tongue.

"I've done well since we last crossed paths, Bradford," Veronique said with a sly smile.

"So I see," Bradford said. "I can't wait to hear all about it."

"Of course, darling. We'll talk soon."

Bradford reached into his inside breast pocket, pulled out one of his business cards, and gave it to Veronique. Barbara stiffened as the baroness snapped a finger and handed the card to one of her servants when he magically appeared at her side. It was looking more and more like there was some shady history between these two. And knowing Bradford, it probably included sex. Dammit. She was hav-ing so much fun tonight. Why did Bradford have to go and ruin it for her?

"Thank you, Bradford. And it was lovely to meet you, Barbara." Veronique blew a kiss in their direction and slid on to the next couple.

Barbara glared at Bradford. "So, do you mind telling me what that was all about? How do you know the baroness?"

Bradford shrugged nonchalantly. "There's not much to tell. I did some business with her husband down in Atlanta about five years ago. She was simply Veronica Butler back then, married to a man named Guy Butler. I did hear that they divorced. I think Odette is her maiden name."

Barbara relaxed a bit, but not much. She knew Bradford too well to relax when he had any kind of connection to a beautiful, sophisticated woman.

14

*B*ARONESS *V*ERONIQUE *O*DETTE *Valentine de Marjolais and Jo-lene Brown quickly became the best of friends and allies. Together, they set out to destroy one snobby family after the other in Silver Lake, starting with the Bentleys. They plotted to ruin Bradford's business, then laughed as Barbara and Bradford were forced to sell their mansion and move to the slums in inner P.G. County.*

Then one day, while sipping champagne in Veronique's salon, the baroness told Jolene that she'd heard a rumor that Barbara had had her Louis Vuitton bag snatched as she walked to her car in the hood. Jolene threw her head back and laughed so hard she nearly spilled her drink all over her St. John suit.

Jolene jumped and opened her eyes. She blinked. Fuck! She'd woken up in the middle of the best part of her dream about Barbara and Bradford Bentley. What a pity. She sighed, tossed the covers back, and threw her feet over the edge of the bed.

Then she thought about the party at the baroness's house the night before and smiled as she stretched. She thought about the $5 million she'd won just a few days earlier and her smile grew bigger. What a fabulous week. First she'd won the money. Then she'd shopped all day with no thought to how much she was spending. Finally, she had attended the most glamorous party ever. She had even managed to corner the baroness and talk to her privately for at least fifteen minutes toward the end of the night. That was longer than Veronique seemed to linger with any of her other guests, including the Bentleys.

Jolene found Veronique's account of how she had met and married European royalty fascinating. The baroness said that she was originally from Atlanta, Georgia, where her first husband had been a successful software developer. They had lived comfortably in a neighborhood similar to Silver Lake until their marriage collapsed.

After the divorce was final, Veronique decided to take an extended vacation to Europe to get away from it all. It was while relaxing in the south of France that she had met Baron Pierre Valentine de Marjolais. He was from a tiny European municipality with a long complex name and he was also on vacation. They fell in love and married within "six short, sweet weeks," according to the baroness. But recently Veronique had found herself missing America and she had convinced Pierre to build her a small "bungalow" in the States.

Bungalow? Yeah, right, Jolene thought as she poured her first cup of coffee. She had oohed and aahed in all the right places while the baroness regaled her with some of the most fascinating tales Jolene had ever heard. For a while, as she listened to Veronique, she thought seriously of ditching Silver Lake and heading for Europe to find *her own* Prince Charming. But she could never do that as long as Juliette was in school.

At least she and the baroness had hit it off. Jolene thought they had a lot in common. They both had style and lots of flair, unlike the dowdy matrons of Silver Lake such as Barbara Bentley. And she and the baroness both had millions.

Jolene was confident that with just a little work she could make friends with the baroness. And if she was good at anything besides sex, it was "working it." She would plan a small gathering of her friends who lived outside Silver Lake and invite her new neighbor. Maybe she would eventually get an invitation from Veronique to visit her estate in Europe. Now that would be *something*.

She took her coffee cup to the family room and sat at the computer. Thank God she no longer had to go into that crappy office in town, she thought, as she searched the drawers for her good stationery. Fifteen minutes after winning the lottery she had called her boss and quit, refusing to even give the customary two-week notice. Why should she? She didn't need them any longer and never would again.

Jolene picked up her new sapphire blue Waterman fountain pen, with its 18-karat gold nib and 23-karat gold-plated trim. Now, should the first invitation be for afternoon tea? Jolene shook her head. No, that was too corny. Besides, the baroness was not British royalty.

She would throw a small luncheon on Sunday two weeks from today and hire a caterer to fix an extravagant meal. She would invite Veronique and a few girlfriends, and she'd have the invitations hand-delivered just like Veronique had. Then she would make sure the word got around to Barbara and all the others in Silver Lake who had snubbed her over the past year that the baroness was coming to her house for lunch. And they weren't.

15

PEARL LOOKED UP from her client's head and noticed a Rolls-Royce parking in front of her hair salon. She frowned. She had only one client who owned a Rolls-Royce, and she was not expected today. Pearl stared as the driver got out of the Rolls and walked around to the rear passenger door. *None* of her clients had chauffeurs. How odd, Pearl thought.

Then she gasped aloud as Baroness Veronique Valentine alighted from the car.

"Ooh," gushed Mary from beneath the blow dryer in Pearl's hand. "Isn't that the baroness who just moved to Silver Lake?" Mary reached for the eyeglasses dangling from the ends of the strap around her neck and slipped them on. "Yep, that's her."

Pearl shut off the dryer and watched as the baroness strolled toward the door of the salon. "So it is," she said, trying to sound calm as she wiped her hands on her white smock. Then she realized that her hands were already dry. Nerves, she thought wryly, and shook her head. Well, it wasn't every day that royalty visited her salon.

She supposed everyone in Silver Lake knew about the baroness living in their midst. Then she remembered that Mary didn't live in Silver Lake or Prince George's County for that matter. She lived in the next county over. News sure traveled fast.

The chauffeur opened the door to the salon and the baroness stepped in, all smiles. She was wearing a snugly fitting crepe silk dress and matching jacket in a beautiful aquamarine that complemented her coppery complexion and womanly figure. Pearl rushed up and extended her hand. This was so exciting. She had to remind herself not to do something stupid, like curtsy.

"Good afternoon, Baroness, and welcome to my salon."

"Thank you. You must be Pearl."

Pearl blinked and nodded excitedly. "Yes I am."

"I heard that you're the best around when it comes to hair color."

Pearl felt her cheeks go hot. She waved an arm, trying to appear nonchalant. "Oh, shoot. I don't know about that. But thanks anyway. What can I do for you?"

"I'm in desperate need of a touch-up around my roots and a trim. Do you think you can match the color?"

Pearl walked around Veronique slowly. She might gush like a schoolgirl about royalty entering her salon, but when it came to hair she was all business. "It's a beautiful color. Sort of an almond or honey blond, isn't it?"

The baroness smiled. "Oui. C'est miel blond."

Pearl nodded even though she barely understood what the baroness had just said. "I should be able to come very close."

The baroness smiled warmly. "Wonderful. When can you get to it?"

"You're in luck. I had a cancellation today. As soon as I'm done with Mary here I can get to yours. Do you mind waiting about fifteen minutes? There's a nice coffee shop next door and . . ."

"That's fine. And I'll wait right here. It will give us a chance to talk." She settled herself into one of Pearl's waiting chairs, crossed her legs, and picked up a copy of *Essence* magazine as Pearl went back to Mary.

Pearl smiled as she picked up the hair dryer. The baroness might be royalty now, but Pearl had heard that she was from Atlanta, Georgia, and she was starting to think that despite all the elegance and flair, deep down inside the baroness was still just a good old southern sister at heart.

"By the way," Pearl said. "This is Mary Rivers. And Mary this is, um . . ." Pearl hesitated. "I'm not exactly sure what I should call you, Baroness."

"Oh, just call me Veronique."

"Pearl's the best," said Mary. "And I'm so pleased to meet you."

Veronique nodded. "Were you at my party last week, Mary? Forgive me if you were, but I invited most of Silver Lake and I didn't get around to meeting everyone there."

Mary shook her head. "I don't live in Silver Lake," she said. "But I heard about it."

"Mary lives in Montgomery County," Pearl explained. "That's right next door to Prince George's."

"So your services are popular far and wide, Pearl. Next time I'll have to extend an invitation to those in Montgomery County. It feels so good to be back in the States after several years living abroad."

"Do you like living in Europe?" Mary asked.

Veronique nodded. "I love it. But I do miss some things about living here. Like southern cooking. I love to cook but rarely get a chance to these days. Not that I need to with all the help I have."

"I was just about to say," Mary said, "why on earth would you be cooking with all the servants you probably have?"

"Pierre and I have a very busy social life, and you're right. It's hard to find the time when I don't have to do it."

Pearl smiled. "I love to cook, too."

"I miss it so much at times," Veronique said. "I make a mean sweet potato pie. My husband loves my pies, but I haven't made one for him in years."

Pearl laughed. "Cakes are my specialty. I used to have a catering service before I opened this salon."

"Pearl makes the best-tasting rum cake this side of the Mississippi River," Mary said.

"You seem to be very enterprising, Pearl," Veronique said. "I admire that. I'm glad the Silver Lake Neighborhood Association called and suggested that I add you to my invitation list for the party."

"That was some party," Pearl said, as she picked up a bottle of her homemade hair oil and applied a generous portion to Mary's newly curled and styled locks.

"I met so many wonderful people there," Veronique said.

"Did you get a chance to talk to the Bentleys?" Pearl asked. "Barbara is very well known in Silver Lake. She's the one who called the association for me."

Veronique nodded. "Bradford and I go way back to my days in Atlanta. He also knew my ex-husband."

"Oh?" Mary said. "They were in business together or friends?"

"Business."

Pearl was surprised at this news. Barbara had never mentioned anything about this to her. Maybe it was news to Barbara, too. Barbara was a very private person and didn't talk much about personal matters. But everyone in Silver Lake knew that Bradford had a roving eye and that Barbara had an off-and-on-again drinking problem because of it. She hoped that the relationship between Bradford and Veronique had been all business. The last thing Barbara needed in her life was more bimbo drama.

"What kind of business was that?" Mary asked.

"Software," Veronique said.

"Bradford Bentley is still in software as far as I know," Mary said. "Does he have an office down in Atlanta?"

Pearl tugged Mary's hair gently as she ran the oil through it. The woman was asking too darn many questions. Couldn't she tell that the baroness seemed a little uneasy? Maybe she didn't want to talk about her ex, and Pearl didn't like it when her clients felt uncomfortable, especially not this client.

"Uh, have you been to the country club?" Pearl asked.

"Not yet. But Jolene Brown mentioned it. She's been very nice to me. She invited me to her house for a luncheon next Sunday."

Pearl didn't say a thing. She didn't think she would ever hear the words "Jolene" and "nice" together in the same sentence.

"I've heard about that Jolene Brown," Mary said. "Didn't she just win ten million dollars in the lottery?"

"She won the lottery," Pearl said. "But it was more like five million."

"I've never met her," Mary said. "But from what I'm told you might want to be careful around her. Especially with your husband."

Veronique frowned. "Why is that?"

"She can't be trusted," Mary said. "I know she had an affair with Bradford Bentley last summer, and it was a mess when Barbara and Jolene's husband found out about it. That's why Patrick left her. Isn't that right, Pearl?"

Pearl cleared her throat. "My mama always said if you got nothing nice to say, don't say nothing. I think I'll keep my lips zipped on this." Pearl smiled slyly. "But you two can carry on."

Veronique and Mary laughed. "Hmm," said Veronique. "I admit that there is something about Jolene that doesn't feel quite right. I'm not sure what it is."

"People say she's a sneaky social climber," Mary said. "A big wannabe."

Veronique narrowed her eyes in thought. "Now that I think

about it, when I mentioned to Jolene that I was coming here to get my hair colored, she got a strange look on her face and said that I could do better. She recommended another salon in Washington, D.C."

Pearl tightened her lips. How dare Jolene do that. Pearl had never done a single thing to hurt that woman. Not one thing. Why was she always so mean? Pearl had planned to keep her mouth shut but she couldn't after hearing this.

"She's nothing but a troublemaker," Pearl said. "She's the most conniving woman I've ever . . ." Pearl paused and tried to calm herself. "I just stay as far away from her as I can."

"Probably good advice," Mary added. " 'Cause that woman is bad news."

Veronique nodded. "I hear you. I'm going back to Europe for a short visit the Monday after her luncheon, and Lord knows I've got enough on my plate to do to get ready. I haven't responded to her yet so I'm not obligated. We'll see."

Pearl nodded.

"Pearl, if you're not busy next Saturday, do you think you could stop by and show me how to make that famous rum cake of yours? I'd like to surprise Pierre with it when I go back to Europe."

"I'd love to show you, but I'll be here at the salon all day on Saturday. Only days I'm free are Sunday and Monday."

"Hmm." The baroness thought for a moment. "How's Sunday, early afternoon then?"

Pearl nodded. "You're on. I'll be there right after church and I'll bring everything we need to make the cake."

Veronique shook her head. "I insist that you make out a list and I'll have one of my guys pick up everything. You should come too, Mary. We'll have a ball."

"I'd love to," Mary said, clasping her hands together.

Pearl smiled. Minute by minute, the baroness was sounding more and more like a homegrown sister.

16

"MA! PHONE!" JULIETTE yelled from upstairs. Jolene looked up from the dining room table, where she and Darlene Dunn, the party planner she had hired for her luncheon that coming weekend, were poring over menus and decorations as they made the final preparations. Jolene rolled her eyes to the ceiling. Teenagers, she thought. All the effort she had put in over the years to try to make Juliette a graceful young lady sometimes seemed to have had no impact whatsoever.

She stood and walked to the bottom of the stairs, where the strains of the hip-hop music blaring from Juliette's room became unbearable. "Will you please not shout all over the house," she yelled. "And turn that damn music down. I have company."

"Sorry, Mother," came Juliette's voice from inside her bedroom.

"Who is it?" Jolene asked as soon as the music died down.

"That lady named Veronique from across the street."

Jolene's eyes popped wide open. Thank God, it was the baroness finally calling to RSVP. And to think she'd heard that awful music when Juliette picked up the phone. Jolene ran into the living room, her new pair of animal-print mules flapping on her feet, and picked up the antique phone sitting on the mahogany end table. "It's the baroness," she said in a loud whisper to Darlene as she covered the mouthpiece. "I'm sure she's calling to accept my invitation."

Darlene gave Jolene a thumbs-up.

"Hello," Jolene said in as refined a voice as she could muster.

"This is Veronique Valentine from across the street. Is this Jolene?"

"Why, yes it is. And how are you, Veronique?"

"I'm good. And you?"

"Très bien," Jolene responded, barely containing the excitement in her voice. She was speaking French to a baroness! It didn't get much more exciting than this.

Veronique laughed lightly. "Yes, well, I got your invitation for lunch on Sunday. It's already Wednesday, and I'm sorry to be so late calling to respond."

"Oh, don't worry about it. Better late than never I always say. And don't bother to bring anything with you. Just come and enjoy . . ."

"Ah, excuse me, Jolene."

Jolene paused and wrinkled her brow. Something didn't feel quite right. "Yes?"

"I don't mean to interrupt you, and I thank you for the invitation, but I'm afraid I won't be able to attend your luncheon."

Jolene nearly dropped the receiver. She couldn't believe it. Who the hell waited until four days before a social event to decline? Was this some European shit? "Um, but I . . . I'm so sorry to hear that." Goddammit. How the fuck did this happen?

"So am I," Veronique said. "I'll let you go now. I'm sure you're very busy."

Jolene stomped her foot, and Darlene glanced up from the party menus on the dining room table with a startled expression on her face. "Veronique, may I ask why you can't come? I was really counting on introducing you to some of my friends."

Silence. Perhaps she was out of line asking the baroness such a question but Jolene thought she had a right to know why Veronique was turning down the invitation. Jolene's whole reason for throwing this stupid luncheon was to have an excuse to invite Veronique over.

"Well, actually, Jolene, I've accepted another invitation the same day from Pearl."

Jolene held the receiver in front of her face and stared at it in disbelief. She what?! It took every ounce of restraint she could muster not to throw the phone on the floor and smash it with her heel.

"Pearl Jackson?" Jolene almost choked getting the name out.

"Yes."

Jolene bit her bottom lip. Her head felt like it would explode any second. "Very well," she said between clenched teeth. "I'm sorry you can't make it."

Jolene slammed the phone down. "Fuck!" She couldn't believe the baroness was turning her down to accept an invitation from that frumpy-assed bitch. Oh, the agony! She clenched her fists and screamed at the top of her lungs.

Darlene jumped up and raced into the living room, her heels clicking loudly on the wood floor. "Is everything all right, Jolene?"

"No!"

"Is there anything I can do?" Darlene asked, her café au lait complexion looking flushed as she stared at Jolene with concern.

Jolene didn't say a word. She ran across the floor to the Henredon coffee table, grabbed the crystal flower vase, and hurled it into the fireplace.

Darlene gasped and backed slowly out of the room as the vase smashed into tiny pieces. Jolene paced up and down the Oriental carpet as Darlene stared at her with a look of total fear in her eyes. Jolene didn't care. This was a disaster. She had been bragging to anyone who would listen that the baroness would likely be coming to her luncheon. And now this. Turned down in favor of Pearl.

"Ha!" She howled with laughter. Out of the corner of her eye, she glimpsed Darlene slipping her petite frame into her size 6 suit jacket, then gathering her things from the table and hastily shoving them into her canvas tote bag. Still, Jolene couldn't stop laughing. She sank down onto the couch, holding her stomach in a mad fit of giggles. This shit was so fucking unbelievable it was actually funny. She shook her head.

"Don't bother to get up. I'll let myself out," Darlene said as she dashed across the living room carpet. "I'll call you tomorrow."

Jolene's eyes followed Darlene's feet darting across the rug, and she thought of the French Aubusson carpet she had ordered to replace this antique one, so she could impress Veronique. She had paid extra to have it rush-delivered and it was due to arrive tomorrow. Now the baroness wouldn't even see it.

"You do that," Jolene said to Darlene without even looking up as the front door opened and shut. She couldn't stand Darlene anyway. The tiny bitch was a snob like all the rest.

Jolene squeezed her head with her hands. Her party was ruined. *Ruined.* All because of Pearl.

She jumped up and paced the carpet again. That bitch was going to pay for this. No one did this kind of shit to her and got away with it. She didn't know how she would get back at Pearl but she would think of something.

BARBARA WAS SLIPPING into her terry-cloth bathrobe when Bradford walked into the bedroom wearing one of his favorite Brioni suits and bearing a tray covered with a white linen napkin. On the tray sat their finest bone china, piled high with bacon, eggs Benedict, wheat toast, and freshly squeezed orange juice. The smell of her favorite coffee, Jamaica Blue Mountain, filled the air. In the center of the tray was a sterling silver bud vase with a single red rose.

"Oh, my," Barbara exclaimed, as she hopped back onto the bed. She clasped her hands together as he carefully placed the tray in front of her. "This is so sweet of you."

He leaned down and kissed her on the lips. "Happy birthday, sweetheart."

Barbara smiled. "Thank you. I wasn't expecting anything special today. You already gave me the car."

"Never underestimate your old man." He removed a small Tiffany box from the inside pocket of his suit and presented it to her with a grand bow.

"Goodness, Bradford. You didn't!" She opened the box to find a pair of platinum and diamond stud earrings. "Oh, they're precious."

"Two carats each," he said with pride as he sat on the edge of the bed. "Like 'em?"

"I love them."

"Good. 'Cause they go with this." He reached into another pocket and pulled out a second Tiffany box, this one long and narrow.

Barbara put her hand over her heart. "I don't believe you, Bradford."

He smiled at her as she opened the long narrow box and lifted out a platinum and diamond tennis bracelet. She gasped. "Oh, Bradford. It's gorgeous."

"Here, let me help you put it on." He took the bracelet from her, and she held out her arm. After he fastened the clasp, she held the bracelet up and admired it. "Thank you. It's lovely. Did you fix all of this food yourself?"

"Let's not go that far," Bradford said as he straightened his red silk necktie.

Barbara chuckled and took a sip of coffee. "Oh, so Phyllis did the cooking?"

"Hey, I supervised. I planned the menu. I picked out the gifts."

"Well, it's the thought that counts. Thank you, again, Bradford. This is the best birthday I've had in ages."

He sat down next to her on the bed and gently took her hands. "I know I'm not the easiest man to live with, Barb. Sometimes I get so wrapped up in my work, it must seem like I forget about you, but I don't." He squeezed her hands. "So, what do you have planned for your fifty-first birthday?"

Barbara blinked. The question took her by surprise. Bradford rarely asked her how she was going to spend her day. She was also startled to hear the age fifty-one mentioned along with her name. It sounded strange. She shivered. "Ugh. Don't remind me. I can't believe I'm . . . um . . . that age."

"Don't worry about it. You don't look a day over thirty-five, Barb. It's uncanny how young you still look."

"Thank you, Bradford. I work hard at it."

He released her hands. "So? What are your plans for today?"

"Oh, right. Well, normally I'd be going to the club to work out and then to the office. But I'm going to stay in today and catch up on some reading. I may go to Pearl's salon later for a pedicure."

"What about that literary board you sit on that usually meets in D.C. around the first week of the month?"

"That's tomorrow. Today I want to relax and pamper myself."

"Good." He kissed her on the forehead and stood up. "Enjoy your breakfast and the rest of your day, sweetheart. I'm having an early dinner with a client, but I want us to spend a nice romantic evening together. Maybe pop a bottle of Cristal."

So he had a dinner meeting? Well, that wasn't really unusual. Bradford was always meeting clients. "Sounds good to me. I look forward to it."

He leaned over and kissed her again, and Barbara watched as he strolled across the carpet and out the door. She held up her new bracelet. It was moments like this that reminded her why she had stayed with Bradford through all the ups and downs. He could be so sweet and generous when he wanted to be.

She finished her breakfast and reached into her nightstand for a fresh pack of Benson & Hedges. The phone rang and she wiped her hands on the linen napkin and picked the phone up.

"Hi, Mom, happy birthday." It was her eldest daughter, Robin.

"Hi, baby. And thanks. Are you at work?"

"Yes. How would you and Dad like to come into D.C. for dinner this evening to celebrate your birthday?"

Barbara smiled. Robin had just started working in downtown D.C. after completing her master's degree at the University of Maryland. Bradford had wanted Robin to come and work for him at his company, Digitech, but Robin wanted to strike out on her own. She'd found a job at an information technology firm and bought a condo near Chinatown. It was probably one of Bradford's biggest disappointments, since he almost always got what he wanted one way or the other.

Barbara secretly admired Robin's independence. Barbara had gotten married before finishing college and was pregnant with Robin within a month. She had worked briefly when she and Bradford were first married while he got his business off the ground. But when he landed his first million-dollar contract, she quit work to stay home with the children.

"Your father is meeting a client for dinner, but I'd love to come."

"Good. Rebecca's leaving work early, so she can stop by and pick you up. We'll go someplace special for dinner. Maybe B. Smith's since that's your favorite restaurant."

Rebecca was the baby, although heaven help Barbara if Rebecca ever heard her say that. She was twenty-six years old and had been married for two years now. She and her husband had just bought a small house in Lake Arbor, not far from Silver Lake.

"Wonderful. It'll give me an excuse to wear the new diamond bracelet and earrings your father just gave me."

"Another set?" Robin said teasingly. "You're going to have to open a jewelry boutique if this keeps up."

Barbara laughed. "A woman can never have too much jewelry. What time do you want us to meet you downtown?"

"Say six o'clock? At B. Smith's?"

Barbara hung up the phone feeling like the luckiest woman alive. She had a husband who was really trying to make their lives better and two attentive daughters. And she was sober. This was the best birthday she could remember in years. It was perfect, maybe too perfect.

Barbara shook that thought from her head. She would see if Pearl could take her at the last minute for a manicure and pedicure, then she'd call Rebecca. Maybe she could even get a little shopping done before she hooked up with the girls.

J OLENE UNDID THE top button to her St. John pantsuit and leaned forward in front of the full-length mirror in her dressing room. She smiled approvingly at herself. She was showing just the right amount of cleavage for a dinner date with an ex-husband whom she was trying to steal back from his mistress.

The black suit, with silver-toned accessories, was one of her favorites in her vast collection of St. John suits. Most of the designer's outfits had gold-toned accessories, so this one was a rare find. She knew she had to have it the minute she spotted it on the rack at Neiman Marcus.

Jolene turned from side to side to admire herself. She had put on a few pounds but still had her hourglass figure. Not bad for a thirty-something-year-old broad, as Terrence would have said. It had been ages since she'd thought of Terrence, a former lover from a distant time and place.

Forget all those ex-lovers. She wanted her husband back. She hated Pearl Jackson. Not only had she stolen Patrick by sneaking in sideways right after they separated; she had stolen the baroness and ruined Jolene's well-planned luncheon. A few women had shown up, but that didn't make up for the baroness not being there. Pearl was going to have to pay for that.

Jolene knew Patrick well enough to know that her newly found wealth and the promise of some good sex weren't enough to get him back into her life. She would have to use all the ammunition she could find, from Juliette needing him at home to the history they shared together as a family—all things lacking in his relationship with Pearl Jackson.

Jolene had devised the perfect plan. She had finally persuaded Patrick to have dinner with her and Juliette, for Juliette's sake, of course. Once Patrick arrived, she would break the news that Juliette had been invited to a sleepover with her girlfriends at the last minute.

She fastened on a pair of white gold earrings and checked herself once more in the mirror. She left the master bedroom suite and walked down the hallway toward Juliette's room, her black Manolo Blahnik slingbacks clacking on the hardwood floor.

Juliette had her own bedroom suite with a master bath and two rooms. One was where she did her studying, gossiped on the phone, listened to hip-hop music, and entertained her friends. The other was where she slept.

Jolene entered smiling, but as soon as she saw the outfit Juliette was wearing the smile fell off her face. Juliette's jeans that were so tight and low-cut that Jolene could see her red thong and part of her ass. And she had on a skimpy red midriff top with the words TAKE ME written across her perky little breasts. Jolene was stunned. Whatever happened to her sweet, innocent little girl?

"Take that junk off right now," Jolene said, trying to keep her voice steady. She was tempted to tear the trashy outfit right off.

Juliette eyed her mother defiantly. "Why?"

"Because I said so, that's why. It's too revealing. You look like a tramp."

Juliette pursed her lips. "I've peeped you wearing a lot less," she said smartly.

Jolene caught her breath. What had gotten into this child? She put her hands on her hips. "Don't you dare talk to me that way. I'm your mother. When you're my age you can wear whatever you damn well want. But you're only fifteen, so take that outfit off."

Juliette crossed her arms stubbornly. "But all my girlfriends are gonna be dressed like this and—"

"I don't give a damn how they're going to be dressed. You are not going out of this house looking like that. Maybe you need a different set of friends. I can see your butt and I don't want boys looking at it, too!"

"Aw, chill, Ma. It's a sleepover. It's just us girls."

Jolene narrowed her eyes. "I wasn't born yesterday. I know boys hang out at these things."

A sly smile crossed Juliette's lips and she lowered her eyes.

"Uh-huh. Got nothing to say now, do you?"

"Can I just wear the top if I put on different jeans? Please?"

"No. You're not wearing a top with that trashy slogan written on it."

"Dammit." Juliette yanked the top over her head and got up in her mother's face. "You're ruining my fucking life."

Jolene gasped and slapped Juliette solidly across the cheek.

Juliette stuck out her bottom lip and held her face. "I don't believe it. You just hit me."

"And I'll do it again if you ever talk to me like that again." Jolene had no doubt that all this defiant behavior was the result of Juliette's spending so much time around that thug Lee. She was going to have to talk to Patrick about this.

She looked through Juliette's closet and found another pair of blue jeans and threw them on the bed. "Wear those," she said firmly. "And find another top. You can throw everything you have on in the trash. And hurry up and get dressed. Your father will be here to take you to Monica's any minute."

Juliette ran to her dresser, yanked a drawer open, and pulled out another skimpy top, this one off-white. Jolene grabbed it and held it at arm's length, while Juliette put her hands on her hips and tapped her bare foot impatiently. Jolene ignored her daughter's cheeky behavior as she carefully examined the top. This one was just as bare as the other but had no dirty slogan written on it. She ought to ban this one, too, but she felt a little guilty after slapping Juliette, and she wanted to make amends.

"That's all right," Jolene said and handed the top back to Juliette.

"You treat me like a baby half the time," Juliette said in a calmer voice. "You say you want me to grow up but then you won't let me wear what I want. It's contradictory."

Jolene sighed. "I want you to grow up to be a strong, confident woman, not a slut. And I—"

The door bell rang and Jolene paused. "That's your father now," she said as she headed out the bedroom door. "And you still have your hair to do."

Juliette flipped her hair. "It's a weave, Mother, just like yours. There's nothing to do."

"Fine but I want you downstairs in ten minutes." Jolene strolled down the staircase and opened the door to see Patrick standing there looking very handsome in a smart gray blazer and brown slacks. It wasn't exactly Armani, but he still looked good.

"You look nice," she said as he kissed her on the cheek.

"And you look beautiful as always." He looked her up and down. "New suit?"

She nodded. "Sort of. Juliette's still getting dressed," she added before he could ask how much she had spent on the suit. She knew her ex-husband, and any outfit that cost more than a few hundred bucks was a waste of money. It wouldn't matter to him that she was now a millionaire. "Um, why don't you come on in for a minute and sit down while we wait for Juliette?"

Patrick blinked and glanced at his watch. "If we're going to make the reservation at seven, we should leave now."

"She'll be down any minute. I have some things to talk about before we leave."

Patrick glanced at her suspiciously as he followed her into the family room. They sat on the black couch and she turned to him.

"You know how she is these days. She takes forever to get ready. And prepare yourself. She's dressed kind of scantily."

He smiled knowingly. "Like mother, like daughter it's turning out. Don't let her go too far."

"I made her change, but she's a teenager. She has to be able to express herself a bit."

He nodded. "I'm surprised you're dressed and all ready to go before she is."

"I wanted to talk to you about something. You see, Monica invited Juliette to a sleepover at the last minute, and she really wants to go. So she won't be coming to dinner with us."

Patrick's face fell. "Damn. I was looking forward to us spending some time together before I take her to my house for the weekend."

"Oh, I know, honey," Jolene said as she reached out to pat his knee. "She was looking forward to it, too. But this just came up and, well . . ."

"You could have called me on my cell phone. We could have arranged to have dinner another time when she was free."

That's exactly why she *hadn't* called, Jolene thought. She knew Patrick would want to postpone getting together until Juliette was free. "Uh, well, I started to," she said. "But then I thought you and I could still go out and enjoy ourselves." She touched his knee again playfully. "You know, sort of like old times."

He frowned and clearly looked puzzled. He didn't seem to have a clue that his ex-wife was flirting with him. Maybe she was coming on too fast. Back up, Jolene. Give him a little more time.

She cleared her throat. "I thought it would give us a chance to celebrate my winning the lottery," she said brightly.

"That's very exciting and I'm very happy for you, but—"

"Um, I also thought it would give us a chance to talk about some of Juliette's behavior lately," she said, interrupting him. She knew where this was going. He was trying to wiggle out of dinner. "I'm really getting worried. She cursed at me today. The f-word."

Patrick sat up. He looked genuinely concerned. "That doesn't sound like Juliette."

"Some of it is just, you know, growing up. But she's also bitter about our divorce. At least we can talk freely during dinner if she's not there. And it will help if she sees us getting along." The Juliette angle always seemed to work with Patrick. He was full of guilt for leaving his daughter behind when he left Jolene.

"You're probably right," he said nodding. "And since we're both dressed and ready, we might as well go."

"Good. I'll go up and see what's keeping her. We can drop her off on the way." Jolene stood up and paused. "Um, Patrick, do me a favor, hon. Don't say anything to her about her changing her plans. She feels bad about not going with us. She was worried it would hurt your feelings."

He nodded. "I understand."

Jolene breathed a sigh of relief. Her little scheme to get Patrick out to dinner alone was moving along just as planned.

19

BARBARA AND REBECCA walked through the bar area of B. Smith's and entered the dining room to wait for Robin to arrive. The restaurant sat in a corner of Washington, D.C.'s Union Station, a complex of restaurants, shops, and the train station. B. Smith's was elegantly decorated in the Beaux Arts style, and the down-home cooking was a mix of southern, Cajun, and Creole, with dishes such as jambalaya and lemon-pepper catfish. Barbara loved dining there.

"I have some news to tell you both after Robin gets here," Rebecca said, all smiles as they sat in the waiting area.

"Oh?" Barbara said. "Good news, judging from the look on your face."

Rebecca nodded. "But I'll wait until Robin gets here and tell you at the same time."

Barbara nodded just as she noticed Baroness Veronique Valentine walk through the main entrance, looking gorgeous in an elegant black silk suit that showed off her figure. The baroness spotted Barbara in the small waiting area and approached with a warm smile. Barbara stood.

"Why hello, Barbara," Veronique said as they exchanged air kisses. "Small world."

"It seems that way," Barbara said. "How are you?"

"Very well, thank you, Barbara."

Robin rushed up and kissed her mother on the cheek. "Sorry I'm late. I got held up at the office."

"Veronique, I want you to meet my daughters," Barbara said, gesturing with pride. "Robin and Rebecca. Girls, this is Baroness Veronique Valentine."

They all shook hands.

"Your daughters are lovely, Barbara. They're both spitting images of you. Although I see a touch of Bradford in Robin."

"Thank you," Barbara said.

"How is Bradford?"

"He's fine."

"Good. I'm told this is a very nice place to eat," Veronique said. "And if you're here, I'm assuming it must be true."

Barbara nodded toward her daughters. "They brought me here to celebrate my birthday."

"Oh, happy birthday, Barbara."

"Thanks. Are you dining alone?" Barbara asked as the maître d' walked up and told her their table was ready. "If so, we'd love to have you join us."

"No, I'm meeting a friend. But thank you for the invitation." Veronique slipped a beautifully bejeweled hand into her Louis Vuitton bag and pulled out a gold-and-diamond card case. She handed a card to Barbara. "Why don't you call me and we'll get together for lunch."

"I'll do that," Barbara said. She glanced at the crème-colored card, with its delicately engraved black script, then slipped it into her Fendi shoulder bag.

"Enjoy your celebration, Barbara."

"Thank you, Veronique. I'm sure we will."

Barbara and her daughters followed the maître d' to her favorite table in the colonnade. As Robin summoned the waiter, Rebecca leaned close to her mother.

"Is she really a baroness?" Rebecca asked eagerly.

Barbara nodded. "She's American, but she married a European baron."

"She seems normal enough," Rebecca said.

"She *is* normal," Robin said. "I mean, it's only a title."

"Well, yes, but it's still exciting," Rebecca said. She stood up and excused herself to go to the ladies' room as the waiter approached.

"I'd like three glasses of sparkling water in champagne glasses, please," Robin said to the waiter.

"Go ahead and order real champagne for yourself and Rebecca," Barbara said.

"No," Robin insisted. "Water is fine."

Barbara didn't press. It was better for her not to be tempted, as Robin was all too aware.

The waiter brought the drinks, and as soon as Rebecca returned Robin raised her glass. "To the best mother a girl could hope for and to the next fifty-one years."

"I'll drink to that," Rebecca added. "If I can be half the mother you are, I'll be happy."

Barbara raised her glass to her lips. She was proud of these two beautiful young ladies. Robin, the fiercely independent, go-get-'em warrior, and Rebecca, a happily wed wife.

Rebecca sniffed her glass. "Is this water or wine?" she asked.

"Water," Robin responded.

"Why? What's wrong?" Barbara asked.

"Nothing," Rebecca said, a small smile forming on her lips. "Just being careful. In my condition I shouldn't have alcohol."

Barbara gasped and held her breath. "What do you mean, 'your condition'? Is this what you had to tell us?"

"You're pregnant?" Robin guessed with wide eyes.

Rebecca smiled and nodded happily.

Barbara put her hand over her heart. "Oh, Rebecca! That's the best news, honey."

Barbara hugged Rebecca as Robin took one of her sister's hands and squeezed it. "Congratulations, sis," Robin said. "It's what you've always wanted."

"What *she's* wanted?" Barbara said. "I've waited two years to hear this. How far along are you?"

"A little over a month. So don't go around blabbing to everyone yet, Mom. I want to get a little farther along first. Anything can happen in the first trimester."

"That's probably the smart thing to do," Robin said. "Although I'm sure you'll be fine."

"Of course she'll be fine," Barbara insisted. "But if that's what you want, we'll keep it quiet. You have to let me go shopping for the baby, though. In fact, why don't we drive over to Saks in Friendship Heights next weekend?"

"I don't even know if it's a boy or a girl yet."

"So," Robin said. "We can get white."

"Fine. Fine," Rebecca said. "As long as you don't tell anybody until I'm at least three months along."

"I promise," Barbara said. "I won't tell a soul except your father until you're ready. He's going to be thrilled. He'll probably—"

"Speaking of Daddy," Robin said. "He just walked in."

Barbara nearly leaped out of her seat. "Your father? He's here? Where?"

Barbara and Rebecca turned to look in the direction that Robin was facing. Robin nodded toward the doorway leading from the colonnade into the main dining room. "I just saw him go by to be seated."

"He must be here with a client," Barbara said, trying to keep her voice calm. Could it be more than a coincidence that the baroness was also here? Barbara was tempted to jump up and run into the main dining room to see who Bradford was with. But she didn't want to start acting the part of a fool in front of her daughters.

"I'll go tell him we're here," Robin said as she placed her napkin on the table and stood up.

"Ask him to stop by our table for a minute so we can tell him about the baby," Rebecca said.

Robin nodded. "I'll be right back."

The waitress brought their appetizers just as Robin walked off, but Barbara had lost her appetite. She picked up a fork and fiddled with her salad.

"Keith is so excited about becoming a dad," Rebecca said as she picked up her spoon. "Last week he bought paint and brushes. He's going to paint the baby's bedroom pink and blue this weekend."

Barbara put on a smile and squeezed Rebecca's hand. "I'm so happy for you and Keith."

Robin came back, sat down abruptly, and grabbed her napkin off the table. She didn't utter a word, just picked up her spoon and began shoving gumbo into her mouth.

Barbara wasn't entirely surprised by the change in Robin's demeanor. Bradford was up to his old tricks, she knew it.

"What's wrong with you?" Rebecca asked Robin. "What happened?"

"Nothing."

"It's got to be something," Rebecca prodded. "Where's Daddy?"

Robin was tight-lipped.

"Did you see him?" Rebecca asked. "Is he here?"

Robin nodded slowly.

"Is he all right?"

"Yes, yes, he's fine, Rebecca," Robin said. "But I don't think we should bother him. Let's just eat."

Not only had Robin's behavior changed dramatically since she went to greet her father, she now avoided looking into Barbara's eyes. Barbara placed her fork down, dropped her napkin on the table, and stood up.

Robin glanced up at her mother anxiously. "I wouldn't go over there if I were you," she said softly.

"Well, you're not me."

Robin looked down at her plate as Rebecca stood to follow her mother, but Barbara put a firm hand on her daughter's shoulder. "You stay here."

"But I want to tell Daddy about—"

"I said stay here, Rebecca. I'll be right back."

Rebecca sat back down as Barbara took a deep breath and strode through the doorway into the main dining room. She hated being so abrupt with Rebecca. Of course her daughter wanted to see her father and tell him the good news about the baby. But Barbara had a sinking feeling that she needed to see Bradford for herself first.

She looked around the large dining room until she spotted Bradford sitting at a table near the back. She took one step in that direction and then froze. Seated across from Bradford was not Veronique but Sabrina, Bradford's former office assistant and mistress from two summers ago. This was the woman who had driven onto their lawn and crashed into the tent at Rebecca's wedding reception. This was the little bitch who had grabbed a knife from the reception buffet table and brandished it at Barbara until Bradford tackled her. And all because she was upset that she wasn't invited to the wedding.

Barbara's eyes flashed red. So the player was still up to his old tricks. Damn that man.

She marched toward him, dodging in and out between the tables. Bradford looked up and saw her just as she approached, and a guilty smile played around his lips. Barbara stopped at the edge of the table and glared at him without saying a word.

"Barbara," Bradford said, trying to sound pleased to see her. He dabbed his lips with his napkin and stood. "What brings you here? I thought you were staying out in Silver Lake today."

"I'll bet you did," she snapped. *You bastard.* She wanted to scream, but too many people were around, and the last thing she wanted was to cause a scene.

"Um, you remember Sabrina, don't you, Barbara?"

Remember her? How the hell could she forget the woman? Bradford had sworn that his affair with Sabrina was history and that he never wanted to see her again. And now here he was, having dinner with the woman at *her* favorite restaurant.

Barbara was tempted to yank Sabrina's drink off the table and throw it in her face. Instead, she coolly ignored the woman. Still, she had seen enough to notice that Sabrina had folded her shapely petite figure into an expensive-looking designer suit. Where on earth did a twenty-five-year-old secretary get the money for a suit like that? Why she was even younger than Noah. Way younger than Noah.

"What are you doing here, Bradford?" Barbara hissed quietly. "With that." Barbara jerked her head in Sabrina's direction.

Sabrina jumped up. "How dare you talk to me like that," she yelled. A few nearby heads turned in their direction.

"I wasn't talking to you," Barbara said calmly. "I was talking *about* you. So why don't you mind your business?"

Sabrina jabbed a finger in Barbara's direction. "Bradford, you do something about her or—"

"Do something about *me*?" Barbara said indignantly. She turned to face Sabrina head-on. "Why you little—"

"Wait a minute," Bradford said, holding his hands out to interrupt them. "Both of you calm down. Barbara, all we're doing is talking over dinner."

"You expect me to believe that?" Barbara said as Sabrina sat back down and rearranged her napkin in her lap. "And even if it's true, did you have to come *here* with her?" Barbara continued. "This is my favorite restaurant, Bradford. You know that. And in case you've forgotten, she pointed a knife at me at Rebecca's—"

"This happens to be *my* favorite restaurant, too," Sabrina said smartly.

Barbara glared at her. "You mean after KFC or—"

Sabrina jumped up again. "I don't have to take this."

"Barbara, stop it," Bradford said. "Listen to me."

"No, *you* stop. I'm tired of this. This is why you were so interested in what I had planned for today. You wanted to know if I was coming into town because you wanted to be free and clear to come to my favorite restaurant and entertain your little tramp."

"That's it," Sabrina said. "I'll wait for you at the bar, Brad." With that, she turned on her heels and fled across the dining room.

By now, everyone near the table was stealing glances and whispering loudly. Barbara caught a glimpse of Veronique's honey blond hair three tables away, but she was past the point of caring what others thought.

"Go ahead," she yelled at Bradford. "Run and get her."

"Barbara, I'll talk to you when we get home. People are staring. Someone might recognize us."

"Ha! Well, you should have thought about that before you came in here with your mistress, don't you think? I'm sick of talking about it anyway. Nothing ever changes with you." She fumbled with the clasp on her new diamond bracelet.

"I should have wondered why you were buying me so many expensive presents for my birthday."

She yanked the bracelet off her wrist and threw it on the table. It landed in his champagne glass with a splash.

"Barbara, you'll ruin . . ."

She ignored him and whirled around on her heels. Then she remembered the earrings and stopped. She removed them from her ears, stormed back to the table, and threw them at him. He ducked out of the way then stared at her with eyes wide open. She turned and flew.

Barbara reached the table in the colonnade and grabbed her purse. "Come on, girls," she said to Robin and Rebecca. "We're leaving." Barbara signaled the waiter, planning to pay and cancel the rest of their meal.

"We've already done that," Robin said quietly.

They had known what was coming the minute she had jumped up out of her seat, Barbara realized, because they had seen this scene or others like it countless times over the years. Barbara felt a pang of shame as she marched out of the restaurant with her daughters in tow.

J OLENE AND PATRICK dropped Juliette off at Monica's house,
then drove down to K Street for a night at Georgia Brown's.
Jolene couldn't have asked for a more romantic setting. It was a
perfectly clear evening with a deep blue sky, and this was one of her
favorite restaurants. The food was low-country cuisine, with dishes
such as fried green tomatoes served in an elegant dining area with
high ceilings and sparkling chandeliers.

After a dinner of crab soup and southern fried chicken salad, she
and Patrick settled back with crème brûlée and brandy. By the time
Jolene ordered a second round of drinks for them, Patrick seemed
more relaxed with her than he'd been since they had split up. They
talked freely about everything, their conversation drifting from Juliette's teen behavior to Jolene's lottery winnings and plans for the future. It was wonderful to have Patrick laughing and agreeing with
her for a change instead of arguing.

As Patrick chatted on about his job, Jolene smiled and nodded. Once in a while she leaned over just enough to give him a good look down her low-cut suit jacket. She pretended to sip her brandy but she really just let it grace her lips much of the time. She had ordered a second round to get Patrick loosened up, but she wanted to keep a clear head herself. She had big plans for the two of them later that night.

She touched his leg gently under the table with the toe of her Manolo. It was a light touch, probably barely noticeable, but it let him know that she was available. He smiled at her. Maybe he was finally getting the message.

If all went well, Patrick would wake up in her bed tomorrow morning and many mornings afterward. She would see how Pearl felt about *that*.

Following brandy and dessert, they climbed into Patrick's Nissan Maxima and chatted and laughed all the way home. When they pulled up in front of Jolene's house, she gently put her hand on his thigh. "Why don't you come in for a cup of coffee?"

He nodded in agreement so quickly that it surprised Jolene. She had expected to have to do some persuading, especially since Pearl had called him on his cell phone as they were leaving the restaurant. Maybe things between Patrick and fatso weren't going so well after all. Or maybe he still found his ex-wife too hard to resist.

She poured them both glasses of sherry instead of coffee, as Patrick unbuttoned his jacket and settled on the couch in the family room. She wanted him to feel that they could get along again as a couple, and the looser Patrick was the easier that would be. She thought if she could just get him into her bed overnight, the rest would come easy.

"Sometimes I wish we could go back," she said as she sat down beside him.

"Go back where?" he asked as he sipped his drink.

She kicked off her heels and tucked her feet up under her. "To the way things were when we were first married."

Patrick sighed with nostalgia. "Remember when we brought Juliette home from the hospital?"

Jolene nodded and smiled. "You held her almost all night while I got some rest. Wasn't that special? What happened to us?"

"Different goals, different needs. You were always more money and power hungry than I was. Although money's obviously not a problem for you anymore."

"No it's not, thank God. But lots of couples disagree about money. It doesn't mean they have to break up."

"True. But it's different if one of them is also screwing the other's boss."

Jolene was silent for a moment. He'd said it in a lighthearted way, but still. He *would* have to bring that up. She hit him playfully in an attempt to break the sudden tension in the air. "Don't go there. I know I screwed up. I don't know what I was thinking."

She wasn't going to remind him that he had cheated on her during the early years of their marriage. He had even fathered a child from the affair, a daughter he'd had nothing to do with until about a year ago. But she couldn't fault him entirely for that. He hadn't even known about Lee until she had shown up on their doorstep last summer.

"Neither of us was exactly an angel," she said. "Let's leave it at that."

"If you're talking about Lee, the affair with her mother was the only time I was unfaithful to you. You were so depressed about losing your first baby and your family rejecting you that I thought our marriage was doomed from the start. But then I decided that it was wrong to get involved with someone else and I broke it off after only a few weeks. I wanted to do everything I could to work things out with you."

He paused and shook his head. "I was crazy about you then. But nothing I did made you happy. You always wanted more—a bigger house, a fancier car. And that got to me eventually. I guess we're just not right for each other."

She touched his arm. "Don't say that. We were both so young when we got married. I was too immature and stubborn to see how good you were for me. But I'm older and wiser now and I really regret some of the things I did. Men don't come any better than you, Patrick." She slid closer to him on the couch until their shoulders touched.

He smiled down at her in appreciation and they sat together silently for a moment. She noticed that his caramel complexion was flushed with alcohol. He didn't appear to be intoxicated, just very relaxed. She touched his cheek gently. "We get along much better now. Notice?"

"Yes. You know, I still find you very attractive."

A tingle traveled down her back. "Thank you."

She placed her glass on the coffee table, then took his glass and set it down. She swung a leg over his thighs and straddled him.

"Jolene, I don't know about this."

She ignored his protests and licked his ear with her tongue. He closed his eyes, moaned, and leaned his head back. She knew she had him.

She smothered his face with kisses as she removed his jacket and tossed it onto the floor. She had just reached for the top button to his shirt when a phone rang, piercing the hot and heavy air like a dagger into flesh.

Jolene jumped. "Where the hell is that coming from?"

Patrick pushed her off his lap and back onto the couch and grabbed his jacket off the floor. He reached into the inside pocket and pulled out his cell phone.

"Yeah," he muttered into the receiver.

Jolene exhaled with frustration as she straightened her suit jacket. She crossed her ankles and listened.

"Hey," Patrick said softly. "No. I shouldn't be much longer. Will you still be there?"

Jolene rolled her eyes to the ceiling. That was Pearl, no doubt.

Who did she think she was, calling and checking up on him every fucking five minutes? Meddlesome cow.

"Mm-hmm," Patrick said glancing at his watch. "About ten minutes?"

Dammit. What the hell was he talking about? Ten minutes? They needed *way* more time than that.

Jolene crossed her legs at the knees and bounced her foot up and down. It was all she could do to keep from yelling at Patrick. She couldn't stand being ignored, especially when she was horny.

"OK. I'll see you then, baby."

This was too much, Jolene thought as she hastily brushed imaginary lint off her jacket. Now he was calling Pearl "baby." She ought to yank the goddamn phone out of his hand. How dare he carry on like that in front of her.

Patrick said good-bye and hung up. He glanced at Jolene out of the corner of his eye. "Sorry about that."

"Pfft. Why does she have to call you all the time?"

"She's at the house with Lee. I told her I would be back by ten o'clock and it's after eleven."

"So now she's got you on curfew?" Jolene said sarcastically.

"Don't be silly. She's just wondering how much longer I'll be."

All damn night if I have my way, Jolene thought. "Let's not talk about her now," Jolene said. "I don't want to argue. Where were we before we got interrupted?" She threw her leg back over him, but he grabbed her by the waist and sat her back firmly on the couch.

"What's wrong?"

"I really need to go." He stood up, slipped his arms into his jacket, and placed his cell phone back in the pocket.

Jolene stared at him. She was flabbergasted. "You're leaving? *Now?*"

He smiled down at her. "I'm afraid so."

Shit. He was leaving her to go to Pearl? Un-fucking-believable. But she had to stay calm. She had to strategize if she wanted to win

Patrick back. She still believed there was a chance and she wasn't going to give up yet. It was just going to take more work than she had thought.

She stood and straightened her suit. "Well, I'm real disappointed that we were interrupted and now you have to run off. I mean, we were just getting started."

"I'm sorry. I . . . we should never have let things get as far as they did. I don't know what came over me, or you, for that matter."

She grabbed the lapels of his jacket. "Well, *I* know what came over us. You wanted me, Patrick. I could feel it."

"I won't deny that I still find you attractive, Jolene. I already said that. But I doubt things would ever work out between us. We're too different."

"Differences are good for a relationship. They keep it exciting."

He chuckled uncomfortably and gently removed her hands from his lapels. "Sometimes maybe a little *too* exciting for me."

She grabbed his lapels again. "Patrick, please. Listen to me, honey. I've changed, and I really miss you. Juliette does, too, and I know you miss her."

A look of sadness came over Patrick's face at the mention of Juliette. "That is my biggest regret about things not working out between us."

"Then come back to us, Patrick. Come home."

He sighed. "It's not that simple, Jo."

"Isn't it? We were a family before. We can be a family again. All you have to do is move back in with us. Only this time, things will be a lot better. We won't have financial problems like before. Think of all the things we can do with the money I won. Think of Juliette."

He took her hands and cupped them in his own, and Jolene's heart pumped faster.

"I don't know, Jo. And I don't want you getting your hopes up and especially Juliette's if things don't work out."

If things don't work out? That meant he was thinking about it and that maybe things *could* work out. She had to reassure him about Juliette. "I wouldn't tell her about us unless it was a sure thing. You know I would never intentionally do anything to hurt her."

He nodded. "If there is one thing I've always admired about you, it's that you're a damn good mother to my daughter. The best." He squeezed her hands.

She smiled. "Thank you."

"OK. Maybe I'll come by in a couple of weeks, one day after work, and we can talk more. I'll call to make sure Juliette will be around."

"I'll do my best to make sure she is," Jolene said sweetly. If anything, she was going to make sure Juliette was *not* around.

"Good," he said. "But no promises. Understood? We're just talking at this point."

"Right. Just talking." Jolene smiled sweetly as she walked him to the front door. With any luck, the end of the next date would turn out a lot better than this one. She didn't care if she had to lie, connive, and cheat, she was going to get her man back from that bitch.

PEARL TAPPED HER foot as she sat on the couch in Patrick's house and flipped through the pages of *Jet*. She sighed deeply, closed the magazine, and dropped it on the glass coffee table. She placed her hands in her lap. She felt silly sitting in that position, so she picked up the magazine and flipped through it again.

She looked up. She wasn't seeing any of the pages, not really. She couldn't stop worrying about Patrick and when he was going to get back. She glanced at her watch. It had been ten minutes, no, more like fifteen, since she had called over to Jolene's place and Patrick said he was on his way home. And Jolene lived less than half a mile away.

Pearl dropped the magazine back on the coffee table. She was acting like a jealous fool. Patrick had every right to have dinner with his baby's mama. So why was she behaving like this?

Perhaps because his child's mama was Jolene Brown, and Pearl didn't trust that woman at all. They had never gotten along and never would.

If all that wasn't enough, Jolene was also a big flirt. She walked around looking and acting like an expensively dressed whore, always wearing low-cut tops with her boobs hanging out. Not to mention all that fake hair and makeup.

Still, Pearl knew that she had to trust Patrick if this relationship was going to work. She *did* trust Patrick. She just had to remind herself of that every now and then. She picked up the remote control from the coffee table, turned the television on, and flipped through the channels. She soon realized she was doing the same thing with the television that she had been doing with the magazine—not paying attention. Was there any hope for her?

She was placing the remote on the coffee table when she heard the front door open and shut. It was about time. She jumped up just as Patrick walked into the living room.

"Sorry about that," Patrick said as he brushed her cheek with a kiss.

"That's all right," Pearl said, waving her hand in an effort to sound nonchalant. "So how was dinner?"

"It was fine."

"Where did you go?"

"Georgia Brown's."

"Oh?" They had driven *that* far together? "Where is Juliette? I thought she was coming back home with you."

He moved toward the couch and unbuttoned his gray blazer. "Juliette didn't go to dinner with us. She was invited to a sleepover at one of her girlfriend's at the last minute."

"Oh," Pearl said. Her heart began to pound a little faster. So he and Jolene had driven all the way into town for dinner alone. Pearl didn't like the sound of that. "And, um, how is Jolene?"

"Good, good." He stretched his legs. "So, what did you do for dinner?" There was something about the way he quickly changed the subject that didn't sit right with Pearl. His answers to her questions were short, almost curt. But she didn't want to think about that now. It was probably just her imagination.

"I ate at home and then I came over here about nine-thirty, since you said you would be back by ten."

He nodded.

Lordy, Pearl thought. The short blunt responses had turned into no response. She sighed and glanced at her watch. "It's almost midnight and I have to open the salon for an appointment at nine. I should get going."

He stood up. "Fine. Is Lee asleep?"

Pearl blinked as she stood. In the past he had always tried to talk her into staying overnight. Something was definitely different. "She's in her room. She was on the phone the last time I was up there."

"I see." Patrick took Pearl's arm. "I'll walk you to your car."

Pearl smiled stiffly. "Thank you."

There was an odd sound in the air as she picked her shoulder bag up off the stuffed armchair. They walked out the front door and down to the curb. By the time they reached her minivan, she knew what the odd sound was. Silence. In all the months they had been dating, Pearl could never remember such a lengthy silence between them.

He opened the door to the minivan for her and shut it after she climbed in. She rolled down the window slowly and awkwardly, since the little round knob had broken off, and inserted the key into the ignition.

He leaned down and smiled at her through the window. "When are you going to get around to replacing this old clunker?"

So that was how it was? He was spending all his time with his millionaire ex-wife eating at fancy restaurants, and now her van was a clunker. "When I get the money," she said curtly.

His head jerked back. "Sorry. I was only teasing."

Her comment wasn't really fair, she thought. He had been bugging her to replace the minivan for months. "I know," she said. "I'm just tired I guess." She was more upset than tired, but she didn't want to show it. She needed to get away and think. "I'm going now."

He stood up abruptly. "I'll call you tomorrow, OK?"

She blinked, startled that he hadn't kissed her good-bye as usual, and rolled the window back up. She pulled off and looked into the rearview mirror, expecting to see him standing there in the driveway waving at her like he always did. But he was gone.

She hit the steering wheel with her fist. Darn it! He'd slept with her. She *knew* it. The air was thick with something fishy. That had to be it.

Patrick and Jolene driving into town together and dining all alone. Patrick and Jolene going back to Jolene's place all alone. Patrick acting stiff and distant with her. She could put two and two together. Jolene had seduced him.

She pulled the minivan over to the curb and put it in park. She put her hand on her chest and tried to regulate the pace of her breathing. In, out. Slowly.

After her divorce, Pearl had dropped out of the social scene for years and focused on raising Kenyatta. She hadn't wanted the distraction of a man keeping her from doing a good job of raising her son. Then one day she looked up and Kenyatta was an adult waving good-bye, and Patrick was smiling down at her.

She weighed even more back then than she did now, and she couldn't believe that this successful, good-looking man was interested in her chubby self. But he was still married to Jolene then, even if they were separated, and for a while Pearl kept turning him away. He kept calling and stopping by the salon, making her laugh with his wry sense of humor, and eventually she'd given in and gone out with him. They had been a couple ever since.

Now it looked like his ex-wife wanted him back.

Pearl tightened her lips with determination. She banged her fists on the steering wheel. Dammit! Ms. Thang wasn't going to get him back without a fight. When her ex-husband had started messing around with his young white secretary all those years ago, she had given him up without so much as a whimper. That wasn't going to happen with Patrick. This time she was going to fight for her man.

She swung the minivan around and pointed it back toward Patrick's house.

"DID YOU FORGET something?" Patrick asked when he opened the front door and saw her standing there.

Pearl entered and turned to face him. "Actually, it was *you* who forgot something," she said, her hands planted firmly on her hips.

He knitted his brow, obviously puzzled, as he shut the door. "Me? What?"

"This." She reached out, pulled him close, and kissed him on the lips.

B ARBARA LOOKED UP from her desk to see Noah standing before her wearing black jeans and a white cotton shirt. He was holding a single lilac-colored rose in his hand.

"Welcome back," she said.

"Thanks." He held the flower out toward her, and Barbara thought he looked so sweet. "That's a happy belated birthday wish and an apology," he added. "Still friends?"

She smiled as she accepted the rose. "Thank you, Noah. But you don't need to apologize. We're fine."

He shrugged. "I think I stepped over a boundary last time I saw you."

You certainly did, Barbara thought wryly. She had thought about their tender kiss often since that night a few weeks ago, especially after catching Bradford with Sabrina. Sometimes, just before falling off to sleep, she'd found herself wondering what it would be like to make love to a younger man like Noah.

But to act on those feelings would be monumentally stupid. Their lifestyles were so different, and nothing could ever come of a relationship with Noah except sex. She wasn't like Bradford. She couldn't get intimately involved with someone unless she thought there was a possible future in it. Besides, if she got involved with Noah she could lose a friend and a coworker whom she could always count on to help her out.

She waved her hand nonchalantly. "Don't worry about it. Like you said that night, let's pretend it never happened." She held the rose to her nose and inhaled. "Mmm. This was very thoughtful of you. I'm surprised you remembered my birthday. Isn't this a sterling rose?"

Noah nodded and sat in the chair in front of Barbara's desk. "They can be tricky to find."

"They're very hard to grow, even in our greenhouse. Emilio, my gardener, hasn't had much luck."

"Greenhouse, gardener. You lead a charmed life, Barbara."

Yes, but it wasn't without its pitfalls, Barbara thought. It came at the price of a philandering husband who barely noticed her much of the time. She eyed Noah sitting in front of her in snug-fitting jeans and felt her stomach tingle.

"Um, how was Jamaica?" she asked.

"Nice. Saw a lot of my relatives. Perfect weather the whole trip."

She couldn't count the number of times since she last saw him that she had pictured Noah in swimming trunks on a beach, his chestnut complexion glistening in the sun.

"Good. Have you had a chance to check in with Bernice since you got back?" She needed to change the subject to business and clear her head of all the sensual thoughts of Noah. Get ahold of yourself, girl, she thought.

"That's what I came in to tell you. She and Bernard are back together."

Barbara rolled her eyes to the ceiling.

"At least they're still in the market for a house," he said. "And since it's for both of them, they're willing to spend up to two mil."

"Fantastic. Does this mean that Bernice has stopped flirting with you?" Barbara said it teasingly, but immediately regretted the remark. It made her sound jealous. Then she realized that she *was* jealous.

He flipped his hand back and forth. "It depends. Unless her husband's around, it's the same old thing. That's just her way."

Barbara was silent for a moment. She had to stop the jealousy. She had no right to feel that way about Noah. "It's your call."

"No worries. I can manage her just fine. We went to Virginia this weekend. She likes Beacon Hill, but the husband thinks that's too far out. He prefers your neighborhood in North Silver Lake."

"At least they're back together, and you still have a client."

"You mean *we* still have a client. We split the commission on this one. Unless they break up again." He shook his head. "Strange couple. He cheated on her, right?"

"That's what she told me."

"So why does she keep going back to him? I don't understand it."

Barbara smiled thinly. She knew the deal with the Wrights all too well. She had the same love-hate, on-and-off thing going on with Bradford. When he was being good, or she at least thought he was, they got along fine. Then out of the blue, another mistress would pop up and their relationship would quickly speed downhill. Like now.

The night she had caught Bradford with Sabrina at B. Smith's, he came home around midnight. Barbara had been in bed for an hour, tossing and turning, but as soon as she heard Bradford, she switched the lamp off and turned to face away from his side of the bed. She heard his footsteps coming up the stairs and closed her eyes.

"Barbara, are you awake?" he asked softly as he sat on his side of the bed.

She didn't say a word, didn't budge. She was in no mood to deal with him.

"Barb, I think we need to talk about what happened this evening."

She shut her eyes tighter.

"I know you're awake, Barbara. You're a very light sleeper. You probably have the wrong impression about what you saw. Will you sit up and talk to me for a minute?"

Her lips tightened.

"Fine. We can talk in the morning when you've had some time to come to your senses, but I'm telling you nothing is going on with Sabrina. We talk from time to time, that's all. If you had calmed down, I could have had her explain that to you."

There he goes, Barbara thought. Trying to make it seem like she was a jealous fool who needed to calm down and think rationally. Like *she* was the one with the problem. Barbara was sick and tired of this. She had never cheated on Bradford a day in her life, yet he'd had so many affairs she'd lost track of the number. *He* had probably lost track. Sometimes she wondered why Bradford wanted to stay married to her. Why not dump her and be free to fool around as much as he wanted with no wife to worry about?

She opened her eyes but kept her back stiffly toward him. "Bradford, tell me why we shouldn't just get a divorce. Give me one good reason."

"A divorce? Don't be foolish, Barbara. You saw me in a restaurant having dinner with a woman and now you're talking divorce?"

"Not just *any* woman. A former mistress."

"Exactly. Key word there, Barbara, 'former.' "

"Are you sure she's a former mistress? I have a hard time believing that, which is sad in itself. Maybe you're telling the truth, but I can't trust you because you've lied so many times before."

"Look, I told you, those days are over. I'm not running around like that anymore. I have no need to lie. If I had something to hide with Sabrina, do you think I would have taken her to B. Smith's of all places?"

"That's why you were asking me all those questions this morning. You wanted to be sure the coast was clear for your little rendezvous."

Bradford let out a big gust of air. "Barbara, you're imagining things, and I understand why. I haven't been the most faithful husband in the past. But I've changed. Have you seen real signs of anyone else recently?"

"Maybe you're just doing a better job of hiding them."

"Or maybe I have nothing to hide."

She turned onto her back and looked up at the ceiling. "And what about us? We have sex, what? Maybe once every couple of months."

He loosened his necktie and removed it. "I'm not getting any younger, Barb. Things have slowed down."

"All the more reason why you shouldn't try to please more than one woman at a time anymore."

"Barb, please. There is no one else. Only you."

She turned back away from him and pulled the sheet up over her shoulders. "I'm tired, Bradford. I'm going to sleep."

"Fine. 'Cause there's really nothing more to talk about. I've said what I wanted to say."

Her thought exactly. It was pointless. She was done talking. She was done listening. But she still wasn't willing to leave him. Why? What the hell was wrong with her? And with Bernice and all the wives who stayed with husbands who cheated compulsively?

"It's hard to explain," she said to Noah. "But it's difficult to leave someone you've been with for so long. You have history and memories. You have children together, friends, property. You can't just walk away from all that the way you can a girlfriend or boyfriend or even a live-in lover. Bernice probably feels that her life with Bernard is better than it would be without him, even with all his faults."

Noah looked directly into her eyes. "You say that like you've been there."

Barbara arched a brow as Noah rested his elbows on the arms of the chair and cupped his fists under his chin. But she said nothing.

"So why not have some fun of your own?" he asked. "Or do you?"

Barbara blinked. "Some do, and it's tempting for the rest of us but . . ." Barbara paused. Was she revealing too much to him? No, she didn't think so. Somehow she felt comfortable sharing this with Noah. She trusted that it would never leave the room, something she didn't always feel with her girlfriends.

"But what?" he asked. "It seems so unfair not to."

"It probably looks that way on the outside. But I . . . the women probably feel they're getting something in return, a certain lifestyle maybe."

"So it's about money?"

"Not just money. Security, comfort, status . . . Look," she said, smiling awkwardly. "Can we change the conversation? I've already said more to you than I intended to."

"I didn't mean to make you feel . . ." He paused as someone knocked at the office door, and Barbara glanced at her watch.

It was nearly twelve-thirty and she remembered that Veronique was supposed to meet her at the office at noon and then they were going to lunch together. Veronique had called Barbara a few days after the episode at B. Smith's and suggested they do lunch. Barbara was surprised by the call but thought, why not? She had been embarrassed by the scene with Bradford at B. Smith's but she was also curious about the baroness and especially about her past with Bradford.

"Come in," Barbara said.

The door opened and Veronique strolled in wearing a tight-fitting pair of gold lamé jeans that were obviously not from the Gap and a stylish Chanel tweed jacket unbuttoned just enough to reveal a hint of cleavage. On her feet were a pair of three-inch-high black stilettos.

"Hello, Barbara, I'm sorry to be . . ." Veronique paused and glanced from Barbara to Noah and back to Barbara. "I hope I'm not interrupting anything."

"No, not at all," Barbara said as Noah stood and buttoned his sports jacket. "This is Noah Woods, one of my associates here. Noah, this is Baroness Veronique Valentine."

Veronique extended a hand toward Noah.

"A baroness?" Noah said. He took her hand and kissed it. "Fascinating."

"Oh, he's hot, Barbara," Veronique said, smiling at Noah. "Now I'm hoping that I *did* interrupt something." She winked at Barbara.

Noah blushed as bright as his chestnut brown complexion would allow. All the women seemed to develop an instant crush on Noah, Barbara thought. First Bernice, now the baroness. But this was the first time she had seen Noah blush around another woman. Veronique walked in and *poof!* Noah was glowing like a schoolboy.

Barbara smiled. "He has quite an effect on all the women."

"Oh, I don't doubt it," Veronique said.

"You ladies are going to have to stop this," Noah said, laughing. "It's embarrassing."

"Would you like to join us for lunch, Noah?" Barbara asked as she retrieved her purse from a bottom desk drawer. "You can tell us all about Jamaica."

"No, thanks," he said as he glanced at his watch. "I have to meet a client in Silver Spring in about an hour. You two go on and have fun." He smiled shyly at Veronique. "It was nice meeting you."

"Likewise," Veronique said, extending her hand again. "And I'm very sorry you won't be joining us."

Noah bent over and kissed Veronique's hand again. Barbara noticed that he seemed to like doing that. As he backed out of the office, his eyes never left Veronique, and it seemed to Barbara that he had forgotten she was even in the room.

"SO, TELL ME, Veronique," Barbara said as she dipped a shrimp into her cocktail sauce. "How did you meet Bradford?"

"We met in Atlanta," Veronique said as she ate a bit of her Beluga caviar. "He and my ex-husband had some business dealings together and . . ."

"Software?"

Veronique nodded. "Guy's company was much smaller than Bradford's, and Bradford loaned him the money to expand, quite a sum from what I remember."

"You said Guy's company 'was' smaller than Bradford's. He no longer has the company?"

"No."

Barbara wanted to ask what had happened to her ex-husband's business, but something about Veronique's blunt 'no' made her hold back. Guy was an ex, so there could be bad blood between the two of them. It wasn't business that Barbara was concerned about anyway.

"How well did you and Guy know Bradford?"

Veronique put her fork down and dabbed her lips with her napkin. "Barbara, given what I knew about Bradford back then and what happened at B. Smith's last week, I think I know what all of the questions are about."

Barbara stiffened.

"And I can assure you that I don't get involved with married men. I don't need to bother with them when there are so many single men out there who come without a lot of baggage. I hope you believe that."

Barbara relaxed. The baroness sounded truthful. Why would Veronique go to the trouble of befriending the wife of a man she'd had an affair with? It didn't make sense. "Thank you for telling me that, Veronique."

The baroness nodded. "I want us to be friends and I know we can't unless you feel you can trust me. Ask me anything you'd like."

"There is just one other thing. You said, 'given what you knew about Bradford back then.' What does that mean?"

"Well, Barbara. Let's see, how should I put this?"

"You can tell me the truth. I doubt it's anything I haven't heard before. And, besides, this was five years ago, right?"

Veronique inhaled. "Yes, but it's not a pretty picture."

"With Bradford, it rarely is."

Veronique nodded with understanding. "He was coming to Atlanta a lot back then. He had a branch office there."

"Yes. He closed it down a few years ago."

"Well, when I was in Atlanta, there were rumors that he was seeing several women down there."

Women? Barbara thought. Plural? She twisted her lips in disgust.

"Two of whom I knew personally, and both were married. So there was at least some truth to the rumors."

Barbara twirled a shrimp between her fingers. "I see."

"I'm so sorry," Veronique said, knitting her brows with concern.

"No, it's fine. I'm not surprised. Really." Barbara had always suspected something like that had been going on in Atlanta. Bradford had spent a lot of time traveling back and forth during those years, and it was then that her drinking problem was at its worst.

"Can we please change the subject?" Veronique asked, smiling. "I want to talk about something fun."

"Of course."

"Let's talk about Noah." Veronique winked.

Barbara was surprised. Was Veronique interested in Noah? "What about him?"

"He's a real honey, and I saw the way you look at him."

Barbara waved her hand. "Oh, please. I was going to say the same thing about the way he looked at *you*."

Veronique laughed. "With me, I think the attraction is mainly the title half the time."

"Well, Noah and I are just coworkers." Barbara paused as Veronique gave her a "You can't fool me, girl, so don't even try" look.

"I'm serious," Barbara protested. "Whenever I get clients who want to look at houses in Northern Virginia, he shows them around since I'm not licensed in Virginia and he is."

"You mean he's never made a pass at you?" Veronique looked genuinely surprised.

"Um." Barbara paused. She hadn't told a soul about "the kiss," not even Marilyn. It was too private and it was embarrassing that she hadn't resisted more forcefully. She didn't know Veronique well at all, but in a way that made it easier to talk to her, and she was dying to tell someone.

"He tried to kiss me once but I shoved him away. He's only thirty-eight. Compared to me, he's a schoolboy."

"The baron is thirty-four, and I have a feeling that I've got a few years on you."

Barbara blinked. It sounded like Veronique was almost old enough to be the baron's mother.

Veronique tossed her head. "Oh, don't look so shocked. Europeans are much more sophisticated about these things than we Americans generally are. Age is only a number."

"You're right." Barbara shrugged. "Anyway, I probably scared Noah off."

Veronique studied Barbara for a moment, then leaned in close. "Would you want him to try again?"

"Are you suggesting that I have an affair with Noah?"

"Well, why not? Have you ever had one?"

Barbara laughed nervously. "Absolutely not."

"You should. You're an attractive woman."

Barbara sighed with annoyance. Not at the comments coming from Veronique, but because she knew it would be difficult to explain why she'd never had an affair to a woman who knew Bradford's history. "I honestly can't justify it except to say that I would probably feel guilty."

"Barbara, forgive me for what I'm about to say. I don't know what Bradford's been up to recently, but I do know what he was like in Atlanta. And once a cheater, always a cheater has been my experience."

Barbara nodded reluctantly. "Still, it's not just that. Noah and I are so different. The baron may be younger than you are, but you have similar lifestyles, I'm sure. Noah is into blue jeans and baseball caps and hip-hop. I haven't worn a pair of jeans in twenty years and I'm about to become a grandmother."

"We're talking about an affair, darlin', not marriage. You're already married. And you still haven't answered my question. Would you want Noah to make another pass at you? Would you handle it any differently if he did?"

"Would I want . . . Um, well . . . I guess." The fact that she had admitted it out loud likely surprised Barbara more than it did

Veronique. But she had thought of Noah constantly since they kissed. She had hoped her feelings would go away during his vacation, but they hadn't.

"Yes, yes, I would," Barbara stated more firmly.

"Then do something about it."

Barbara leaned in and whispered. "Like what? I'm not the type to make a pass at a man. I wasn't even before I got married."

"Oh, I'm with you there. I'm old-fashioned enough to think that the first pass is the man's job. But women aren't completely helpless. There are things you can do to let Noah know that, well, you've changed your tune about him."

"Such as?"

"You could start with your wardrobe."

"What's wrong with my clothes?" Oddly enough Barbara wasn't insulted by this woman she barely knew asking her probing questions and criticizing her wardrobe. The baroness always looked so young and fresh without looking childish, and Noah had been captivated by her. Barbara was eager to hear whatever Veronique had to say on the subject.

"Don't get me wrong, Barbara. You always look wonderful and I love your Fendi bag. But just because you're almost a grandmother doesn't mean you shouldn't look sexy. And congratulations, by the way."

Barbara smiled. "Thank you."

"Now, what other designers are you wearing?"

"The suit is Dana Buchman, and the shoes are Ferragamo."

Veronique smacked her lips. "Ferragamo? Oh, Barbara. Instead of Ferragamo you should be wearing—"

"What's wrong with Ferragamo for an office shoe?" Barbara interrupted. "I wear the more upper-end designers when I go out someplace special, but—"

"Ferragamo's just too damn practical, darling. You should be wearing Jimmy Choo or Manolo Blahnik on your feet at all times. Prada,

Gucci. And nothing works on a man like a little décolletage. If you've got it, flaunt it."

Veronique looked Barbara up and down then continued. "Now, that watch you have on is nice, but what is it?"

Barbara held her wrist out. "Um, Ebel."

Veronique nodded. "One of the more basic models, I'll bet. A decent watch, but how about an eighteen-karat white gold and diamond Piaget? Something like this." Veronique extended her wrist gracefully. "I noticed at the party that Bradford wears a very nice Rolex."

Barbara focused anew at the diamond jewelry flashing on Veronique's wrist and hands. "It's lovely, Veronique, but all that's never really been me."

"Well it should be. Men love sexy, feminine things on a woman, and Bradford certainly can afford to buy you the best. Frankly, Barbara, after all he's put you through over the years, you've earned whatever you want."

Barbara sighed deeply. She was beginning to like the idea of spicing up her wardrobe but didn't have a clue how to begin. "I wouldn't know where to start looking for those kinds of things or how to pick them out. I'm used to shopping at—"

"Leave it to me, darling. As soon as we're done here, I'll have my driver take us to Friendship Heights. We'll hit Saks-Jandel and a few other shops out there. Maybe even take a drive up to New York one day soon. It's really very simple, Barbara. A change in your wardrobe and hair . . ."

Barbara shook her head vigorously. "No, I'm not changing my hair."

"Fine. Just the wardrobe for now. And I'll give you a few pointers on flirting—subtly of course. Trust me. You'll have Noah eating out of the palm of your hand in no time at all."

"OH, MY," MARILYN said, her eyes growing wide as she looked up from a stack of real estate listings. Barbara walked into the office, dropped her new Louis Vuitton bag on her desk, and twirled around slowly to show off her new outfit, from the snugly fitting black St. John jeans to the tweed Chanel jacket. At least someone appreciated her new look, Barbara thought. Bradford hadn't so much as glanced at her that morning when they passed each other in the kitchen.

But then they weren't talking much these days. In the past, such a lengthy freeze in their relationship would have been a sure route to the bottle for Barbara. But now she had her morning workouts, a job, and a brand-new look, thanks to the baroness and a few shopping sprees over the past week.

"You look fabulous, girl," Marilyn gushed as she batted her eyelashes with surprise.

"It's not too flashy?" Barbara paused with her hands on her hips and struck a pose.

"Not at all. It's stunning. And I love the new reddish hair color."

Barbara touched her hair. Veronique had finally persuaded her to take a trip to Pearl's salon to lighten her drab brown color. When she first got a look at it in the mirror of the salon, she had almost cried, it was such a startling change. And when Bradford had seen it that night and hadn't uttered a word, Barbara was certain she'd made a terrible mistake. She had called Veronique and Pearl, practically sobbing on the phone. They both assured her that the new color was perfect for her, and each day she had liked it more. Still, for your husband not to even notice such a drastic change, or at least pretend not to notice, was a huge blow.

So Marilyn's vote of approval was more than welcome. If Marilyn liked it, that meant the changes were stylish without being overboard, and she could relax. She and Marilyn had known each other for years and had similar taste. And although Marilyn had always been more of a clotheshorse than she was, Barbara trusted her old friend's judgment. Marilyn lived in Fort Washington, just south of Silver Lake, but she used the Silver Lake Country Club twice a week as a guest of Barbara's. That was where they talked about any- and everything, and Marilyn was always full of good advice.

It was Marilyn who had saved her when she was at a real low point in terms of self-esteem about a year ago. Barbara had just discovered that Bradford was having an affair with Jolene Brown. It was the first time he had cheated with someone Barbara knew, and she had taken up the bottle after months of sobriety. Good old Mr. Belvedere had become her constant companion once again. Marilyn finally stepped into the picture and helped her regain her confidence by introducing her to real estate sales.

Marilyn stood, walked up to Barbara, and gestured toward the diamond studs in her ears. "How many carats?"

Barbara touched her ears. "Two each," she said, smiling guiltily.

"Bradford bought them for me, but I usually just wear them when I dress up to go out."

"Well, well. So what brought all this on?"

Barbara shrugged. "Sometimes a girl just needs a change."

"Yes, but I didn't know you had it in you, Barbara."

Barbara folded her arms across her waist. "And what is that supposed to mean?" she asked teasingly.

"Nothing. It's just such a dramatic change for you."

"I did have some help. The baroness."

Marilyn nodded with understanding. "Ah. Now I get it."

Barbara sat at her desk just as a tap came at the door, and they both looked up to see Noah standing in the archway.

"Good morning, ladies," he said, nodding in the direction of each of them.

Barbara smiled. Just the man she wanted to see. "Morning."

Noah looked at Barbara. "I wanted you to know that I'm taking Bernice and Bernard back out to Beacon Hill to look at houses today."

Barbara nodded and stood. She wanted to make sure he got a good look at the new her. "So they're still together, I take it."

He smiled. "Still together."

"Good luck."

"Thanks." Noah waved good-bye and disappeared.

"I'm surprised he didn't say anything about your new look," Marilyn said as she picked up her coffee mug. "He's usually so observant."

Barbara stared ahead as Marilyn left the office with her coffee cup. Marilyn couldn't be any more surprised than she was. Maybe her new look wasn't so appealing to men after all. First Bradford had ignored her, now Noah. Men. Would she ever be able to figure them out?

Barbara had just sunk back down into her chair when she heard another knock at the door. She glanced up to see Noah standing there again. He leaned against the doorjamb and folded his arms across his chest.

"By the way, Barbara, that new look is off the chain."

Barbara raised her brows in puzzlement. "Off the chain? I hope that means you like it."

"Very much. I didn't want to start babbling like a teenager in front of Marilyn, but you nearly knocked me off my feet."

"Now, Noah, I can't picture you babbling about anything. But thanks." She smiled and turned to her computer as he disappeared again. Now *that* was what she needed to hear, she thought. He had no idea how much.

"Um, so . . ."

She looked toward the doorway. Noah was back. "Yes?"

"Hmm," he said, staring at her as he shoved his hands into the pockets of his jeans.

She lifted her brow. "Yes, what is it?"

He shook his head. "Nothing. Just that you look very nice. I already said that, didn't I?"

Barbara was tempted to giggle. She had never seen Noah act like this around her. She had never seen *any* man act this way around her. Maybe Veronique really knew what she was doing.

Barbara smiled seductively. "Yes, Noah, you did."

Noah looked slightly embarrassed and backed away from the door. Barbara's face fell as he disappeared around the corner. What happened? Was it her smile? Something she had said or didn't say? Had she scared him so badly when she rejected his kiss that he was afraid to make another move?

She closed her eyes and rubbed her forehead. This was all so confusing. She felt a headache coming on. The phone rang and she picked it up just as Marilyn reentered the office with a fresh cup of coffee and sat at her desk across the room.

"Barbara?" It was Veronique calling. "How's it going at the office? Did you dazzle them?"

Barbara sighed forlornly. "Hello, Veronique."

"What's wrong?"

Good question, Barbara thought. What *was* wrong with her? She was acting like a fool, batting her eyelashes and flirting with a younger man at the office. Ridiculous.

"Say something, Barbara. Has Noah seen you?"

"Yes."

"And?"

"He saw it. He liked it. End of story."

"Hmm. What did he say?"

"Not much."

"You're awfully tight-lipped about this. When I talked to you last night you were so excited about wearing one of your new outfits and seeing him. Did I call at a bad time?"

Barbara glanced at Marilyn. She was talking on the phone and deep into a Realtor website on her computer. "No, not at all. It just wasn't the reaction I expected. I think I scared him off for good. But that's fine. I—"

"I see. So you're disappointed."

"Yes, and that's annoying. I don't think this is right for me."

"Don't give up so easily. Give it some time. Getting a man to ask you out during office hours can be tricky."

"Do you understand what I'm saying, Veronique? It doesn't matter. *No* time is good for me. In the office or out of the office."

"Oh, Barbara. Don't say that. You have to have more confidence in yourself than that. Although it looks like you might have to make the first move after all."

"No. There's no way I'm going to do that. I—"

"For goodness' sakes, Barbara," Veronique said, cutting Barbara off. "Do you think for a minute that Bradford would hesitate if it were someone he found attractive? Just ask Noah out for lunch or something. What's the big deal?"

Barbara was surprised by the sudden harshness in Veronique's tone. She was always blunt but also calm and collected. Now she seemed to be losing her patience with Barbara. Still, Barbara had her limits. "I'm not ready for that, not even close."

Veronique sighed deeply into the phone. "Fine, Barbara. We'll have to think of something to get the two of you away from that office. Let me think. Oh, I know. Perhaps it's time I went house hunting again, this time in Northern Virginia."

PATRICK WAS COMING over for dinner again, and as Jolene pulled a slinky black dress over her head she couldn't remember being so excited about anything in ages. She slipped her feet into a pair of Gucci heels and checked herself in the mirror.

She had practically shoved Juliette out the door for her double date with some guy named Phillip. Like the teenager she was, Juliette spent more than an hour getting dressed, and even after her friends arrived to pick her up she was still changing. Jolene finally had to insist that she decide on an outfit and be done with it. She wanted Juliette out of the house before Patrick arrived.

Jolene dabbed a touch of Joy Parfum between her breasts then wiggled her dress up and put a little between her thighs. It was Patrick's favorite perfume but only because he had no idea that the spicy scent cost her $400 dollars an ounce at Nordstrom. If he knew that, he'd probably learn to hate it. Patrick could be so cheap, and it used to annoy her to no end.

Jolene glanced at her watch. It was seven o'clock, and Patrick was already thirty minutes late. She skipped down the stairs, ran to the living room window, and peeked out between the drapes to see if his car had pulled up. She stretched her neck and looked up and down the block. No sign of him. She took a deep breath. She hoped Pearl wasn't holding him up. The last time they had gone out together all it had taken was a simple phone call from Pearl to get him up and running off. What he saw in that woman was beyond her understanding.

She heard a car pull into the driveway and lifted the drapes again to see Patrick's Nissan Maxima. A shiver ran down her spine and she tugged the dress's cowl neckline down farther off her shoulders. Black strapless bra, black G-string, everything in place. Maybe later that evening she would give him a little striptease. After dating chunky Pearl, he needed to be reminded what an attractive woman looked like.

She put on her sexiest smile and opened the door. Patrick was standing there holding a single red rose. He looked so handsome in a gray suit and blue silk necktie.

She took the rose and inhaled the scent. "Thank you. That's so sweet of you."

He smiled awkwardly and Jolene thought he actually looked a little shy. She took his hand and led him into the dining room. White candles flickered in the windowsills, Barry White crooned in the background, and the table was decorated with her Tiffany bone china and crystal. She had spent more than an hour setting the right mood. She wanted everything to be perfect for him.

Patrick stopped at the entrance to the room. "Whoa. You did all this for me?"

She nodded. "You like?"

Patrick blinked, and Jolene put her hands on her hips playfully. "You *don't* like?"

"Uh, yes. It's nice. But I wasn't expecting dinner let alone all this."
Jolene almost dropped the rose. "But you said . . . you said—"

"I said I would stop by to talk. We said nothing about dinner. And
where's Juliette? You said she would be here."

"Um, she went to a movie with some friends." Jolene shrugged.
"Last-minute thing."

Patrick pursed his lips. "Not again? You couldn't have had her
wait just a little while to see me?"

"Don't get mad, Patrick. I assumed since it was dinnertime that
you would stay and eat, and then you could see her when she got
back later tonight."

He shook his head with disbelief. "Did it ever occur to you that I
might not be here later tonight? Or that I might have other plans?"

No. It never occurred to her. "How can you have other plans
when you can have *me*? Dammit, Patrick, do you remember what
happened when we went out to dinner a couple of weeks ago? In
case you forgot, we were that far from making love." She held her
thumb and forefinger an inch apart.

"I also remember telling you that things should never have gone
that far. I let myself get carried away, and if I misled you, I'm sorry.
But this has to stop now."

Jolene wanted to scream. This wasn't going at all as she had
planned. She had thought for sure that they would cross the line this
time. And now he was dishing out this crap. How could they have
been so far apart on their thinking about tonight?

She bit her bottom lip. She had to stay calm. OK, so they were on
different tracks now. That didn't mean she couldn't get him back on
her track. All she had to do was lay on the charm. She could work it
like the best of them. She could remember when just the right smile
from her would turn Patrick on like a water hose.

She placed the rose on the sideboard and looked at him solemnly.
"OK. I'm sure you didn't mean to mislead me. It's just that I was so
excited about us spending some time together. When we went out

to dinner, I got to thinking about the way things used to be with us. You, me, Juliette. I spent a lot of time fixing all this for you."

He nodded. "I can see that. But Juliette's not even here."

"I know. If you want I can call her on her cell phone and get her to come home early. Say by about nine? We should be finished eating by then, and the movie—"

"I can't stay that long. Pearl is expecting me later tonight."

Jolene shut her eyes briefly and pretended she hadn't heard that name. She walked up to Patrick and laid her hands on his chest. "Stay for just a bite, then. It's pot roast. One of your favorites."

He looked down at her. "You don't give up easily, do you?"

"No. You know that."

"Man, don't I." He smiled at her. "It's obvious you went to a lot of trouble, so maybe I'll stay and have just a taste."

"Oh? A taste?" she said teasingly and moved closer to him.

"The pot roast, I mean."

"Fine. We'll save the best for dessert." She gave him a seductive look, picked up the rose, and turned toward the kitchen. "I'll go put this in water and fix us some drinks."

Jolene walked into the kitchen and pumped her fist. "Yeah!" she said softly. She had him right where she wanted him. It had taken a bit of work, but that didn't matter now. He was hers for the night. She would see to it.

She opened a cabinet and reached for the bud vase. Just as she placed it on the countertop, she heard an unfamiliar phone ring, probably Patrick's cell. Something told her that she needed to check this out. She walked back into the dining room still holding the rose just as Patrick hung up his cell phone. He looked at her.

"Um . . ." He shook his head. "I'm afraid I won't be able to stay at all."

"Why not? You just said you would stay."

"I know." He sighed. "But Pearl wants me to come now, and uh, really, I think that's best."

Jolene threw the rose at his feet. She had had it with that woman screwing up her plans. Pearl this, Pearl that. "Shit. Don't talk about that bitch in my house. You're here with *me* now."

He backed away nervously. "I'll just see myself out."

He turned and Jolene darted around in front of him. "What the hell is wrong with you? You're going to pass me up for that . . . that fat-assed . . ."

He pointed a finger at her. "Don't go there," he said sharply.

"Well, excuse me, Patrick. But it's true. She's overweight and she combs and presses hair, for God's sake. She looks like something out of—"

"She has a big heart," Patrick snapped. "She's sweet and generous and knows how to treat a man. She raised her son on her own, and she's good with Lee and Juliette. You can make fun of her beauty salon if you want, but she built it from the ground up and it's very successful. I admire so much about her."

Jolene scoffed. "Please. Spare me the sermon."

"Fine. I'm out of here. I made my point. And by the way," he said, pointing at the rose on the floor, "I brought that for Juliette."

He reached out to open the front door, but she planted herself firmly in front of him. "Wait, Patrick. I can't believe you're doing this. You used to be crazy about me. Now you act like you hate my guts. What happened?"

"I don't hate you, Jolene. It's just that I'm looking for something different now, and I don't think you can give it to me. Yes, you're prettier, and, yes, you're more educated and glamorous. You're loaded now, too. But that stuff isn't important to me anymore."

"Well, what else is there?"

"Unconditional love, to start."

"Oh, well, I told you I've changed. I—"

"Look, I didn't come here to get into this. I'll just go."

"What about Juliette? You know how much this divorce has hurt her. Don't you even care about her anymore?" Jolene knew what she was saying was utter nonsense. She was grasping at straws, but she couldn't help it. Patrick was about to walk out on her *again*.

"The fact that you would say something like that tells me a lot. You're not thinking of Juliette or me for that matter. You're thinking of yourself. As always. Now move out of my way."

Tears welled up in her eyes and that startled her. She hadn't cried in years. Then again, she hadn't felt this miserable in years. She had been so certain that she could win him back.

"Please, Patrick, don't do this."

"Move out of my way or I'll move you myself."

He said it so coldly, as if he were speaking to a stranger on the street. She searched his face and for the first time realized that it was void of expression. The loving way he had once looked at her was gone. She stepped aside and in an instant he was gone.

She marched across the floor, stomped on the red rose, and squished it into the carpet with her heel. "Bastard!" she yelled. "Bitch! You can both go to hell for all I care."

The way Patrick blabbed on and on about that woman and her stinking salon made Jolene sick to her stomach. So Pearl fixed hair. Big damn deal. Jolene Brown was a fucking millionaire. She could probably buy that stupid salon ten times over.

Pearl had him mesmerized with that fat pussy of hers. That had to be it. What else could he see in her?

One way or the other Jolene would make that fat bitch pay.

PEARL FLIPPED THROUGH the pages of *Jet* magazine. It was the same one she had been flipping through when Patrick was out with Jolene before. She would have to bring something more up-to-date to read next time she came to visit Patrick. It seemed to Pearl that he was spending a lot more time at Jolene's these days while she sat around and waited.

She dropped the magazine on the table and sat back. Why did he need to spend so much time over there when he had a woman waiting for him at home? There were times when she could swear he was sleeping with Jolene again. Then he would flash that sweet smile—the one that had hooked her in the first place—and she was sure he would never cheat on her. She sighed.

"What you looking so pissed about?"

Pearl jumped and looked up to see Lee standing in the middle of the floor of the living room with her hands on her hips. She wore her usual baggy jeans and baseball cap.

"I look angry?"

"You look like you ready to blow someone's head off."

Pearl shrugged. "It's nothing."

"Daddy ain't home from work yet?"

Pearl winced at Lee's language. "No. He's not here yet. And you know he doesn't like you saying 'ain't.' "

Lee shrugged and glanced at her watch. "He been coming home late a lot. Where is he?"

"He stopped by Jolene's on his way from the office."

"Oh, so that's what you so down about. Figures." Lee chuckled. "For what it's worth, I can't stand that bitch either. Or her stupid daughter. Thinks she's all *that*."

"Look, Lee. I don't want you talking like that around me. Juliette is your dad's daughter, too."

"I call it like I see it."

"What do you have against Juliette?"

"She's a snob, and I don't like the way she looks at my man."

"Who? Phillip?" Pearl smiled. "I didn't know he was your boyfriend, but he seems like a real nice guy."

Lee smiled with pride. "But not the kind I would be messing with, right?"

"I didn't say that. You're a very pretty girl, Lee. I just wish you would dress, um, a little nicer."

Lee spread her arms out and looked down at her baggy jeans. "What's wrong with the way I dress?"

"Nothing, unless you want to look like a boy."

"This is me. You ain't never going to get me in some frilly dress."

Pearl grimaced. "How about a nice denim skirt?"

Lee shook her head. "Uh-uh. Forget that."

"Or jeans that fit? That would be a start. And you could come to my salon and let me do your hair. Something besides cornrows would be nice for a change."

Lee laughed as if she thought Pearl was losing her mind. "No, no, and no."

"All right. But if you ever change your mind, let me know. Does Phillip like you dressing like that?"

"He likes it just fine."

Pearl smiled. "If you say so."

Lee shrugged. "Anyway, I don't trust that bi . . . , uh, witch, Juliette. Every time he comes here, she's all over him."

"I think she's just being friendly."

"Humph. That's too friendly if you ask me. I got my eye on her."

"Probably not a bad idea," Pearl admitted. "But don't act too possessive. Guys don't like that."

"I hear you," Lee said. "Got to walk a fine line. Well, I'm going to work on my summer school paper now." She turned and Pearl shook her head as the baggy jeans disappeared around the corner. Whatever happened to cute dresses and pumps? Girls these days wanted to look too much like guys. Or whores. Pearl was all for women's rights but there had to be limits. She wanted to be equal to a man, not *be* a man. She didn't want to look like a whore either.

But it was nice chatting with Lee. That was the first time they had talked to each other at length when they didn't have to. Maybe Lee was getting used to having her around.

Pearl heard the door open and glanced up to see Patrick step in carrying a dry cleaning bag over his arm and his briefcase in one hand. She was tempted to look at her watch to see how late he was but she didn't want him to feel like she was timing his arrivals.

She went to the door, took his briefcase and placed it on the floor, and kissed him on the lips. Not one of those short quick pecks that they used to exchange when they greeted each other. But one of the big heartfelt kisses that were common when they first started dating and that she had reintroduced the night he had dinner with Jolene a couple of weeks ago.

"So," he said when she let him go. "What have I done to deserve all this sweetness lately?"

She smiled at him. "Nothing special. Can't I kiss my man when I want to?"

He laughed.

She was dying to ask what had happened at Jolene's but she didn't want to appear anxious. "You want some dinner?"

He nodded eagerly. "I'm starving. What did you fix?"

"Pasta and a salad."

"Sounds good," he said as he tossed the dry cleaner bag over the arm of the couch. "Where's Lee?"

"She's upstairs doing her homework. She already ate, but I waited for you. I'll go heat our plates up."

Pearl turned toward the kitchen, but he reached out and grabbed her around the waist. He pulled her close, wrapped his arms around her and looked into her eyes. "I really appreciate how you come around here and help out when you don't have to work late at the salon."

She smiled. "Well, you know me. I aim to please."

"And that you do well." He kissed her on the lips, a long, passionate kiss. Now that really felt like old times, she thought.

"I like it when I come home and you're here. Or did I just tell you that?"

She laughed. "You did, sort of, but that's all right. I love hearing you say things like that."

He kissed her again. It had been weeks since he had been so affectionate with her. She should stop worrying about Jolene and savor the moment. But she couldn't just yet.

"So," she said after the kiss as they stood holding each other. "How is she?"

"How is who? Jolene?"

Pearl nodded.

"She's fine. I stopped by for a few minutes, then I ran some errands. We had some things to work out."

"Oh?"

"I'll tell you about it after we eat."

Pearl let him go and folded her arms. "I've got a better idea. I'll get your dinner after you tell me."

Patrick smiled and pointed at the couch. "Let's sit down."

They sat next to each other and he put his arm around her. "Let's see. How should I put this?"

"Just come out with it."

"OK. Jolene was kind of wanting us to get back together or something, mostly for Juliette's sake. Or that's what she said."

"Uh-huh." So she had been right all along. She knew something like that was up. "And?" Pearl held her breath and waited for his answer.

"And I told her it wasn't going to happen. It would never work out. 'Sides, I got all the woman I need right here." He squeezed her gently.

Thank God, Pearl thought. She looked up at him. "You got that right."

BARBARA CLIMBED THE stairs to the front door of
Veronique's mansion and rang the bell. The butler opened
the door almost immediately and escorted Barbara down a
hallway lined with what appeared to be photographs of the baroness
with her family and friends. In many of the photos Veronique was
posing in exotic locations with celebrities. There was even one of
her and a handsome thirty-something white man standing inside the
White House with President Clinton. Barbara assumed that the
young man was Veronique's second husband, the baron.

The interesting photos helped to calm Barbara's nerves. She had
spent two hours dressing that afternoon and had even called
Veronique twice to get advice. She finally settled on a pair of sleek
white Escada slacks and a lightweight pale pink leather jacket, perfect
for a late June afternoon.

Barbara wasn't even sure why she was here. The baroness had invited her and Noah to a casual lunch under the pretext of discussing houses in Northern Virginia, but Barbara had no idea what to expect. She had come close to backing out at least half a dozen times but had finally decided to come. The worst that could happen would be that she would enjoy a meal talking with friends.

The butler stopped at a set of double doors and opened them to reveal a sunny parlor with a huge fireplace and antique French furniture. Veronique was reclining on a yellow chaise longue in a pair of black silk slacks and a flowing aqua top that contrasted vividly with her hair and skin tones. Noah sat across from her on a small elegantly carved sofa dressed in a casual gray summer slacks and black tee shirt. They both stood as the butler slowly backed out of the room.

"There you are, Barbara," Veronique said as she stood up. The two of them hugged warmly, and Noah stood and clasped Barbara's hands.

"Noah was just telling me about some of the communities in Northern Virginia," Veronique said as she settled back on the chaise longue. Barbara and Noah sat at either ends of the sofa.

"I was describing Beacon Hill to her," Noah said.

"We have another client who is looking at Beacon Hill," Barbara said, thinking of Bernice. "The homes there are custom-built but smaller than what you may be used to, Veronique."

"I'm looking for something smaller than this," Veronique said, waving her arm about. "Something that can be managed with one or two servants when I want to get away but not have to travel too far."

"Great Falls is another area," Noah said.

"Yes," Barbara said. "It has some beautiful views of the Potomac River. Noah knows both areas very well."

Veronique nodded and glanced at her watch. "I'm sure we'll work something out." She stood and Noah immediately rose from his seat. "But now, if you'll both excuse me for a moment, I need to make an overseas call, and as soon as I'm done we'll go in and have lunch. We can talk more then."

When Veronique was sure that Noah couldn't see her face, she gave Barbara a big private wink and slipped out of the room.

Noah sat back down beside Barbara. "She's a fascinating woman."

"Yes, she is," Barbara said as she brushed away an imaginary piece of lint from her slacks.

He swung one foot up over his knee and they sat silently. Now what the hell was supposed to happen? What had she gotten herself into? She used to feel so comfortable around Noah, and they were never at a loss for words. But things felt so different lately.

"Um, how was your weekend?" he finally asked.

"Good," she said. Bradford was out of town so there had been no arguments about other women and that was a good weekend, she thought. "And yours? Another party?"

"Yeah, I partied all weekend."

Of course, Barbara thought. He was young and attractive.

"Not really," he said. "I was kidding. I went out for a drink Saturday night with a couple of dudes from my neighborhood. On Sunday, I went by Blockbuster and rented a video, came home and popped in a microwave dinner. Pasta with shrimp if I remember correctly. They all begin to taste the same after a while. Pretty exciting, huh?"

Barbara laughed. It sounded better than what her evenings were generally like, she thought. Eat dinner with cheating husband when he was home. Eat alone when he wasn't. Argue with cheating husband.

"Sounds to me like you need a good home-cooked meal." Barbara's heart skipped a beat. That sounded so flirtatious, she was surprised by how easily it rolled out. She had definitely extended a line to Noah. What if he didn't bite? She shut her eyes tightly and listened.

"You offering?"

She opened her eyes. Now was the time to back out before she got in too deep for her own good. Go back to sanity, Barbara. Go back to your dull life. Or . . .

"I'd love to fix you a nice home-cooked meal if you're up for it. I make a mean meat loaf." Or she used to when she and Bradford were first married. She wondered if she still remembered how to make it.

"I'm more than up for it."

She smiled with relief. Then she panicked and her heart began to flutter. What had she just gotten herself into?

"When's a good time for you?" he asked.

"Um, when is good for you?"

"How about Friday evening? Day after tomorrow. My place after work?"

"I'll be there." Had she just made a date with a man? A part of her wanted to jump up and run screaming out of the room to the security of her home. She and Noah were starting to engage in an elaborate dance, and their relationship had just taken a sharp turn.

As Barbara searched for a parking space in front of Noah's house near the corner of Fourteenth and U Streets in D.C., she drove past storefront galleries, bookstores, and small coffee shops. The crowded and colorful blocks reminded her how far she had stepped out of her comfort zone. All her close friends lived in big houses, most on large estates in Maryland, and Barbara couldn't remember the last time she had visited someone in the city or someone who rented her home.

This area of town was undergoing a revival, and the air was a lot more funky and congested than what she was used to. Blacks and whites wore their hair in locks and gay couples strolled hand in hand. The suburbs were bland in comparison, with mile after mile of driveways and manicured lawns. She always felt so alive when she came down here, and couldn't think why she didn't get into town more often.

She freshened her lipstick in the mirror above the steering wheel and popped a breath mint into her mouth. Noah hated her smoking almost as much as her daughters did, and she didn't want him to smell on her breath the cigarette she had just stubbed out.

She walked the block to his row house and climbed the short flight of stairs. Just before ringing the bell, she glanced up and down the block, although she wasn't sure why. She certainly didn't have to worry about running into anyone she knew in this part of town.

She tightened the sash at the waistline of her blue denim skirt, raised her hand and knocked softly. Then she closed her eyes and ordered the jitters in her stomach to settle down. She was just beginning to relax a little when Noah opened the door, and in an instant the jitters bounced from her stomach to her throat.

Noah took both of Barbara's hands, led her into the house, and leaned down to kiss her on the mouth. She quickly turned and gave him her cheek. He was going to have to slow down. Yes, it was obvious why she had come, but she was out of practice. She needed to ease in slowly.

"I can't believe you're here," he said as he shut the door behind her. He looked fresh and relaxed in neatly pressed black jeans and a champagne pullover.

"Neither can I." She looked around. Anything to avoid his eyes. "Nice place you have here, Noah. Not at all what I expected."

The furnishings were modern and in good taste. In the living room sat a gray leather couch and plush black armchairs. Brightly colored suede pillows were strewn about the furniture and on the floor. Two end tables were adorned with sleek metal lamps, and a huge, brightly colored abstract painting hung above the fireplace.

On one wall was a built-in shelf where he kept the television, CD player, and piles of CDs. Jazz played softly in the background, and Barbara suspected that the music had been selected for her. The one time she had ridden in Noah's car with him, a rap song blasted from the radio when he started the engine.

"What were you expecting?" he asked. "More of a junky bachelor pad? Loud hip-hop music?"

She laughed. "Probably. Did you furnish it yourself?"

He nodded. "My ex-wife was a decorator, so I learned a thing or two from her. The only things I haven't gotten around to doing are something for the windows, and I need some kind of rug in here. But between teaching school and selling real estate, I'm always working."

"I don't see how you do it all. But you have very nice taste."

"Thanks. I really like the area and I'm hoping to buy this house with the money I make selling real estate. The owner wants to put it on the market now, but I persuaded her to give me a few more months to come up with the down payment."

"What percentage are you planning to put down?"

"I need to put down twenty percent to be able to handle the mortgage. That's another reason I'm not spending any more money decorating right now. Every free dime I get goes toward that down payment. I hope the commission on the Wright house will come through for us soon."

Barbara didn't ask, but she figured this house would probably sell in about the half-million-dollar range given the up-and-coming neighborhood. That meant he needed $100,000 for the down payment, a lot on a teacher's salary. Now she understood why he worked so many hours selling real estate on the side and why he put up with Bernice's constant flirting. She'd had no idea that Noah was depending on the commission from the Wright sale to stay in his home.

"What will you do if the deal doesn't go through?"

He shook his head. "I'll have to move. It's as simple as that. I sell a lot of houses but most of them are under half a million, way under half a million. I'd have to sell five or six more of them to get what I'd get on the Wright house. But I'm not worried. We *will* sell a house to the Wrights."

She smiled. She liked his positive attitude. And if they sold a house to the Wrights, she was going to let Noah keep the entire commission. He obviously needed the money more than she did. If she knew Noah at all, he would object to such an arrangement. So she would wait until they made a deal with the Wrights and then refuse to accept any part of the commission.

"Can I get you something to drink, Barbara? Soda or water, right, since you don't drink liquor?"

"You're right, I don't drink alcohol. Soda will be fine."

"Neither do I really. I just keep a bottle of wine handy for company. Ginger ale okay?"

"That would be nice."

He waved her into the kitchen. "Come on back with me."

"Did you get the things for dinner?" she asked as she followed him. "I should get started on that meat loaf I promised you."

"What you should do is relax, Barbara. Dinner is taken care of. I'll explain in a minute."

Barbara frowned as he removed two chilled mugs filled with ice cubes from the freezer and filled them with ginger ale. He handed one mug to her and shooed her back into the living room.

"I'm waiting," Barbara said as she took a sip.

"Let's sit down first." He picked up two animal-print pillows from a corner of the room and tossed them down in front of the fireplace. "Will this be okay?"

Barbara looked down at the pillows and smiled. She hadn't sat on the floor in ages, probably since Robin and Rebecca were toddlers. But what the heck. She was so far out of her comfort zone now, it didn't matter. "This is fine," she said. She pulled off her shoes and they both sat down.

"Okay," he said once they had settled across from each other on the floor. "About dinner. I got to thinking after we talked at Veronique's and decided that I didn't want you slaving away in my kitchen the first time you came to visit me. I mean, it was very nice of you to offer but . . ."

"I don't mind, really."

"I know and I appreciate it." He touched her knee lightly and briefly startled Barbara. Goodness, she thought. If she was going to get all worked up about him touching her on the knee, what was going to happen if he tried to kiss her full on the lips again? She'd faint at this rate.

"I went ahead and picked up meat loaf from Boston Market instead," he continued. "Is that okay? It's pretty good stuff, to me at least. But what do I know. My usual is microwave dinners."

"I doubt it's as good as my meat loaf, but it should be fine."

"You can cook next time," he said.

Barbara cleared her throat. Next time? Just let me get through this first visit without passing out, she thought. She was sitting on the floor in a young single man's apartment and drinking soda with no idea what would happen next. That she had made it this far was a miracle.

"There's that look again," Noah said.

She blinked. "What look?"

"That faraway look. The one that got me in trouble before."

"Oh, right." She looked away.

"Relax," he said. "No worries when you're here, okay?"

No worries? That was easy for him to say since he wasn't married. And it had been so long since she had been in a romantic situation with a man other than Bradford. Actually, it had been ages since she'd been in a romantic situation *with* Bradford.

In a way she envied Noah. He was young and free, with only himself to think about—no spouse, no children. When he was attracted to someone he could just go for it without worrying about all the consequences because there were none, except maybe getting your feelings hurt.

Still, she hadn't expected to be so nervous with Noah. She wanted to reach out and touch him, to grab some of that youth and freedom. Instead, she took a sip of her soda. "It's all good," she said, using an expression that she'd heard Noah use before.

"Here, let me help you relax." He placed his mug on the floor, got up on his knees, and scrambled behind her. He planted his hands firmly on her shoulders and began to massage them slowly.

"How's that?" he asked.

She closed her eyes. "Mmm. Good."

He rubbed her shoulders and back for about ten minutes, and they began to feel like jelly under his touch. He looked at her and smiled. "You certainly look a lot more relaxed."

"I feel like a new woman," she said, and meant it.

"That's what I like to hear. So, ready for the big tour now?"

So much for relaxing. She wondered how many women he had given this so-called tour and exactly what it included, but she pushed all those thoughts out of her head. Enjoy the moment, girl. It didn't matter how many other women he'd given it to. *She* was here now. "I'd like that."

He stood up and extended his hand to help her up. "Well, this here is the living room," he announced with a wave of his arm.

She laughed. "Lovely."

"And that there is the fireplace. And here, we have the TV, and . . ."

He took her hand and led her around the room, briefly describing the things in it. She found his descriptions of the people in the photographs around the room particularly interesting. Noah had told her that he was born in Florida and that he had moved to the D.C. area to attend Howard University and stayed. She also knew that his parents had divorced when he was only four years old and his older sister, Debbie, was fourteen. But she knew little else about him, since their conversations usually revolved around real estate.

One of the photos sitting on the mantelpiece was of his mother and Debbie, both still living in Florida. Another was of his father, who had been born in Jamaica and had moved back there after the divorce. Noah and his sister had spent their early years shuttling back and forth between Florida and Jamaica two and three times a year. Debbie had been his rock during those times, and they were still very close.

"That's one of the reasons I want to stay here," he said. "I hate moving around now."

Barbara nodded and he led her into the kitchen and pointed to the microwave oven.

"One of my most prized possessions," he said.

Barbara laughed out loud. By the time he led her back across the living room floor and up the stairs, it seemed the most natural thing in the world.

"And this is the bedroom," he said as soon as they entered. It was sparsely furnished but tidy like the rest of the house. He walked around and explained each piece, one by one—the bookcase full of books by authors from Toni Morrison to Eric Jerome Dickey, the patchwork quilt handmade by his mother, the first tennis racket given to him by his father. He pointed to the treadmill in a corner of the room and explained that he used it for an hour each morning before going in to his teaching job.

As he moved around, Barbara noticed that he skipped over the king-size bed, easily the biggest object in the room. Perhaps he was just as nervous about this as she was.

Finally he stopped and turned to face her. He took both of her hands in his and squeezed her fingers. Maybe he wasn't so nervous after all, Barbara thought.

"And this is the bed."

"Hmm," she said softly.

"And this is a boy." He pointed to himself without letting her hands go.

"And this is a girl."

Barbara closed her eyes. It was corny as hell and straight from a movie she had seen a long time ago. She couldn't remember which one. Still, it was the first time anyone had recited the lines to her and it felt very romantic.

She looked up at him, and this time when he leaned in to kiss her, she didn't resist.

JOLENE GOT DOWN on her hands and knees and searched under
the bed of the Capitol Holiday Inn for her G-string. Not there.
She stood and immediately noticed Brian sitting in the chair
near the window in his red boxer shorts and dangling it. She
snatched it from him.

"Damn," he said. "Just trying to help."

She smacked her lips with annoyance. She could feel his eyes
watching her every move as she pulled the G-string up over her
hips, and it disgusted her. *He* disgusted her. But one thing about
Brian, he was always even hornier than she was and that was saying
a lot.

He licked his forefinger and ran it across the table top next to
him, picking up the last remnants of coke they had snorted earlier.
He stuck his finger in his mouth.

She reached down to the floor, grabbed his blue jeans, and threw them at him. "You need to get up off your lazy ass and get dressed," she said quietly but firmly. "And clean that shit up," she said, pointing to the small empty baggie and straw sitting on the tabletop.

"What the hell kind of way is that to treat me," he said as he slipped into his jeans. "When you called a couple of hours ago, I couldn't get over here fast enough for you. Now you ready to kick my ass out. Women. Sheesh."

"I'm not kicking you out," she said. "But I don't have all day."

"Fine with me. Never liked no cheap-ass Holiday Inn anyhow. Air conditioner don't even work half right and it's hot as hell. Don't know why you can't spring for something a little nicer when we meet, all that money you got now."

Jolene was tempted to remind him that the Holiday Inn was probably nicer than his apartment, wherever the hell that was. She couldn't risk running into someone she knew at any of the nicer hotels. But she bit her tongue. There was no need to be uncivil. Brian filled a huge void in her life and he did a damn good job of it. Besides, she needed him to help carry out her plan.

"You didn't mind being hot a minute ago," she said teasingly as she fastened her bra.

He smiled at her as he pulled his T-shirt over his head. "I guess I'll get on back to the office then. Give me a call anytime you want to have some fun."

"Wait." She reached out and touched him. "I'm not ready for you to leave just yet."

He looked her up and down. "You going to dance for me again?"

She smiled wryly. "You should be so lucky. Sit down a minute. I want to talk to you about something."

They sat across from each other in the two chairs next to the window, and he leaned back and stretched his legs. He had on dirty work boots and jeans that were littered with specks of dry paint, yet he looked sexy to her. It was strange how Brian repulsed and attracted her at the same time.

When she won the lottery and quit her job, she'd sworn to herself she was through with Brian. But she couldn't get him out of her system. After Patrick brushed her off a couple of months ago, she began calling Brian again. Sometimes she thought she wasn't right in the head.

"You not gonna propose to me, are you?"

Jolene couldn't help but chuckle. "Stop being silly, Brian. You're good, but not that good."

He lit a Marlboro without even asking if she would mind. Jolene normally never let anyone smoke in her presence but she just fanned the smoke as he blew it into the air. She could make an exception just this once, considering what she was about to ask Brian to do to Pearl Jackson.

P EARL SET THREE Giant grocery bags on the countertop and dropped her shoulder bag in a chair. As she removed the wheat bread and placed it in a drawer, she heard a loud thud. She paused and cocked her head to the side. What on earth was that? In all the months she had been coming to Patrick's house she had never once heard that sound.

Thump! There it was again. It seemed to be coming from the basement, and she wondered if it could be a burglar. She was reluctant to investigate since it was Monday and Patrick wasn't home from work yet. But the girls should be home and her concern for them overcame her fear.

She opened a lower cabinet and removed a cast-iron skillet. Not that she expected to be able to overpower an intruder, but it gave her a small sense of security. She walked briskly out of the kitchen to the top of the basement stairs, paused and listened. Silence.

She held the skillet out in both hands and took a few steps down. Then she paused and listened again. She heard nothing and took a few more steps. As soon as she reached the basement landing she heard a loud clash. She turned in the direction of the sound and saw Lee and Juliette circling each other like two angry cats.

Suddenly Lee lunged and grabbed Juliette's head. She held it in a lock and yanked at the hair weave. Juliette's arms flung about wildly as she struggled to free herself, and together they crashed into the big-screen television set.

Pearl lowered the skillet to the floor and ran to them.

"Stop that!" she yelled. "Stop fighting before you break something."

The girls ignored Pearl. Juliette used the best weapon she had available—her long gel fingernails—to scratch and claw at her enemy. Lee let Juliette loose, then grabbed Juliette's weave at the ends and jerked her around like a rag doll.

Pearl caught Lee from behind as Juliette flung her arms about wildly. Pearl pulled Lee hard, trying to get her to release Juliette.

"Let her go!" Pearl shouted.

Suddenly Lee released Juliette, swung around and smacked Pearl in the eye. Pearl jumped back and held her face.

Lee covered her mouth with her hands. "Oh shit!" she exclaimed. "I'm sorry. I didn't mean to hit you, Pearl."

Pearl didn't say a word. She was stunned. She couldn't believe this child had just smacked her upside the head.

"Are you OK?" Lee asked. She reached out to look at Pearl's eye, but Pearl brushed her hand away.

"What is going on down here?" Pearl asked.

"She attacked me!" Juliette screamed. She was nearly in tears as she pointed an accusing finger at Lee with one hand and rubbed her head with the other.

"I told you to quit messing with my man," Lee said.

Uh-oh, Pearl thought.

"It's not my fault you can't hold on to your boyfriend," Juliette retorted.

Lee lunged after Juliette, and Pearl stepped in between them. Lord knew she didn't want to get hit again, but this fighting over some boy had to end.

"For God's sake. Both of you stop this now. I can't believe you're down here carrying on like this about a guy. I thought there was a burglar in the house." She stared at Lee. "You ought to be ashamed of yourself, beating on her like that."

"Tell her to stop messing with my boyfriend," Lee said, pouting.

"Ghetto bitch," Juliette hissed as she tried to put her weave back into place.

Pearl stuck a finger in Juliette's face. "And you, Miss Smarty Pants, shut your mouth now." She looked at both of them. "Wait until I tell your father about this. He's going to be very upset to hear you two were carrying on like this about some boy. Is it Phillip?"

"She's been seeing him behind my back," Lee said.

Pearl looked at Juliette. "Is that true?"

Juliette swallowed hard.

"Don't lie," Lee snapped. "Two people done told me."

Juliette shrugged. "We went out a few times, but only 'cause he told me he broke up with you."

"That's a damn lie," Lee shrieked.

"Well, he's the one lying, not me. If you're still seeing him I don't want to have anything else to do with him. But he definitely told me he broke up with you, probably 'cause you're so ghetto and . . ."

Lee jumped toward her, and Pearl stepped between them again.

"Stop it, Lee," Pearl said. "Let me handle this."

Pearl took Juliette's hand and pulled her aside while Lee stood with her arms folded angrily. "Don't let me ever hear you call her ghetto again. Do you understand?"

Juliette rolled her eyes and tapped her foot defiantly.

"You're lucky your parents could take good care of you, and raise you in good style. Some kids aren't so fortunate. But that's no excuse to make fun of them. That's just plain mean. And if I ever hear you calling her ghetto again, I'll smack that smirk right off your face. Do I make myself clear?"

Juliette blinked, obviously startled that Pearl would threaten to hit her. "My mother would never approve of you talking to me like that."

"Well, your mama ain't here right now, is she?"

Juliette stuck out her bottom lip.

"Now apologize to Lee," Pearl said firmly.

"For what?" Juliette protested. "It's not my fault she can't keep her man. I don't want him anyway."

"I'm talking about for calling her a ghetto bitch."

Juliette sighed and walked slowly across the room. "I'm sorry for—"

"I want to be able to hear it loud and clear from over here," Pearl said, interrupting her.

"I'm sorry for calling you a ghetto bitch," Juliette shouted.

Lee cut her eyes and looked away.

Pearl looked at Lee. "What do you say to her?"

"I don't have nothing to say to her," Lee said stubbornly.

"Accept her apology. Or do you want me to tell your daddy you beat her up?"

"Apology accepted," Lee blurted.

"She should apologize for messing up my hair," Juliette pouted. "It'll cost a fortune to get this fixed."

Pearl had to fight to keep a smile off her face. Strands of Juliette's brown hair weave were dangling loose all over her head. "She's right, Lee. Apologize."

"I didn't mean to mess up your hair," Lee said.

"Good," Pearl said. "Now go on upstairs, Juliette."

They both headed toward the stairs, but Pearl reached out and touched Lee's arm. "You stay here. I want to talk to you."

"But—"

"But nothing. Come sit down."

They walked over to the couch in front of the TV, and Lee

flopped down. Pearl sat beside her. "Listen. I thought this Phillip was a nice guy. You probably did, too. But if he's telling Juliette he broke up with you and—"

"She's lying. He didn't tell her that."

"I find it hard to believe that she would lie. Have you talked to Phillip about it?"

"I don't need to. And even if he did say that, she didn't have to go mess with him."

"I agree. But you should ask him about it before you accuse her of lying."

Lee jumped up. "I don't want to talk about it no more."

"Sometimes it helps to talk about these things."

Lee kept her back to Pearl, and Pearl thought she heard a sniffle. "Are you crying?"

Lee shook her head. "I'm fine."

Pearl stood, put a hand on Lee's shoulder, and patted it gently. Suddenly Lee turned and hugged Pearl tightly, and Pearl could feel her body shaking with sobs. Pearl was surprised at the sudden change in Lee but glad she could be there to comfort her.

"It's OK," she said softly as she patted Lee on the back. "Go ahead and let it out."

Lee jumped back and wiped her nose with the back of her hand. "But I don't want to cry," she said between sobs. "I told myself I would never cry over some stupid dude." She sniffed and Pearl looked around for some tissue.

"Oh, girl," Pearl said. "Sometimes the worst thing you can do is keep things bottled up inside." She found a few napkins on a side table and handed them to Lee.

Lee dabbed her eyes. "I was wondering why he stopped calling me. Shoot. I'm never gonna bother with dudes no more."

"Don't say that. You're a very pretty girl. Someone else will come along in no time."

"And then what? He'll just dump me for Juliette or a carbon copy of her. No thanks."

Pearl took Lee's hand and patted it. "You know what? I think you could use a little pampering. And school starts in a couple of weeks. Why don't you come down to my salon? I'll fix your hair, do your nails and . . ."

Lee pulled her hand out of Pearl's grasp and backed up. "Unh-uh. You ain't getting me in there."

"Just listen. I know you don't want to look too girlie. And I'm not trying to do that. But baby, I have a son and I know for a fact that men . . . boys . . . like girls to look a certain way."

"Too bad. You're not making me a carbon copy of Juliette."

"I would never do that. You don't have to wear a long weave. We could cut your hair into something short and nice. It would be cute."

"I'm not cutting my hair for some dude."

"It wouldn't be for a dude, baby. Do it for yourself."

Lee wiped her nose with the napkins. "I don't know."

"You don't have to decide now. Just come to the salon with me one Sunday afternoon and look around. I have lots of pictures of pretty hairstyles. If you see something you like, we'll do it. If not, we won't. Simple as that."

Lee shrugged. "I'll go over there with you but I'm not promising nothing."

"Fine," Pearl said. "You just might have fun."

"Can I come?"

They both turned to see Juliette standing at the bottom of the stairs. She had changed into a fresh pair of hip-hugging blue jeans and pinned her hair up neatly at the back of her head in an elegant twist.

Lee took one look and rolled her eyes to the ceiling.

"How long have you been standing there listening to us?" Pearl said, smiling.

"Please?" Juliette pleaded. "I could definitely use some help up here after what she did to me." She pointed to her hair.

Pearl looked at Lee. "It's up to you. This is going to be your treat. I can always take Juliette to the salon another day."

Lee narrowed her eyes. "Uh . . ."

"It would be a nice gesture to let her go with us," Pearl added.

"Tell you what," Lee said. "She can come, I don't care, if you promise not to tell Daddy that we were fighting."

Pearl folded her arms across her waist and pretended to think about it for a moment. "It's a deal. I won't say anything to your daddy as long as you two behave from now on. But if I ever catch you fighting again, the deal's off. You're sisters, for God's sake. Don't waste your time fighting over boys. There are more than enough of them to go around, OK? Now shake on it."

They nodded and shook hands.

"**Y**OU WANT *WHAT*?" Brian asked. He sat up in his chair and turned to face Jolene.

"You heard me," Jolene said as she crossed her legs at the knees.

"Let me make sure I have this right. You want somebody's beauty salon busted up?"

Jolene nodded. She had given this a lot of thought. In fact, it was practically all she had thought about since Patrick rejected her advances a couple of months ago. And Brian was the only one she knew who might be able to pull it off.

"Damn. What the bitch do to you, Jolene?"

"Don't get me started. Just tell me, do you know someone who can pull it off?"

Brian shook his head and slowly exhaled smoke from his cigarette.

"Not offhand, I don't. But I can ask around. You serious about this? 'Cause once you get something like this moving, ain't no turning back, baby."

"I'm dead serious."

Brian stared ahead silently. Jolene could see his brain ticking rapidly. "I'll pay good money."

"Hell, yeah, you will. Shit like this don't come cheap. How much you paying?"

She had no idea what something like this went for. "What's a job like this normally cost?"

"Considering you just want her salon smashed up—"

"Destroy it," she said. "Patrick seems to think the earth moves under that bitch's feet just because she started her own beauty salon." But that would all change if Jolene had her way.

"Er, destroyed then," Brian said. "I'd say several thousand, low five figures."

"Fine. And they can take anything they want, but don't hurt Pearl or anyone in the salon."

"You sure you don't want her thrown around a bit?"

"Yes, I'm sure. I'm not *that* evil. I just want to ruin her business, not harm her physically. Now that I think about it, do it on a Sunday or Monday when the salon is closed. I don't want to take any chances."

"Shouldn't be a problem. Shit. If that's all you want and you paying that kinda money, I can probably handle it my damn self."

Jolene shook her head emphatically. "No, no, no. I don't want you anywhere near that salon. You can be connected to me too easily if you get caught."

"I don't plan on getting caught."

"No, Brian. It's too damn risky. I'll give you a twenty percent finder's fee after the job is done but I want you to get somebody else to do it."

"Yeah, yeah. Fine. It's your money."

"How soon can you find someone?" Jolene's heart was racing at the thought that she might be able to pull this off. That bitch was going to get it good, right where it would hurt the most. She leaned forward, flipped her weave, and tapped the toe of her shoes on the carpet. "The sooner the better."

"Whoa. Take it easy. I'll have to ask around. I should know something within the week."

"Fine. And Brian?"

"Yeah?" he said as he stood up to leave.

"Don't mention my name to anyone. Are we clear on that?"

"Hey, you and me, we got something sweet going on here. But holy shit. What you're talking about now with this woman Pearl . . ." He shook his head. "I didn't know you had it in you."

Jolene smiled slyly. "Now you know."

32

BARBARA HELD THE door open to the Gap for Marilyn, but as soon as they stepped in, Barbara immediately felt twenty years older. It had been years since she'd entered one of these jeans outlets. It was noisy and crowded and assaulted her nerve endings. But Noah wanted to take her to an out-of-the-way restaurant in Frederick, Maryland, that evening and he said the place was cozy and laid-back. She wanted to wear something a little less ritzy than St. John jeans.

Barbara smiled as she thought about Noah and their first night together. And the second and third. In the six weeks they had been together, she hadn't gotten around to cooking for him yet. They spent almost all their time together talking about everything from real estate to books when they weren't getting to know each other's bodies from head to toe. Noah liked to explore in bed, and she had discovered that she liked being explored.

Noah was sweet and attentive. And he made her feel so special. From the moment she stepped into his house until she'd left, all of his attention was focused on her. He was always trying to get her to smile or relax. And, most exciting, he wanted to please her in bed. It had been ages since Bradford had tried to please her. She had forgotten what it felt like until now.

"Barbara?"

She snapped to attention at the sound of Marilyn calling her name and looked to see her friend holding up a pair of blue jeans.

"Sorry," Barbara said. "My mind wandered."

"I'll bet," Marilyn said wryly. "Girl, you are hopeless."

Barbara smiled with embarrassment. She knew that Marilyn only halfheartedly approved of her affair with Noah. Although Marilyn said she understood why Barbara might get involved with another man given Bradford's history with other women, Marilyn thought that Noah was far too young for Barbara.

Barbara looked at the jeans Marilyn was holding. "I don't think they're right for me. They're cut too low on the hips."

"Well, that's all you're going to find in here," Marilyn said as she replaced the jeans. "That's what kids wear nowadays, you know."

Barbara ignored the "I told you he's too young for you" tone in her friend's voice, but as they searched the clothing racks, Barbara began to see that Marilyn was right about low-cut jeans being all she would find at the Gap. How depressing. They spent thirty minutes searching, until finally Barbara found a pair of waist-level jeans with a slender leg cut. She decided to buy two pairs, since it seemed they were a rarity. She also picked out several casual tops.

"Lunch?" Marilyn asked as they left the store.

Barbara shook her head as she glanced at her watch. "Sorry, but I need to get back. I'm meeting Noah in a couple of hours."

Marilyn didn't say anything. She didn't have to. Her silent look of disapproval and the tightening of her lips spoke volumes. Barbara was beginning to regret telling Marilyn about Noah. But she and Marilyn had been the best of friends for so long. They shared everything, and it wouldn't have felt right hiding the relationship with Noah from her closest friend.

"Barbara Bradford?"

Barbara looked around to see Ellen Johnson, one of her neighbors in Silver Lake. Ellen lived on a huge estate near the Silver Lake Country Club. She was always immaculately dressed and coiffed, and today was no exception.

"Hello, Ellen. How are you?"

"I'm fine. And you?"

"Just great," Barbara said, and introduced Ellen to Marilyn. All the while, Barbara couldn't help but notice that Ellen was checking her out thoroughly, from the designer jeans to the casual sandals. "Well, you're certainly looking different these days, Barbara. You look so fresh. And happy."

"Thank you."

Ellen glanced down at the Gap bags Barbara was toting. "Shopping for Rebecca and Robin?" she asked.

Barbara gripped the bag handles tightly. "Um, yes, as a matter of fact, I am," Barbara said, relieved that Ellen had answered her own question and saved Barbara from having to think up a lie.

"Well, tell them I said hello. And Bradford. How is he?"

"Oh, he's fine," Barbara said. "Tell Marlon and the kids I said hi."

They walked in opposite directions, and Barbara breathed a sigh of relief. "Nosy busybody," Barbara muttered under her breath.

"Well, what do you expect?" Marilyn said. "You've changed, Barbara. You even look different. People are going to ask questions."

"I deserve some happiness, Marilyn," Barbara said firmly.

Marilyn sighed. "Of course you do. I just worry about what it will do to you in the long run. All new clothes and now you're risking meeting him in public places. Even if you're going to out-of-the-way places, you and Bradford are so well known. Does anyone else know about you and Noah?"

"Only Veronique."

"You told *her*? You barely know her."

"We've become friends lately."

Marilyn sighed deeply. "What does she think about it?"

"She's happy for me. She helped us get together."

Marilyn frowned. "That explains a lot. She's influencing you."

Barbara shook her head. "Absolutely not. I'm an adult. I can make up my own mind."

"Well, can you trust her to keep her mouth shut? What if she tells someone and it gets back to Bradford? Have you thought about that?"

"Veronique wouldn't do that."

"I hope you're right."

33

PEARL UNLOCKED THE door to her salon, and Lee and Juliette ran inside, giggling like schoolgirls at a pajama party. They called them sleepovers now, but to Pearl they were still plain old pajama parties.

"Wow, this is nice," Juliette said as she slipped out of her jacket and looked around.

"Not bad," Lee agreed.

Pearl smiled proudly. She had worked in many salons owned by others while Kenyatta was growing up. When she had finally saved enough to start her own, she found an old building in a strip mall not far from Silver Lake and had it renovated with all of the best features from the salons where she had worked before. One wall was covered with mirrors from floor to ceiling, and she had stations for three other salon workers, all with the finest equipment. She had an area for manicures and pedicures, with two luxurious leather vibrating chairs.

Juliette hopped up onto one of the leather chairs. "This is what I want."

"We'll do one thing at a time," Pearl said. "Hair first, then foot massages. OK, Lee. Hop on up." She patted the back of her salon chair. "You're getting a perm, cut, and style."

Lee looked reluctant as she ran her hands over her cornrows. "I don't know about this."

"It can't get much worse," Juliette said, only half joking.

"Don't start that," Pearl said sternly. "You want your turn?"

"Sorry," Juliette said.

Lee cut her eyes at Juliette and slid into the chair. Pearl threw a smock around her.

"Don't make me look like no hootchie mama up in here," Lee said.

Pearl laughed. "Now why would I do that?"

"Can we get color?" Juliette pleaded. "I wanna be a blonde when I go back to school."

Lee rolled her eyes skyward.

"No," Pearl said firmly. "You're too young for that, and I don't want your mama coming after me."

"She wouldn't care," Juliette said.

"Well, I do," Pearl said. "No color."

Pearl unbraided Lee's hair and let it fall. Lee had a nice head of thick dark hair, but it looked like she hadn't had a professional cut recently, if ever.

Pearl proceeded to transform Lee's hair as Juliette stood beside her chatting and giving pointers and tips. An hour later, Pearl was working on Juliette as Lee sat under the hair dryer and flipped through the September issue of *Essence* magazine.

After Pearl finished with the hair and the foot massages, Juliette reached into her purse and pulled out a little red bag of cosmetics.

"You carry all that crap around with you?" Lee asked as Juliette removed foundation, loose powder, blush, eye shadow, mascara, and lipstick from the bag.

"Watch the mouth," Pearl said.

"Sorry," Lee said.

"I never leave home without it," Juliette said. "You need to start carrying a purse, too, girl. You should always have lipstick. Want me to do your face? I'm good."

"Pft. No way."

"Let her do it," Pearl said. "You can always wash it off and, who knows, you might like it."

"OK, but I'm letting you put this gook on me just this one time."

Juliette worked on Lee's face and then her own as Pearl washed out the sink and swept the floor. Then Juliette and Lee stood in front of the mirror oohing and aahing over how they looked. Pearl watched and smiled. They both looked lovely, and it was nice to see them making an effort to be nice to each other for a change. She had given Lee a short sassy cut that matched her fiery personality, and she had cleaned up Juliette's weave. Juliette had begged nonstop for color the whole time Pearl worked on Lee, and Pearl finally relented and gave her a few soft blond highlights.

"You're a diva now," Juliette said. "They won't even know you when we go back to school next week."

"Oh, please," Lee said, primping her hair. "I do look kinda hot, don't I?"

Pearl rolled her eyes to the ceiling. "Oh, no. What have I done? Created two monsters?"

After pedicures, they walked back to the car with Juliette and Lee laughing and chatting about their new hairdos. Pearl drove them to Jasper's for lunch.

"I'm glad to see you two getting along better now," Pearl said after they had ordered from the menu. "And I know your daddy is happy about that, too."

"It took me a while to get used to Lee," Juliette said. "But she's all right."

"Likewise," Lee said to Juliette. "We're nothing alike. But you're not so bad. At least, I found out that I couldn't trust Phillip when he started fooling around with you. I broke up with him."

"So did I," Juliette said. "That's one thing we have in common."

"You have more than that in common, you know," Pearl said. They looked at her doubtfully.

"We're like night and day," Juliette said.

"You have the same father, and he adores you both."

They glanced at each other and smiled.

"I like having a sister," Juliette said. "I never really liked being an only child. I mean, I like the part about being spoiled and all. My mom will get me just about anything I want, but I like having a sister better."

"Well, I was never spoiled, but I have to admit that having a sister is cool."

They finished their meals then piled into Pearl's car for the ride home. They found Patrick waiting for them in the living room. He looked up from the television set as they entered and did a double take.

"Where are my daughters?" he asked as he pretended to look around for them.

Juliette and Lee giggled and Patrick wrapped his arms around them. "You both look beautiful." He ran his hands over Lee's new haircut. "And this is a big change. I can't get over this."

Lee pulled away from him. "Hey, man, watch it," she exclaimed as she patted her hair back into place. "Don't mess up my hair."

"Uh-oh," Patrick said with mock despair. "Now, I've got *two* divas."

"Tell me about it," Pearl said.

Lee and Juliette slapped high fives. "Divas in the house," they exclaimed as they danced around the room.

34

BARBARA LAUGHED SOFTLY into the telephone as Noah told her one of his cute jokes. Bradford had left early that Sunday morning to go to the office—or so he'd said. For all she knew he was with one of his mistresses, but she wasn't going to worry. All she really cared about was that she had some time to chat freely with Noah until Bradford returned and they had to get ready for a dinner party at Marilyn's that night.

They would be out all evening, and Barbara had wanted to hear the sound of Noah's voice before leaving. So she sat in her bathrobe on the white love seat in the sitting room off the master bedroom and dialed Noah's number from the antique phone on the end table. She had planned to talk to him for about ten minutes before stepping into the Jacuzzi for a leisurely soak. That ten minutes had quickly turned into an hour.

"You always crack me up," she whispered.

"Good, 'cause I love to hear you laugh. When am I gonna see you again? Tonight?"

"No, not tonight, I'm afraid. We're going to a dinner party."

"Oh, right. At Marilyn's. Tomorrow afternoon then? After I get off from work at school?"

"I'll try to meet you . . ." Barbara stopped speaking. Bradford had poked his head in the doorway between the sitting room and bedroom and was looking straight at her. Damn stupid carpeting, she thought. She hadn't heard a thing.

"Um, so you think the Wrights might put a contract on that property here in Silver Lake sometime soon?" she said as she sat up straight.

"He's back, right?" Noah whispered into the phone. "Call me later tonight after you get home and he's in bed. We can make love over the phone."

"I'll definitely get back to you later on that. Bye." She hung up and stood, tightening the belt to her bathrobe.

Bradford set his briefcase down on the small white antique desk in the room. "Who was that?"

"That? Oh, um, just Noah from the office."

"On a Sunday evening? You seem to be talking to him an awful lot recently."

"Business is booming."

"Uh-huh. What's gotten into you lately, Barbara?" he asked, turning to look at her.

"What do you mean?"

"You're dressing differently, spending a lot more money on high-end casual clothes, for one thing. Blue jeans, low-cut silk tops. Even when you go to work you look different now."

She shrugged. "I want to look good for my clients and sometimes that means looking younger. Or trying to. Why? Am I going too far with it?"

"Actually, no. It's a nice change. I just wondered why now and why you're talking to Noah on the phone all the time."

Barbara cleared her throat. "Noah thinks Bernice and Bernard may finally have found a house they both like here in Silver Lake. You know the one the developer is building near the country club?"

"Oh, yeah. Nice house. Well, they've been looking—what? Almost six months now?"

"They keep flip-flopping with the divorce, and she's very picky." Barbara strolled toward the bathroom. "I won't be long."

"Wait a minute," Bradford said. "I'm not done yet."

Barbara held her breath. Bradford was obviously getting suspicious. Maybe someone had seen her somewhere with Noah. They had been very discreet over the past couple of months, spending most of their time together at his place. They had been out together only twice outside of work—to a restaurant and bowling alley, both times way out in Frederick, Maryland. Still, Bradford had friends and business partners all over the place.

"Yes?" she said finally.

"You've also been spending a lot of time on the phone with Veronique lately."

She nodded. "We've become friends."

"I wouldn't have expected that. You have so little in common."

"She's a lot of fun. I like her."

"What do you two talk about?"

Barbara shrugged. "Girl stuff. Shopping, hair." Men, or rather one man in particular, she thought.

"Mm-hmm. Does she say much about Atlanta? Or her ex-husband?"

"Very little. Why?"

"Nothing. Just curious."

Barbara frowned. It was unusual for Bradford to take such an interest in her girlfriends. But then again, Veronique was different from her other friends, and she supposed it could simply be curiosity. "Anything else?"

"Not about that but about a business trip," he said as he sat on the love seat and removed his shoes.

"Yes?"

"I have to go to Seattle for several days."

"Oh?"

He smiled proudly. "A huge telecommunications deal with U.S. West."

"That's wonderful, Bradford."

She used to hate it when Bradford went away on long trips. She always suspected that he was either taking another woman with him or meeting one wherever he traveled, especially if he refused to take her along with him. But things had changed. With Bradford out of town, she would be able to spend whole nights with Noah, rather than only a few hours at a time. He could even come over here in the evening after Phyllis had left for the day and leave in the morning before she arrived.

"So. When will you be leaving?"

"In a few weeks. First Monday in October. I have a meeting that Tuesday morning."

"I see. When will you get back?"

"That Friday or Saturday morning, depending on how things go."

Hmm, Barbara thought. That would leave her at least three nights with Noah and possibly four. "Well, good luck with your meetings. I'm sure everything will turn out fine."

Bradford frowned. "Good luck? That's all? Normally you would be asking if you could tag along to do some shopping."

"Um, well, yes. I do wish I could go. But I promised to show houses to a client that week." That was a lie. Barbara hadn't shown a house in ages and had no plans to do so. She still went to the office once in a while, mainly to see Noah, but she had cut her work hours way back. To be successful at real estate took too much time, time she didn't have, especially now that she was seeing Noah and helping him decorate his house. She had kept up the pretense of still working in real estate only to have excuses to get out of the house to see Noah.

"Postpone it," Bradford said.

"I . . . I don't think that's a good idea. I could lose my client."

"What about Noah? Don't you sometimes fill in for each other?"

"Well, yes, but I don't want to do that with this client. I, um, don't want to split the commission."

"My, my, Barb, getting greedy, are we? It's not like we need the money."

"It's not about the money, Bradford. It's about me closing this deal by myself." Or spending time with Noah, she thought. "You said yourself that I needed to 'think big.'" She made quotation marks with her fingers.

"Is this about the deal with Bernice and Bernard Wright? If it is, I can talk to Bernard. He'll . . ."

"No, Bradford," Barbara snapped, and immediately regretted it. He was already suspicious enough. "It's not Bernard," she said calmly.

"Suit yourself," Bradford said. "I'm just surprised that you'd pass up a chance to shop on Rodeo Drive."

Barbara's eyes lit up. "You didn't say anything about Los Angeles."

"I wasn't planning to go to L.A., but we could stop there for the weekend if you wanted to do some shopping."

Barbara paused. Rodeo Drive was very tempting. And Bradford's sudden interest in taking her along on one of his business trips would have flattered her at one time. But no, she'd take a moment with Noah over all the baubles in L.A. any day.

"Maybe another time, Bradford."

He stared at her with obvious surprise as she left the room and entered the master bath. She shut the door and sat on the edge of the Jacuzzi. Bradford was obviously getting suspicious. Sooner or later she was going to have to come up with a better story than showing houses.

She turned on the water, reached for her bath oil, and poured in a few drops. Did she feel guilty about spending all this time with another man? Yes, in a way she did. Was she going to stop seeing him? No. She was learning to live with the guilt because, frankly, Noah was worth it. He made her feel years younger. He made her feel wanted. Bradford could give her clothes, cars, houses, jewels, and trips all over the world. But he didn't know how to give of himself.

And if she couldn't get what she needed from her husband, she would get it elsewhere. She was tired of doing without. It was as simple as that.

She turned the water off, slipped out of her bathrobe, and sank down into the bubbles. She rested her head on her little white bath pillow, closed her eyes, and pictured Noah in her mind.

J OLENE DECIDED TO take a detour on her way to the mall that
Monday evening just so she could drive past Pearl's hair salon.
She looked out the window of her Bentley and saw the shop sit-
ting there, looking shiny and nice as usual. Even worse, Veronique's
Rolls-Royce was parked outside with her snooty chauffeur snoozing
as he waited. Jolene knew that the salon was normally closed on
Monday, so the baroness must be getting special treatment.

Shit. It had been nearly six weeks since she and Brian had first
talked about her plan. Just when was he going to get the fucking job
done? Brian's cell phone service had recently been cut off because he
hadn't paid his bills, so Jolene dialed her old office on the car phone
and got her former secretary on the line.

"Donna? It's Jolene."

"Jolene. How are you?"

"I've been better. Is Brian Watson there?"

"I haven't seen him, but I saw his supervisor Ricardo painting an office down the hall. Want me to ask him if he's seen Brian?"

"Yes, please. And call me right back on my car phone the minute you hear something."

"Dammit!" she yelled as she pressed the button to hang up the phone. Bastard never got to work on time. And what the hell was taking him so long to find someone to do the job?

She tapped the steering wheel impatiently and pulled her Bentley onto the beltway. She was doing eighty miles an hour by the time the phone rang, and she slowed down to fifty-five as she pressed the button and answered.

"Jolene Brown here," she said into the speakers.

"Hi," Donna said. "Brian just got in. I told him to call you. He said he would as soon as he can get to a phone."

"Good," Jolene said and hung up. She hated having to go through other people to contact Brian. No doubt Donna was wondering why the hell she was calling the office painter when she no longer worked at HUD. But when she wanted something done she expected it to get done promptly.

The phone rang again and she pushed the button to answer.

"Hello?"

"Yeah, you looking for me?"

"What the hell is taking you so damn long?"

"I'm doing the best I can."

"Is there a problem?"

"Yeah, people who do this shit don't exactly grow on fucking trees."

"Very funny, Brian. How much longer will you need?"

"I talked to several people. I think I'm getting close."

"Why don't you just place an ad on the fucking Internet. Exactly how many people did you talk to?"

"Maybe four, five."

Jolene gasped. "Are you mentioning my name?"

" 'Course not. I'm not stupid."

Jolene didn't say anything. She knew better than to push Brian too far. "Well, call me as soon as you get someone. And Brian . . ."

"Yeah?"

"Can we get this going sometime this year?"

"Yeah, yeah."

Jolene hung up and gritted her teeth. She knew that a job like this took careful planning, and she was trying to be patient, but she couldn't stand the sight of that salon much longer. She would give Brian another week, and if he couldn't get the job done she would start looking for someone else. Pearl Jackson had completely ruined her life with Patrick, and that fat bitch was going to pay for it.

She pointed the Bentley toward the fast lane and pressed the accelerator.

PEARL BUTTONED HER wool jacket against the night air as she left Jasper's and headed back toward her salon. She and Veronique had eaten a late leisurely dinner after she finished working on the baroness's hair. Veronique was fun to talk to, and Pearl loved hearing stories about her life in Europe during the private Monday afternoon sessions. She even got a chance to ride in the Rolls-Royce on the way to the restaurant. It was her first time riding in such a fancy car with a chauffeur. She smiled. She could get used to living like that in a hurry.

She was just going to stop back at the salon briefly to straighten up, then she was going to go home and rest to get ready for the upcoming workweek. Barbara Bentley would be visiting tomorrow as soon as she finished her workout at the club, and two women were coming to interview for a position as a stylist.

As she walked by the picture window of the salon, she noticed that the light in the storeroom was on. That was odd, she thought. She could have sworn that she had turned off all the lights before leaving for dinner with Veronique.

She approached the door and rummaged through her purse for the keys. She kept them on a separate key chain since there were so many of them—one for the main entrance, one for the back entrance, which she rarely used, one for the storeroom, and another for a small safe she kept to store cash in until she could get to the bank to deposit it.

She opened the front door and immediately sensed that something was amiss. She stepped inside, flipped the main light switch, and gasped in horror. The place was a mess. All three sinks had been ripped out leaving gaping holes in the wall, and water was everywhere. Jars of hair and nail products had been flung about in piles on the floor. The cushions to her precious velvet couch and leather salon chairs had been ripped to shreds. And the big beautiful mirrors that covered one wall of the room had been smashed to smithereens. Pieces of shattered glass lay everywhere.

Pearl nearly screamed at the sight. For a second, she thought she was in the wrong salon. Then she heard a noise from the back storeroom. Her heart told her to flee but her head held her in place. She had spent a lifetime and fortune building her dream salon. She had to know who was trying to destroy it.

She stepped gingerly through the glass and water on the floor and peeked into the storeroom. Shelves had been knocked over, boxes and bags of supplies were strewn about, and a window had been smashed. She paused, trying to decide whether to go farther or pick up the phone and call the police, when a man holding a crowbar appeared in the doorway.

Pearl stared in horror. "Oh, my God. What are you doing?"

The man sprang toward Pearl, and she jumped aside as he dashed past her and flew out the front door. She chased after him, screaming at the top of her lungs.

"Help! Help! Somebody stop him."

He ran down the block and jumped into an old sedan with chipped blue paint. Pearl tried to get close enough to read the numbers on the Maryland tags, but he flew around the corner before she could make them out.

She sank down to the curb and several people stopped to see what the ruckus was about. An older man ran up to her. "Are you all right? What happened?"

Pearl put her head in her hands and sobbed. "I'm ruined," she said over and over again. "I'm ruined."

PATRICK HELD PEARL'S hand as they stood outside the salon and she answered the police officer's questions. Three police cars were parked in front of the salon, lights flashing, and a small crowd of curiosity seekers had gathered nearby.

"So he was a light-complexioned black male, average height, and probably about thirty-five to forty," the officer said as he wrote on a notepad. "You said he had a crowbar. Anything else you can remember about him?"

"The car. I'm not sure of the make, a Ford maybe. Blue, with the paint peeling off. I know I've seen that car around here before. I just can't remember where now."

"Think about it and call us if it comes back to you. Anything else?"

Pearl shook her head. "No, it all happened so fast."

"I understand."

"What about some of the people here," Patrick said to the officer. "Maybe some of them saw him or the car."

"We have an officer questioning potential witnesses now. A couple of them claim to have gotten a good look at him as he ran off. We'll catch this guy. He doesn't seem too smart."

Pearl choked back a sob at the memory of the man appearing in the doorway of her storeroom wielding a crowbar. Patrick squeezed her fingers in support as the officer handed her a business card. "Take this. And if you think of anything else, give me a call."

Pearl's son, Kenyatta, drove up just as the officer walked toward the crowd of people. He jumped out of his car and hugged his mother. "What happened, Ma?"

"Some dude broke in and trashed everything," Patrick said.

Pearl sniffed and leaned on Patrick's shoulder. "It's terrible. Everything I ever worked for. Gone."

"At least you're safe," Patrick said.

"And you have insurance, Ma," Kenyatta said. "We'll just start over."

Pearl reached out and took Kenyatta's hand. "Oh, baby. It's not that easy. I won't be earning a dime until I open up again."

"I'm just sorry you came back in the middle of it," Patrick said. "He could have harmed you."

"You saw him?" Kenyatta asked, eyes wide with surprise.

Pearl nodded. "Maybe it's a good thing I did. At least I was able to call the police right away and give a description of him and the car. Whoever is responsible for this, I hope to God they catch him and put him away for a long time to come."

J OLENE PEDDLED THE exercise bike faster as she lifted one end of
the white towel draped around her neck and dabbed the sweat
off her forehead. Brian had called yesterday afternoon and said
the job was going down that night. He would call her on her cell
phone Tuesday morning and utter the word "done," if it was successful or "no go" if not, then hang up.

"Just remember, no one gets hurt," she had reminded him. If anyone was injured this would escalate into a whole different game and
a very ugly one at that. Her ass was on the line here and she had to
be sure they were all on the same page—she, Brian, and whoever he
had found to do the job. "Just vandalism. That's all. Understand?"

"I understand. You don't have to worry about a thing. Just sit
your ass tight until you hear from me. Later now."

"Later."

Since Jolene's request, the conversations between her and Brian had gotten shorter and shorter. The thinner the trail between them, the better all around.

For a while it had looked like it was never going to happen. Then suddenly last night someone had popped up. Brian refused to divulge the guy's name in order to protect Jolene if something went wrong, and that was fine with her. She didn't care who did it as long as it wasn't Brian.

Just thinking that they might actually pull this off excited her. This was power and it was exhilarating. Patrick thought Pearl was so damn special because she had her own beauty salon. And Pearl probably thought she was Miss Thang since the baroness had become a regular customer. Well, presto! Not anymore. Not if Jolene had anything to do with it.

She smiled and glanced around the exercise room. She needed to wipe this smirk off her face or people would think she was nuts. But she hadn't felt this good since she had won the lottery. She was even back to exercising three times a week.

She had slacked off with her exercise routine long enough. She was a millionaire and she was going to get back into shape and put her life back together. As soon as Brian's accomplice finished the job on Pearl, she was going to pay Brian his finder's fee and get him out of her life. She deserved a better man than that ignorant jerk.

She was also going to throw the biggest damn party Silver Lake had ever seen, bigger than the one she had two summers ago when she moved into her house, bigger than any of Barbara Bentley's affairs, bigger even than the baroness's.

She reached for the towel and mopped the back of her neck. She glanced at her watch. It was already close to ten o'clock. Why hadn't Brian called yet? Maybe the guy who was supposed to do the job had backed out at the last minute. Or maybe something had gone wrong and the guy got caught. No, no. She wasn't going to think that way. She was going to think positive thoughts. The job had gone down without a hitch, and Pearl's beauty salon had been smashed beyond repair.

Jolene's thoughts were diverted when she noticed Veronique entering the exercise room wearing snugly fitting black workout pants with a bold red stripe down the side and a matching top. Jolene was surprised. Since she had starting coming back to the club she had never seen the baroness. She figured a woman as wealthy as Veronique would have a private workout room in her mansion.

Jolene watched out of the corner of her eye as Veronique strode across the room in her direction. Should she speak? Jolene hadn't been in touch with Veronique since the baroness had called at the last minute to decline the invitation to her luncheon last spring. Jolene smacked her lips at the memory. That had been so rude, but it had happened months ago. Besides, Veronique had replaced Barbara Bentley as the queen bee of Silver Lake, and Jolene would love to have the baroness at her party.

It certainly wouldn't hurt to try speaking to her. "Hello," Jolene said, smiling and slowing the bike down as the baroness walked by. "How are you, Veronique?"

To Jolene's delight, Veronique stopped and smiled broadly.

"Jolene, how nice to see you. I'm doing well. And you?"

Jolene nodded and marveled with envy at how slim and fit the baroness looked. She seemed to have not one ounce of fat anywhere on her body. "I'm just fine," Jolene said. "You look fantastic. Have you been coming here to exercise very long?"

"This is my first time."

"Oh, well, if you need me to show you anything at all, just ask."

"I'll do that, Jolene. Thank you."

"And if you have the time, maybe we could grab a bite to eat at the restaurant here a little later?"

"That sounds fine."

Jolene glanced at her watch. "In say an hour and a half?"

Veronique nodded. "I'll meet you there. I need to run now, though. My aerobics class is starting. See you soon."

"Hell, yeah," Jolene muttered under her breath as the baroness walked off. She was tempted to jump off the exercise bike and dance around the room. But she had to stay calm. After all she was now a wealthy woman like the baroness. A lady of leisure who worked out, dined, and shopped during the day while all the little people went to work.

Jolene's cell phone rang and she grabbed it from the tray near the handlebars and put it to her ear.

"Done."

Jolene sucked her breath in at the word coming from her phone. For a moment she was speechless. She had pulled it off? Just like that? It was scary how easy it was.

"Thanks," she muttered when she found her voice. She was about to hang up when she heard Brian say something else and she hastily put the receiver back to her ear. Dammit, this was not the time to chat.

"What did you say?" she snapped. They had agreed—one word each, no conversation.

"I said there was a problem. Trashed the place like you wanted, even pulled the sinks out of the walls. But . . ." He paused.

Jolene stopped the bike and her heart flipped. "Well, what?"

"The bitch showed up right at the end. She saw me."

Holy crap. Pearl saw Brian? "You went with him? You weren't even supposed to be there," Jolene whispered.

"There was no 'him.' I decided to do it my damn self. I need the money."

"Shit, Brian," she hissed into the phone. Shit, shit, shit. "Are you fucking crazy?"

"What the hell do you care who did it as long as it got done?"

"You were supposed to find someone who has no connection to me. What the hell is wrong with you?" It was all she could do to keep her voice down. She wanted to scream. She wanted to reach through the phone and grab this idiot by the throat.

"I couldn't find anybody I could trust."

She jumped down off the bike and walked to a corner of the room. "Why was she even there? The salon is closed on Mondays."

"Fuck if I know, but she damn sure showed up for some reason."

"You didn't hurt her, did you?"

"Nah, but that bitch saw me, and I don't like that."

"Neither do I, dammit. You have screwed up royally." A woman walked by and stared at Jolene strangely. "I have to go. We'll talk later."

"When do I get my money?"

"When and where we planned," she said. They had agreed to meet briefly at the Holiday Inn the following Tuesday evening so she could pay him the finder's fee. "Or did you fucking forget that, too?"

"Fine. See you later. And be sure to bring the the finder's fee and the dough for doing the job."

Jolene snapped the antenna back into place and closed the phone. She had no intention of meeting that fool anywhere anytime soon. If Pearl or anyone else recognized him during the break-in and an investigation led to him, she had no doubt it would lead straight to her.

How could he be so stupid? How could *she* have been so stupid to trust that fool to do this right? Jolene was tempted to jump up and run out. She needed to get away and think. But she was meeting the baroness for lunch and couldn't possibly miss out on that. She took a deep breath. She would meet Veronique as planned and then go home and think things through carefully. She had to be sure she had covered her tracks.

38

BARBARA SMILED AT Noah from across her hot tub and sipped her ginger ale. He looked so sexy under the light of the moon, with the ends of his dreadlocks dangling in the water. But he also looked uneasy.

"You look uncomfortable," she said, touching his leg with her toe.

"Do I?"

"A little, yes."

He smiled slightly. "Maybe I'm not used to lounging around in Bradford Bentley's hot tub with his wife while he's away on business."

So that was it. He was worried about her husband. Bradford had a hold on her life even when he was twenty-seven hundred miles away. She rubbed Noah's leg with her foot. "Relax. I told you he won't be back for three more days at least."

Noah laughed. "I'm usually the one telling you to relax. Now look at you. Miss Chilling Out."

"That's because I know there's no way Bradford will be back anytime soon."

"You're sure about that? He won't come back early?" Noah grabbed his chest and feigned a heart attack.

"I've never been more certain of anything in my life. Bradford has never returned early from a trip in more than thirty years of marriage. I think I know my husband."

Noah grabbed her foot under the warm water and cupped her toes in his hand. "Hmm. Well, it's worth the risk to spend some time in this hot tub with you."

Barbara leaned back, rested her head on a small plastic pillow, and looked up at the full moon. Bradford was out there having too much fun, probably with a woman, to return early. In the past, she would have been drowning herself in a bottle of booze or lounging around and smoking a pack of cigarettes while he was away. Now she was having fun, too.

It was gorgeous out here with the soft light of the moon shining down on them and the water of the hot tub keeping them warm in the fall night air. She always felt so alive around Noah, so free. Something about him made all her worries disappear, and she barely even thought about cigarettes when she was with him. Maybe it was his way of taking things in stride. She didn't think she'd ever seen him lose his temper, even with some of their most trying clients. One of his favorite sayings was "No worries," and that seemed to be the way he lived his life. Some of it was youth, but a lot of it was just Noah.

"C'mon," she said teasingly, as she wiggled her toes in his hand. "No worries, tonight, huh?"

He smiled wickedly and fumbled beneath the water until he came up with his swimming trunks. He tossed them over the side onto the deck. "As you wish. Now it's your turn."

"Uh-uh. I don't know about that. What if a neighbor sees me?"

"Out here? You can barely see your nearest neighbor's pad. It's so dark and the houses are several acres apart, most with trees hiding them."

"They could have infrared binoculars," she said firmly. "They're nosy people."

Noah shook his head and smiled at her playfully. "You're not worried about them seeing a man with locks get into your hot tub with you, but you're worried about them seeing you toss your swimsuit over the side?"

"It doesn't make much sense if you put it that way, does it? OK, so here it goes." She slipped out of her suit and tossed it up onto the deck.

His smile deepened. "You look beautiful in this light, Barbara."

"Why, thank you, sir. So do you."

"Now, I have just one more request. Can you let your hair down? Or will your neighbors throw a hissy fit about that too?"

"If I don't keep it pinned up the steam will make the ends frizz up."

"So?" He slid over next to her, reached up, and unpinned the French twist at the back of her head. Her hair fell down softly over her bare shoulders. "There," he said. "That's better. You know, sometimes, I don't think you realize how pretty you are."

"It's always wonderful to hear you tell me that."

"I would think you hear it all the time. When you first told me how old you were I was shocked. I always assumed you were about my age, maybe a little older because of the way you dressed. I mean, you always looked nice but in a mature, sophisticated kind of way. I never would have guessed that you were over fifty in a million years, especially now that you're dressing more hip."

Barbara laughed softly. "I'm surprised you didn't run in the other direction when I told you my age."

"Why would I? I've always been attracted to older women.

My last long-term relationship was with a woman in her late forties."

"Really? You never told me that. What attracts you to older women?"

He shrugged. "It probably has to do with my sister. She was a big influence in my life. We were always being shuffled between our folks, and sometimes my grandparents, but Debbie was always there looking out for me. If you were to see her, you would never know how strong she is inside. She's petite and kind of reserved, and people assume that she's meek. Big mistake. She's one tough lady. You're like that, too. On the outside you have this very reserved demeanor. You can be sweet and soft, but there's also a quiet strength about you."

In listening to him describe her, Barbara felt that Noah knew her better than Bradford did. Noah certainly seemed more interested in trying to understand her than Bradford ever had been. With Bradford it was all about Bradford—his business deals, his looks, his golf game. Noah was such a refreshing change.

"How do you feel about *my* age?" he asked. "And the twelve-year difference?"

"Thirteen years," she corrected. "Not that I'm counting."

He laughed.

"Honestly, though, it doesn't bother me as much now as it did at first. I mean, we're both adults. Once people reach their thirties, I think differences in age shrink."

He nodded. "It shouldn't bother you, 'cause it means nothing."

She rested her head on his shoulder. "That's what I like about you, your attitude about life. You're able to let things slide right off your back. I worry about every little thing. I'm trying to learn from you."

"Stick around, kid," he said as he stroked her hair. "I've got a lot to teach you. I just wish we didn't have to sneak around. There are so many places I'd love to be able to go with you. Museums and galleries, bookstores, movies, concerts. I'd even like to travel out of town. I'm getting tired of looking at the four walls of my little house."

"I love your house and that neighborhood. I don't know why, but I feel liberated there. Maybe because it's so far removed from my world. All this can get depressing at times." Barbara stretched out her arms.

Noah looked doubtful. "*This* gets depressing? That's hard to believe. You've got it made here."

She sighed. "I guess it looks that way. But the things you have to put up with. The people can be so rigid and unforgiving if you step outside of the box—if you shop in the wrong stores or drive the wrong car or wear the wrong clothes. And God forgive you if you live in the wrong neighborhood or even if you're just seen there."

"So my place near U Street is an escape for you?"

"Yes. And I mean that in the most positive way."

He nodded. "Glad I can be of help."

"But I thought we could use a change of scenery. That's why I jumped at the chance to invite you here when I found out that Bradford was going to be out of town."

He squeezed her shoulder. "I'm glad you did. What do you think he would do if he came home and caught us?"

"Are you still on that? He's not coming back."

Barbara stood up and reached for her towel. Bradford was the last thing she wanted to talk about now. She had much too little time with Noah as it was. When she was with him she wanted to focus on them. She took his swimming trunks off the deck and held them out toward him.

"C'mon," she said. "Let's go inside."

"What for? It's beautiful out here."

"I'm ready to go upstairs where I can hold you without worrying about the neighbors."

He took the swimming trunks from her and tossed them back onto the deck. He pulled her down on his lap, towel and all. "The neighbors aren't thinking about you," he said softly, his voice a little hoarse. "But I am and I don't want to have to wait until we get upstairs."

39

"I'LL BE LATE coming home tonight," Bradford said as Phyllis poured him a fresh cup of coffee. "I'm taking a client to dinner."

Barbara glanced up from her copy of the *Washington Post*. "I'll be late, too," she said. "I have a showing this evening." Not a total lie, she thought. She would be showing Noah plenty after he got off work.

"How's that going?"

"You mean showing houses? Oh, you know. The market has really slowed down. Lots of looking, little buying."

"Did Bernice and Bernard ever sign a contract on the house here?"

"Yes, finally. They went back and forth for so long that I was beginning to give up. But we go to closing next month."

"Why didn't you tell me? Congratulations. Should be a nice commission."

"Yes it will be, but I'm letting Noah keep my half."

Bradford put down his copy of the *Wall Street Journal* and stared at her, eyes wide. "You're giving him *all* of the commission?"

Barbara nodded.

"May I ask why the hell you're doing that? I brought Bernard to *you*, not him. You don't have to give him a damn thing."

Barbara knew this would anger Bradford, but it was better that she tell him up front. Bernard was likely to mention the sale to Bradford, and Barbara didn't want it to look like she was hiding anything. All their financial accounts were joint, and Bradford, with his ever watchful eyes, would surely wonder what had happened to her commission check. "Noah did almost all of the work for the sale and he needs the money for a down payment on his house or he'll lose it."

"How generous of you," Bradford said sarcastically.

"He needs it a lot more than we do, Bradford."

"That's his problem, not ours. You two seem to have become awfully tight lately."

Barbara swallowed hard. "Well, I mean, we've been working together closely with the Wrights and . . . and now with Veronique."

"Veronique? Veronique Valentine? She's looking for another house?"

Barbara nodded.

"You didn't tell me she was in the market for a house and that you were working with her."

"It's recent and I don't have to tell you everything, Bradford. You almost never express any interest in my work."

"You still should have told me about Veronique."

"Why? You mean like you told me about your dealings with her ex-husband in Atlanta? About lending him money to grow his business?" Barbara also wanted to mention all the women Veronique said he fooled around with down there, but she didn't.

He grimaced. "She told you about that? What else did she say?"

"Not much."

"She runs her mouth too damn much from what I remember about her. She's a troublemaker, always meddling in people's affairs. You've changed since you started spending so much time with her."

"You can never be happy for me, can you, Bradford?"

He frowned. "What the hell does that mean?"

"You don't want me to sell real estate, not to Veronique or anyone else, because it makes me independent."

Bradford sighed, picked up his newspaper, and stood up. "You do whatever you want with your part of the commission. But I wonder why the hell you sell real estate if you're going to give away your commissions to anyone who needs the money."

She took a sip of her coffee. She had made up her mind to help Noah, and the less said on the subject the better.

As soon as he left the kitchen she put her cup down and jumped up. She had a full day with a literary committee meeting that morning, and then she was going to meet Veronique for lunch at the Ritz and shopping at the mall until it was time to hook up with Noah at the Hilton in Tysons Corner, Virginia.

She was a little worried about meeting Noah at a hotel, but it couldn't be helped. He was having his house painted that week, and unless they wanted to wait until the job was finished this was the only alternative. At least Tysons Corner was all the way around the beltway and far from her life in Silver Lake.

Sometimes Barbara felt as if she were addicted to Noah. If she had to go more than a couple of days without seeing him outside of work she felt empty. She could never get enough of him, and it wasn't just the sex. It was the wonderful way he made her feel when she was around him.

She wished they didn't have to be so sneaky. She wanted to tell the world that she was Noah's woman. That she, Barbara Bentley, age fifty-one, was with a man thirteen years her junior and they were crazy about each other.

Thank God she and Bradford were rarely intimate anymore. They had slept together only twice in the four months since she'd started seeing Noah, and that was more than enough as far as she was concerned. Whenever she was with Bradford, she thought about Noah, whether they were having sex, eating together, or out attending a charity event. But not once had she thought about Bradford when she was with Noah unless Noah brought him up.

"SO," VERONIQUE SAID, as she picked up her caviar fork and smiled at Barbara from across the table at the Ritz. "How are things with you and Noah?"

"I can't remember being so happy."

"It shows, Barbara. You're glowing. I'm happy for you."

"We can't stand being apart. We're meeting this evening."

"At his place?"

"Actually, out here at the Hilton. He's having his house painted." As soon as she said it, Barbara worried that she might have revealed too much. But she was so happy about Noah and wanted the world to know. Veronique was the only person with whom she could share all the delicious details of her affair. Marilyn was still her closest friend, but she clammed up whenever Barbara mentioned Noah.

"Oh?" Veronique said, raising an eyebrow. "So that's why you had me meet you all the way out here in Northern Virginia. Lucky you."

Barbara sighed. "At times I'm so confused. He's hinted around that he wants me to move in with him. I want to be with him, too, but that's a big step."

Veronique put down her caviar fork and stared wide-eyed at Barbara. "Whoa. I'm shocked."

"At what? That he wants me to move in with him?"

"That you talk like you're thinking of doing it. This sounds serious."

"I'm definitely falling for him."

"And he for you, obviously. I never thought it would go this far."

Barbara laughed nervously. "That obviously would be a whole different lifestyle. I just don't know."

"Do you still have feelings for Bradford?"

Barbara paused. "Good question. Yes, of course. Not the same feelings we had when we were first married, but I'll always love Bradford in a way. We have so much history together, and he can be very generous. But I'm tired of the lack of emotional attention. And all those years of him fooling around, even if he has stopped or slowed down—it's taken a toll."

Veronique nodded. "I understand what you're saying. Can I offer some advice?"

"Sure."

"You've got a good man in Noah, someone who treats you the way you deserve to be treated. That's so hard to find in this world. Whatever you do, darling, don't let him get away."

40

BARBARA STEPPED INSIDE the lobby of the Hilton in Tysons
Corner, Virginia, and adjusted her big Gucci sunglasses and
mahogany mink coat. She didn't dare remove the glasses all
through check-in, in hopes that they made her more difficult to recognize. And she didn't dare remove her mink coat, as she was wearing nothing beneath.

She got the keys from the clerk and rode the elevator up to the
second floor. Once inside the room, she removed the sunglasses and
tossed them on the bed, along with her black Prada handbag.

She looked around. There wasn't much to see—four walls, a bed,
a couple of chairs and nightstands with lamps, the Bible, and the
bathroom. It was a typical hotel room, the kind she hadn't been inside in years. When Noah mentioned getting a room in Northern
Virginia, she was tempted to suggest that she get them a suite at the

Ritz but thought better of it. The last thing she wanted to do was make Noah feel that his money and choices weren't good enough for her.

She sank down on the edge of the bed and tapped her Gucci boot as she waited for Noah. The enormity of what she was planning to do—greet her lover wearing nothing but a fur coat and boots—hit her like a tidal wave on the beach. She was cheating on Bradford, and in a way, even on Robin and Rebecca since he was their father. It felt sleazy.

She jumped up. It seemed like the four walls of the room were collapsing around her. Had she lost her damn mind? She was nearly naked and sitting in a common hotel room waiting for her lover to come and make her feel good for an hour. She was having wild and crazy sex with a man much younger than she was and loving every minute of it. She was even talking to others about leaving her husband. She was no better than Bradford or one of his sluts.

Her heart beat wildly. How the hell could she even think of leaving Bradford for a younger man who was barely able to support himself? She had to stop this nonsense. She grabbed her glasses and bag and ran to the door. She was going to buy a pack of cigarettes, go home, and talk some sense into herself.

She yanked the door open to see Noah standing there with a smile on his face and a single sterling rose in his hand.

"Hello, beautiful."

She blinked as she stared into his face. Her pulse slowed down, her breath evened out. Seeing him flushed all the anxiety out of her heart. She barely knew this man, really, and yet he had a powerful hold on her.

She took the rose, pulled him into the room, and let her coat fall to the floor.

TWO HOURS LATER, Barbara slipped into her mink, adjusted her sunglasses, and smiled as Noah put on his shoes. She didn't know why she had felt so flustered earlier. Yes, what she and Noah were doing was huge. She had no idea what the future held for them or how things would turn out. But if any man was worth taking a chance on, it was Noah. He had just proved that to her.

"Ready?" he asked.

"Not really. I wish we could stay all night."

He walked up and tilted her shades so he could see into her eyes. "I'll go down and pay the man for ten more nights if you want. Just say the word."

"One of these days I'm going to take you up on that."

"But not tonight, right?"

"I can't."

"You could," Noah said. "You *won't* is a better way to put it."

"What on earth would I tell Bradford on such short notice?"

"I know you can't do it now. But tell him you have to go out of town for a real estate conference next week or the week after that. And then let's go somewhere together. Jamaica, Nassau."

"I've never gone away without Bradford, except back home to visit my family. He would get real suspicious if I went that far without him." She laughed bitterly. "He would probably have me followed."

"Why? He's always going out of town on business without you."

She nodded. "You're right. Maybe I will one day."

He put her glasses back down on her nose. "So, you want to leave first? Or me?"

"I guess I should go first."

He tapped her nose. "Until tomorrow then, beautiful."

Barbara touched the doorknob. She hated parting from him. It felt as if a part of her soul was being ripped away. She turned back to face him and took his hand. "Let's go down together." She wanted to prolong her time with him as much as possible.

He lifted his eyebrows. "You sure?"

She nodded. "I'm sure. We're not going to run into anyone all the way out here."

They rode the elevator together, smiling at each other all the way down. They stepped out and walked across the lobby, and she waited near the main entrance while Noah dropped off the key. He joined her and held the front door open, and she stood aside as he gave their parking tickets to the valet. Then he came and stood beside her.

Relax, Barbara Bentley, she thought as she looked around the hotel entrance. The likelihood of running into someone in Fairfax County was slim. And if she did see someone she knew, she could always say she was leaving a meeting.

As she removed her dark sunshades and smiled up at Noah, out of the corner of her eye she noticed a man exiting the hotel's revolving doors. She turned to look and her heart nearly exploded. It was Bradford.

Barbara gasped so loudly that Noah turned and glanced at her, then in the direction in which Barbara was staring. "Oh, shit," he muttered under his breath.

Noah had never met Bradford but he obviously recognized him, probably from the countless times her husband's face had appeared in newspapers. Barbara licked her lips. Here she was standing naked under a fur coat with another man in front of a hotel. She was tempted to turn and flee through one of the side doors.

That plan vanished when she realized that Bradford had just seen them. The look of shock on his face as his eyes traveled from her to Noah and back to her was something Barbara had never seen before. Bradford rarely lost his composure but he looked like he was going to lose it now.

She stared down at the pavement.

"You, okay?" Noah asked softly.

Barbara nodded as Bradford walked briskly toward them, his beige cashmere coat flapping in the fall breeze. He stopped in front of them and glared at Barbara, then at Noah. Noah squared his shoulders and cleared his throat.

"I thought you were showing houses tonight. What the fuck are you doing here? If this is what it looks like, Barbara, I swear I'll . . ."

Barbara wrapped her coat tightly around her neck as Bradford fumed. She suspected that Bradford was here meeting some woman, but there was no sign of that. So what was there to say? She had been caught red-handed.

Bradford turned to Noah. "Who the hell are you?"

"Uh, I'm—"

"He's a coworker," Barbara said, interrupting. "We were having drinks."

"Drinks? All the way out here?" He laughed sarcastically. "I'll bet."

Bradford grabbed Barbara by the elbow and steered her off to the side. When they were a short distance away, she yanked her arm free.

"What are you doing here with that kid, Barbara? Is that the famous Noah?"

"Yes."

He sneered. "Are you sleeping with him?"

She said nothing, and Bradford grimaced. "All right. So that's it then? That's why you've been spending my money on blue jeans and all that bling lately. How old is he?"

"That's none of your business."

"He looks young enough to be your son."

Barbara rolled her eyes. "Pfft."

"Dammit, Barbara. I can't believe you're doing this."

"And what are *you* doing all the way out here?"

He glanced at his watch. "From the look of things it seems that I'm probably being stood up. I've been waiting here for damn near an hour."

"For one of your sluts, no doubt."

"I have a business meeting, Barbara."

"I'll bet."

"Don't try to turn this around. You're the one coming out of a hotel with another man."

"Now you know how it feels," she said, her voice dripping with sarcasm.

"So that's what this is about? Revenge?"

She unfolded her arms and got right up in his face. "Believe it or not, this has nothing at all to do with you. It's about *me*, Bradford. About *my* feelings and *my* needs. For once."

He blinked.

"Strange concepts, huh?"

"I don't know what that kid has been telling you, Barbara, but you've changed. First your wardrobe, now this. I don't like it, and I won't have my wife out here—"

"I have to go now," she interrupted, as a parking valet drove up with her Benz.

"Like hell you do. You're coming home with me."

"Don't be silly, Bradford. What about my car?"

"Leave it here for the night. I'll get someone to pick it up in the morning. And get rid of that kid."

"Stop calling him a kid."

"I call it as I see it. And you're not leaving here with him."

Just then another valet drove Noah's Honda Civic up and parked it behind Barbara's Benz.

"I wasn't planning on leaving with him. But you go ahead and have fun with whoever you're meeting here, because I've stopped caring one way or the other, Bradford."

"I said I'm here for a business meeting," he shouted as she walked away. "Barbara!"

She ignored Bradford and stopped at Noah's side.

"Will you be all right?" Noah asked quietly.

"I'm fine. I'll call you tomorrow."

He nodded and they both got in their separate cars. Barbara gave Bradford one last look before she drove off.

41

JOLENE SLIPPED INTO her Jacuzzi and sank down beneath the bubbles. It had been more than a month since the break-in, and no one seemed to suspect that she had anything to do with it. When Brian first told her he'd destroyed Pearl's salon himself, she had half expected to hear police sirens come screeching up her driveway at any minute. Mercifully, that hadn't happened, and she was starting to feel confident the she had pulled it off cleanly.

From what Patrick had told her the last time he dropped Juliette off from her weekend visit with him, Pearl was devastated. The break-in had left her badly shaken, and she cried whenever she went to the salon. She was even reluctant to rebuild out of fear that it could happen again. Good, Jolene thought as she closed her eyes. It served that frumpy bitch right. She had gotten exactly what she deserved.

Now it was time to throw her party, a big elegant Christmas bash to let everyone know that Jolene Brown was back on the scene. Before her divorce, she used to throw some of the best parties in Silver Lake. With all the money she had now, she should be able to do even better.

The timing was perfect. Since that first lunch with Veronique at the club, the two of them had started working out together, and Jolene was confident that the baroness would accept her invitation. Perhaps she would even agree to be the guest of honor. Veronique was also friends with Barbara, but Jolene would bet her lottery winnings that she and the baroness had much more in common. Forget Barbara Bentley. She didn't need that snob anymore. She was friends with Veronique.

As soon as she got out of the tub, she would phone her mother and ask her to help plan the party. She and her mother didn't have the best relationship, but Jolene knew that if she dropped the baroness's name, her mother wouldn't be able to resist getting involved. Jolene hoped that planning this party together would give them a chance to make their relationship better.

She supposed she should also invite Pearl and Patrick, just for show. She didn't want to arouse suspicion. With any luck, Pearl wouldn't want to attend a party in her depressed state of mind anyway, and maybe Patrick would come alone.

She stepped out of the tub and dried herself off quickly. She wanted to get dressed and call Darlene Dunn to start planning the menu. Flowers and decorations needed to be ordered, invitations printed.

There was a knock at the bathroom door and she cracked it open.

"Mom, Dad's here," Juliette said, standing there in a mini denim skirt. "I'm going."

Jolene put on her bathrobe. Patrick was here to pick up Juliette for the weekend already? It was earlier than usual.

"Tell him to wait a second. I want to talk to him before you go."

She checked her weave then ran down the stairs. Patrick and Juliette were huddled close at the front door talking quietly. She smiled when she saw them, until she noticed the dour expressions on their faces.

"You're early," she said as she tightened the belt around her robe. "We haven't even had dinner yet. Is everything all right?"

Patrick looked up when he heard her voice. "We were just talking about the salon. Otherwise, everything is fine."

Was that what the depressed faces were all about? She supposed she shouldn't be too surprised. Pearl's salon had been nearly destroyed, her life's work flushed down the drain in one night. How wonderful did the fat bitch look to Patrick now?

Sometimes Jolene shocked herself with how evil she could be. But she was tired of playing second fiddle to Pearl, or to anyone for that matter.

She tried to put on a sad face. "How's Pearl? Any better?"

"Not much," he said. "She's taking it pretty hard."

"I'm so sorry to hear that." Jolene wondered if this was a good time to tell Patrick about the party she was planning. She tried to steer the conversation to something a little more cheerful so she could bring it up. "So, what are you two planning today? A movie? Going out to dinner?"

"We're helping Pearl fix up the salon. Then we'll get a bite to eat."

Jolene gritted her teeth. Now she was really getting annoyed. All Patrick ever wanted to talk about was Pearl and her stupid-ass salon. Enough was enough. "I don't know if I want Juliette over there so soon after what happened," she said curtly.

"But I want to go," Juliette protested.

"What on earth for?" Jolene asked. Juliette had never been particularly fond of Pearl. Why this sudden desire to help her out?

Juliette shrugged. "I feel sorry for her. You should see the salon, Mom. It's really bad."

Jolene blinked bitterly and glanced at Patrick. What the hell kind of bull was he feeding their daughter about Pearl? Juliette needed to feel sorry for her own lonely mother, not her dad's whore.

"I want you to stay here," Jolene said. "That's a job for adults, and you'll just get in the way. Your father can come back and pick you up after he's done over there."

"She'll be fine," Patrick said. "I'll be with her, and Lee is already there helping Pearl."

That tramp was the last person Jolene wanted her daughter hanging around. She shook her head. "No, Patrick. You can just—"

"Why can't I help out?" Juliette argued. "Pearl has been really nice to me. The least I can . . ." Juliette paused as the telephone rang.

"Just a minute," Jolene said. "I'll be right back." She slipped out of the living room and into the kitchen and picked up the phone sitting on the built-in desk.

"Hello?" she said shortly. She would get rid of the caller quickly and return to Patrick and Juliette. She absolutely did not want her daughter helping to clean up Pearl's salon. The irony in that was too much. And Lee would be there too? The less Juliette was around that child, the better as far as Jolene was concerned.

"Yo, what up?" Brian asked.

Jolene shut her eyes tight. How the hell did he get this number? She had gotten all her phone numbers changed a week after the break-in. She wanted to wait to make sure that the police didn't suspect him or her before she had any more dealings with him.

"I told you to stop calling me," she hissed quietly. "It's too soon."

"I've waited more than a month. I want my damn money, bitch."

She opened the French doors and stepped onto the patio off the kitchen to avoid being overheard. She had no intention of meeting Brian or paying him anytime soon. "That's not enough time. And who the hell gave you this number anyway?"

"What difference is it to you? Pay me and I'll get out of your fucking life."

"It's your fault we have to wait. You almost got caught."

"I don't want to hear that crap, bitch. Shit. A deal's a deal. You can't cop out now. It's not my fault that bitch showed up."

"If you had followed my instructions instead of doing it yourself and screwing up, we wouldn't be in this jam. But someone might have seen you, and it's too risky for us to have contact now. Maybe in a few more months if nothing—"

"A few more months shit. And fuck your fucking instructions. It got done, didn't it? Pay me now or I'm calling the cops on your ass."

"Well, that would be pretty damn smart, since you're the one who broke in and tried to rob Pearl's place."

"Rob? It wasn't no robbery and you know it. You asked me to bust it up and I did. Now I want my money or I'm going to the cops."

"Go ahead then, stupid asshole," she sneered. "I'll tell them I had nothing to do with it. It was a botched robbery for all I know. Who do you think they're going to believe? An ex-con or me?"

Jolene slammed the phone down as hard as she could. She couldn't believe Brian had gotten her new unlisted number so quickly. Someone at her old office must have given it to him despite her instructions that it not be given out to anyone without asking her first. If Jolene ever found out who was responsible, she was going to make their life miserable.

She hoped Brian wasn't dumb enough to go to the police. But if he did, she would simply tell them that he must be implicating her because they'd had a short affair and she dumped him.

She had it all covered. Let the jerk go to the cops if he was foolish enough to try that. They didn't have a shred of evidence against her. For now, she had to deal with Patrick and Juliette. She was damned if her daughter was going to help clean up Pearl's salon.

She walked back into the living room to find it empty. Had they left without telling her? She ran into the dining and family rooms, and then the den and solarium. No one was there. She opened the front door and looked up and down the block for Patrick's Nissan.

She didn't see it and slammed the door shut. They had slipped away while she was on the phone.

How dare they. She ran up the stairs toward her bedroom, planning to get dressed and go to the salon and get Juliette. But she stopped in mid-flight. Maybe it would be better to let it go. If that creep Brian really did go to the cops, it would help her look innocent if Juliette had helped Pearl out. Still, she couldn't stand the thought of Juliette over there helping to clean up a mess that she was responsible for.

She strolled into her bedroom and picked up the telephone. She was going to go ahead with her original plans for the day, starting with phone calls to Veronique, Darlene, and her mother. She had a party to organize.

"I TALKED TO PEARL day before yesterday," Barbara said to Marilyn as they worked out together on the treadmills. "She said that when she caught the intruder in her salon he was holding a crowbar."

"My God. Did he hurt her?"

Barbara shook her head. "When he saw her, he ran out and took off in his car."

"Do they have any idea who did it?"

"Pearl said the police have a new lead. She finally remembered that she's seen the getaway car driving around in Silver Lake."

Marilyn raised an eyebrow. "Do you think someone around here did it?"

"I find that hard to believe. But you never know. I just hope they catch him. I've always admired Pearl."

"It's such a shame," Marilyn said. "Where have you been getting your hair done lately?"

"I'm just going to a salon at the mall until Pearl gets back on her feet."

"If you need a recommendation, I go to a woman in Annapolis who—"

"That will be too far for me, since I'm moving in with Noah next week." Barbara said it as calmly as if she were talking about the weather on a sunny day in June. She stared straight ahead and kept walking on the treadmill as Marilyn hurriedly pressed the buttons on her treadmill until it came to a halt.

"You're doing what?" Marilyn exclaimed loudly enough for everyone to hear.

"Shh," Barbara said without stopping. "I don't want Jolene Brown to hear." She nodded in the direction of Jolene and Veronique working out next to each other on the cycles across the aisle.

"You can't be serious, Barbara," Marilyn said as she dabbed her cheeks with the towel draped around her neck. "You're leaving Bradford?"

"Yes, Marilyn, I'm very serious."

"Will you stop that damn thing and talk to me?" Marilyn said. She jumped off her treadmill and waved her hands wildly in front of Barbara.

Barbara stopped her treadmill, and Marilyn grabbed her arm and escorted her to a far corner of the room. She let Barbara go, and Barbara stretched, leaning over and touching her toes.

"Well?" Marilyn asked impatiently, her hands on her hips. "And will you stay still for a minute?"

"Sorry," Barbara said. She stood up straight. "I'm tired of Bradford and all his women. Noah knows how to treat me."

"He's a twenty-year-old kid," Marilyn snapped.

"He's thirty-eight."

"And you're almost fifty-two."

"Noah doesn't seem to mind the age difference."

"I don't believe this. What does Bradford say about all of this?"

Barbara swallowed. She didn't want to mention the things Bradford had said since catching her with Noah. Their arguments after that night had been generally short and nasty.

"What the hell is going on, Barbara? Sometimes I think you've lost your mind. He's a kid compared to you."

"He's more man at thirty-eight than you'll ever be."

"The one thing you had going for you was that you always acted like a lady, even when you were drinking. Now you're acting like a slut. If I had wanted a slut for a wife, I would have married one."

"Why didn't you? You've sure had enough of them to choose from."

Bradford clenched his fists.

"And you don't have to worry about being married to one anymore," she added, *"because I'm leaving."*

Bradford's eyes widened. *"And going where? With him?"*

Barbara was silent.

"Fine, leave. You won't survive for a week."

"He doesn't like it, naturally," Barbara said to Marilyn. "But this isn't about Bradford's feelings. It's about mine."

"My God, Barbara. What's gotten into you?"

"Some common sense."

"I would say just the opposite. This is insane. You're giving up being Mrs. Bradford Bentley to be with some kid. I don't care how cute he is or how good he is in bed. This is nuts."

"Noah really cares about me. He treats me like a queen."

"So keep screwing him on the side, girl. You don't have to leave Bradford."

Barbara smacked her lips impatiently. She was sorry not to have her best friend's blessing but that wasn't going to change her mind. At least Veronique was supportive. Veronique seemed to understand her need to be with Noah in a way that Marilyn didn't.

"Where does Noah live?" Marilyn asked.

"Near Fourteenth and U Streets."

Marilyn laughed out loud. "You've got to be kidding. Barbara, you won't last three days down there."

"You sound like Bradford," Barbara said stiffly. "I've spent a lot of time there with Noah. I happen to like it. It's hip, trendy."

Marilyn threw her hands in the air helplessly. "If you're determined to go through with this, I hope you have a damn good lawyer. You're going to need every dime you can get out of Bradford to live with Noah."

"If there's one thing I've learned while spending time with Noah, it's that there are more important things in the world than money and status," Barbara said.

"Like what?" Marilyn demanded.

Barbara rolled her eyes skyward.

"I WONDER WHAT that's all about," Veronique said as she pedaled the exercise cycle.

Jolene frowned and looked in the direction that Veronique was staring.

"Barbara's friend Marilyn seems to be awfully upset about something," Veronique said. "She just jumped off her treadmill, and she and Barbara walked off together in a huff. Looks like they're in the middle of a heated discussion."

"Interesting," Jolene said. "Barbara's always so staid and controlled. I know the two of you are friends, but I've never gotten along with her all that well."

"So I've heard."

Jolene stiffened. She wondered if Veronique knew about the heated affair she and Bradford had had a couple of summers ago. Knowing how ripe Silver Lake's grapevine was, Jolene wouldn't be surprised. "I have to ask just what you've heard, Veronique."

"Mmm. Well, I don't know if it's true, Jolene, but I believe in being blunt and now that I've gotten to know you I'm sure you'd prefer it that way."

"Go on."

"There are rumors that you and Bradford were—ah, how should I put it?—once an item."

Jolene hesitated. Her first instinct was to deny the rumor. But she decided against that. Veronique was a woman of the world, and if the two of them had anything in common it was that they believed in being up front . . . to a point.

"I regret it, but yes, it's true. Barbara and Bradford's marriage isn't as peachy as it seems to be on the outside, and, well, Bradford is an attractive and powerful man and he was available. In fact, he's strayed so often that I almost feel sorry for Barbara."

"I wouldn't."

Jolene turned and stared at Veronique. "Excuse me?"

Veronique smiled slyly. "Would it surprise you to know that Barbara is having an affair?"

"Yeah, right. And I'm taking my vows to become a nun next week."

Veronique laughed. "It's true."

"Barbara is having an affair? *Barbara Bentley?*"

"The one and only."

"Where did you hear that, Veronique?"

"I've met him. He's a very attractive younger man in his thirties."

Jolene peddled the bike slowly and stared ahead with disbelief. "For the first time in my life, I think I'm speechless."

"Is it really that surprising, given what Barbara's been through with Bradford?"

"Hell yeah. I didn't think the broad had it in her. If Bradford finds out, he'll be pissed."

"I'm sure."

"He counted on Barbara being the dutiful wife no matter how much he fooled around," Jolene said. "Well, well. Sounds like he's getting back some of what he's been dishing out to her for years. Now I feel sorry for Bradford. Payback can be a bitch."

"Yes, it can. But in my opinion, Barbara deserves some happiness. And Bradford, well, he has no one to blame but himself."

PEARL OPENED A locker and tossed her gym bag in. She hadn't been to the club since the break-in, or much of anywhere else except the salon. She couldn't get what happened off her mind, yet thinking about it made her stomach turn. As the cops said, it didn't seem like robbery was the motive. Her safe had been untouched and instead of stealing her valuable equipment and supplies the thug had trashed everything. Why would someone do that to her?

But Patrick was right. She had to get on with her life. Let the cops look for the criminal, let the insurance company pay for the damages. She needed to focus on rebuilding the shop and getting her life back together. Even if she had to get a part-time job until she was up and running again, she couldn't let this thug ruin her life.

She exited the locker room and walked down the hall to the exercise room. All the working out the past year had done wonders for her figure. She was a naturally big woman but now she was down to a size 12, the smallest she had been in years. She still had that to be thankful for, and she wasn't going to let her unhappiness over the break-in ruin that. She'd get back into her exercise routine and look better and better.

She opened the door to the exercise room and spotted Barbara and Marilyn talking in a corner. Barbara saw her immediately and waved her over. They hugged warmly and Barbara reintroduced her to Marilyn.

"I'm so sorry to hear about what happened to your salon," Marilyn said. "It's terrible."

"Thanks," Pearl said. She let out a deep breath. "It's been rough, but I'm hanging in there."

"Any word yet on who did it?" Barbara asked.

"Yesterday one of the officers working the case called and said they had a good lead. He didn't say who."

"Do they know why they did it?" Marilyn asked.

"They don't think it was a robbery 'cause nothing was stolen," Pearl said. "Beyond that . . ." She shrugged.

"So it was just vandalism?" Marilyn asked. "Teenagers?"

"I only saw one man and he wasn't hardly any teenager. He had to be well into his thirties."

Barbara shook her head. "It's so strange. Like I said the other day when we talked, let me know if there's anything I can do to help with the salon."

"Thanks, but I'll manage. I have insurance and a little money saved. If it takes too long to rebuild, I'll have to start looking for another job. I hope they catch whoever did this soon. That's what I really want."

43

JOLENE SAW PEARL walk into the exercise room and her heart picked up a beat. She had definitely not expected to see Pearl back here so soon. She would have thought the woman would be at home sobbing into her pillow.

Jolene was thankful she hadn't heard from Brian for several days now. He had her really worried when he kept calling and bitching about the money. Maybe she'd finally got through to him that exchanging money now was the dumbest thing they could do.

"There's Pearl," Veronique said. "I wonder how she's doing after what happened."

"She looks fine to me," Jolene said.

"As soon as I finish my second twenty minutes here, I'm going to go over and say hello to her."

"Hmm," was all Jolene could manage.

"Did you ever go to her salon before the break-in?"

"Me? No."

"I've always admired people who start their own businesses, and to think she did it while raising a son alone."

Jolene rolled her eyes to the ceiling. Not *that* again, she thought. It seemed that all anyone wanted to talk about these days was Pearl's mighty accomplishments. "The way people always go on and on about that, you'd think she had invented a cure for cellulite."

Veronique gave her a puzzled look, and Jolene regretted the words the minute they'd left her mouth. When the topic was Pearl, she was going to have to do a better job of keeping her fat lips zipped.

She hopped off the bike and wiped her face with her towel. "I've got to run. My mother is meeting me here for lunch. I introduced you to her last week when we ran into you in front of the house."

"Yes, you did. Lovely woman."

"She was thrilled to meet you. She's helping me plan my Christmas party. And thank you again for agreeing to be the guest of honor."

"I look forward to it. I'm always up for a good party."

"I've been out of circulation for a while but I'm back now," Jolene said with pride.

Veronique smiled. "Good for you."

"Well, I'm off," Jolene said. "My mother should be here any moment, and I don't want to keep her waiting."

ALMOST THE MINUTE she walked away from Veronique, Jolene spotted two police officers at the entrance to the exercise room talking to one of the club's receptionists. That was odd. She had never seen police officers in the club before.

One of the officers was a heavyset black man who appeared to be in his thirties; the other was a slim, younger white man. They both looked her way as the receptionist pointed in her direction.

"Oh, shit," Jolene muttered. For a second, she wanted to turn and flee in another direction. But running would only make her look guilty.

The officers approached, and Jolene's heart beat so rapidly she thought it would pop out of her chest.

"Jolene Brown?" the black officer asked.

"Yes?" she said, trying to sound calm.

He held out his badge, and Jolene glanced at it. But her head was spinning and she couldn't focus. He could have been holding out a rat for all she knew. She gripped the ends of the towel around her neck to steady her feet. Get ahold of yourself, girl. There is absolutely no evidence against you.

"I'm Officer Harrison. This is my partner, Officer Byrd. We want you to come down to the station to answer some questions."

For a moment Jolene thought she had fainted. Then she realized she was still standing on her feet. "Um, may I ask what this is about?"

"It's in connection with Brian Watson. He's been arrested for the break-in at Pearl Jackson's hair salon. We want to ask you a few questions."

Jolene reached out and held on to the wall to steady herself. Both officers saw her sway and they jumped forward to lend her a hand. "Are you all right, Mrs. Brown?" Officer Harrison asked.

Jolene waved them away. "I . . . I'm fine. I think I'm a little dizzy from just getting off the exercise bike."

"Are you sure?" Officer Byrd asked. "Would you like some water?"

"Yes, that would be good."

She stood in silence with Officer Harrison as Officer Byrd went to fetch water. Jolene didn't really need the water but she did need time to sort this out and get herself together. How the heck had they connected Brian to the break-in? Had that asshole really gone to the cops?

She thought of calling her lawyer, then decided against that for now. The officer said they wanted her to go down to the station and answer some questions. He didn't say she was being arrested. If she asked to call her lawyer now, it would raise suspicion.

Officer Byrd returned with a small paper cup of water and Jolene took a few sips. "Better?" he asked.

"Yes, thank you." Jolene took another sip to stall for more time. Maybe she could delay this. She *had* to delay this. Her mother was coming and people were beginning to stare.

"Are you ready now?" Officer Harrison asked.

"Um, well, this is really not a good time. You see, my mother is on her way to meet me for lunch. Maybe I could—"

"I would strongly suggest that you postpone your plans, Mrs. Brown," Officer Harrison said firmly.

"Oh. Well, I guess I could do that, although I don't know how much help I would be. I don't even know Pearl all that well. I mean, I heard what happened to her salon. It's awful. And I haven't seen Brian Watson in ages."

"We'd still like you to come down and answer some questions," Officer Harrison said. "When are you supposed to meet your mother?"

Jolene glanced at her watch. "In about twenty minutes. She's coming from Washington, D.C., and she's probably already left home. I can't call her because I don't have her cell number with me." Jolene immediately realized that she should have waited for them to ask her to call her mother before she told that lie. Chill, girl, she told herself. This is no time to lose your cool.

Officer Harrison eyed her with doubt. "Officer Byrd here can wait and bring her down to the station to meet you if you'd like."

Jolene shook her head vehemently. Hell, no. She was on shaky terms with her mother as it was. If her mother was met by a police officer when she arrived, she would probably march straight back to her home on the Gold Coast and write Jolene off for good.

"No, um, if you really need me, I guess I could have a neighbor of mine who's here look out for her."

Officer Harrison nodded, and Jolene looked around for Veronique. That was when she realized that everyone in the club had stopped what they were doing and was watching her. It was as if everything going on in the room had been freeze-framed.

Jolene tried to ignore the attention as she walked toward Veronique. But she was horrified to discover that Veronique, Pearl, Barbara, and Marilyn were all standing together. She had no choice but to approach all four of them. Pearl's eyes looked as if they were about to pop out of her head, and Veronique nodded in stunned silence as Jolene asked to see her privately.

"Those officers want me to go to the station with them for a minute," Jolene said after she and Veronique had stepped away. "Can you meet my mother when she comes and tell her that I won't be able to make lunch?"

Veronique nodded. "Of course, Jolene. Is everything all right?"

Jolene's mind raced to come up with a quick fib. "Um, it seems that the alarm at my house went off or something." She leaned in close to Veronique. "I don't want my mother to get upset. Just tell her that I'll call her as soon as I can."

"Yes, I understand. Don't worry about a thing here."

"Thank you." Jolene turned and walked back toward the officers. "Will I have time for a quick shower?" she asked. "I've been working out for an hour."

"You'll be fine," Officer Harrison said firmly. "Just get your belongings and let's go."

Jolene straightened her back, lifted her chin and tried to ignore all the stares boring down on her as she followed Officers Harrison and Byrd through the door.

"WHAT WAS *THAT* all about?" Barbara asked as soon as Veronique returned to the group.

"She said her burglar alarm went off, and the officers want to take her to the station," Veronique said. "Her mother is meeting her here for lunch, so she asked me to look out for her."

Pearl frowned. "It seems strange that they would take her to the police station about her burglar alarm going off."

"Yes, it does," Marilyn agreed.

Barbara turned to Pearl. "Do you think she may have had something to do with the break-in? I mean, you *are* seeing Patrick."

"I have no idea," Pearl responded. "But the police said that since nothing was taken, the break-in looked personal rather than like a random crime."

Pearl shook her head. Jolene had never liked her much even before she began seeing Patrick. But to think that Jolene would do something this spiteful was truly frightening.

"I had no idea that Jolene was so conniving," Veronique said.

"Let's face it," Barbara said. "She's a bitch."

"I pray that she didn't have anything to do with this, for Juliette's sake," Pearl said.

BARBARA HANDED THE pair of four-carat diamond earrings
back to the blond clerk behind the glass counter at Tiffany's.
She stared at the earrings and thought for a moment while
the clerk waited patiently.

More jewelry was the last thing she needed. But since moving in
with Noah a week earlier, she hadn't had much besides shopping to
fill up her days. Noah was always out teaching or showing houses,
and she was left alone in a tiny house in a strange neighborhood. He
put in more hours selling real estate in the evenings than she had realized.

"I'll take them," she said and whipped out her black American
Express Centurion Card.

The clerk smiled. "Of course, Mrs. Bradford. I'll be right back."

The clerk took the card and jewelry and walked toward the cash register. Barbara realized that she had been in the store so often over the past week that the clerks knew her by name. At least Noah made up for his long absences when he came home. She smiled at the thought of the previous evening when Noah had come in around nine and they'd had pizza by the fireplace and made love until midnight. Then they'd talked until two in the morning, discussing everything from selling houses to which sex positions they'd like to try next. He always made her feel so young and alive.

She glanced at her watch. Another four hours to kill until Noah came home tonight. He had said he would try to get back by seven-thirty, so they could go out to dinner for a nice change. Neither of them cooked much, and if she had to eat another pizza or microwave meal she thought she would go mad.

The clerk returned and stood in front of Barbara. The expression on the young woman's face was a mixture of surprise and annoyance, as if she had caught Barbara dipping her hand behind the glass counter and snatching something.

"I'm afraid I have to take the card, Mrs. Bradford," she said solemnly.

Barbara blinked and stared at her with wide eyes. "Excuse me?"

"The card has been cancelled and I have to keep it."

"What?! That's ridiculous. You can't take my card."

Barbara reached out to snatch the card, and the clerk stepped back quickly as if she expected Barbara to try and strike her. Barbara took a deep breath and tried to calm herself. What the hell was going on? Nothing like this had ever happened before. Bradford always paid the bills on . . .

Bradford. She clenched her fist. He had deliberately cancelled her black American Express Centurion Card. She had three other cards she could try, including a platinum American Express card, but what was the point? She was sure that he had cancelled all of those too and that she would only embarrass herself further.

Barbara avoided the clerk's eyes as she put her Coach wallet back in her Vuitton bag and walked briskly out of the store. As soon as she was outside, she wrapped her silver fox coat around her tightly and practically ran back to her Benz. She jumped in and flew out of the parking lot.

Bastard. How dare he do this to her. She fumed all the way around the beltway. She was going to march right into his office and tell him to back off. Two days ago, she learned he had sabotaged the real estate deal with Bernice and Bradford Wright.

"What's wrong?" she had asked Noah as they sat down together in front of the fireplace with microwaved dinners when he returned from the office. "You seem down about something."

He opened the top buttons of his shirt. "Bad news about Bernice and Bernard."

Barbara frowned. "Don't tell me they changed their minds about buying the house again?"

"No, not exactly."

"Then what?"

He sighed. "They still want the house, but they've decided to use a different agent."

"But why?"

He shrugged. "They claim they can get a better deal with a buyer's agent."

"But . . . but they can't switch agents after you did all that work helping them to find a house."

"They can and they are."

Barbara jumped up. This didn't sound right. "They called you at the office today and told you that? Out of the blue?"

"Actually, Bernard called and told me yesterday. I didn't say anything to you because I thought I could persuade them to come back to us. That's why I was so late getting home."

Barbara paced the floor. Why would Bernard and Bernice change agents at the last minute? Something was not right, and it had Bradford written all over it. He could be ruthless when he thought he had been wronged.

She didn't say any of this to Noah. What would be the point? She was sure Bradford was behind it. As soon as Noah left for work the next morning she grabbed the phone.

"Hello, Bernice. It's Barbara Bentley."

"Barbara. How are you, darling?"

"I'm fine, and you?"

"Oh, I'm good. So tell me, Barbara, where are you living now? I hear you're no longer in Silver Lake."

"Um, no, I'm not. I'm living in D.C."

"So, it's true then? That Noah must be something else for you to leave Bradford."

Barbara ignored that comment. "That's not what I called about, Bernice. I need to ask you something. It's important."

Bernice cleared her throat as if she knew what was coming. "Go ahead."

"Why are you changing agents? And why now?"

Bernice sighed. "It wasn't my idea. I mean, I think Noah is a doll and he's good at what he does. But Bernard works closely with Bradford, and you know how that is."

"So Bradford talked Bernard into changing his mind?"

"No. He didn't have to. Bradford just made it clear that he wasn't happy with what's going on between you and Noah. Naturally, Bernard doesn't want to do anything to make Bradford angry. He depends on Bradford for half his business."

"But that's unfair to Noah, Bernice. He worked his tail off for months to help you find that house."

"I know, and I feel bad, but there's not much I can do about it. We're planning to move to Silver Lake, and no one in their right minds who plans to live in Silver Lake and works with Bradford is going to go up against him. I'm sorry, Barbara."

Barbara had known all along that Bradford would be difficult if she left him. But she never expected him to stoop this low. He was trying to ruin her life and he had to stop.

She hastily pulled the Benz into the parking lot of Bradford's office building without even bothering to straighten the car between the lines. She hopped out, ran by the Digitech sign, her fox coat flapping in the breeze, and flew to the elevators.

She reached his suite on the top floor and marched through the lobby. "Good afternoon, Mrs. Bentley," Bradford's secretary said cheerfully as soon as she approached the entryway to Bradford's office. "Mr. Bentley is . . ."

The secretary stopped mid-sentence when she realized that Barbara was not going to stop as usual. Barbara rounded the desk, opened the door to Bradford's office, and slammed it shut behind her.

Bradford was on the telephone and he looked up and signaled for her to wait. Barbara walked up and stood in front of his desk, tapping her black suede Gucci boot on the carpet as she waited for him to finish his call.

He hung up and stood, fastening the buttons to his navy Brioni suit jacket. "I've been trying to reach you on the phone for days, Barbara. What brings you here?"

"How the hell could you cancel my credit cards, Bradford?"

"Oh, that."

"And what is this with Bernice and Bernard using another agent?"

"I have no idea. Bernard is his own man. He can use whomever he wants."

"Dammit, Bradford, I *know* you had something to do with it."

"Barbara, why don't you sit down." He motioned toward the chair in front of his desk.

Barbara stomped her foot. "I'm not going to sit. I want you to stop this nonsense."

"I tried to call you about the credit cards. But you kept hanging up on me."

"Well, why on earth did you cancel them?"

"We're not living together anymore. Why should I continue to pay your debts?"

"How am I supposed to live if you do this?"

"Let Noah handle your expenses," he said sarcastically and sat back down behind his desk.

"Don't be mean, Bradford. You know, I don't even really care about the credit cards. That only hurts me. But please ask Bernard to use Noah as his Realtor. Noah worked so hard to help them find that house."

"Like I said, Bernard is his own man. But I might be able to persuade him. I could certainly try." He pulled the sleeves of his jacket down over his gold cuff links.

"Thank you, Bradford."

"Provided you come home, where you belong."

Barbara placed her hands on his desk and leaned in toward him. "Are you saying you'll only talk to Bernard if I agree to come home?"

He stared at her pointedly.

"That's not fair, Bradford. Why should I go back? To be miserable while you chase every skirt in town? Or all over the country?"

"I've stopped doing that."

"That's what you said before I caught you with Sabrina."

"I was only having lunch with her. I told you that."

"Why should I believe you? You've lied before."

"But I'm telling the truth now. You have to learn to trust me again instead of running around with younger men. All I want is for us to have a good marriage."

"Then what were you doing at the Hilton all the way out in Tysons Corner?"

He glanced away.

Barbara straightened up. "You can't answer that question, can you? Veronique was right. Once a cheater, always a cheater."

He looked back at her sharply. "She said that to you?"

"That and a whole lot more. She told me all about your philandering down in Atlanta. I always knew you liked the ladies, Bradford, but I had no idea how rampant it was until she told me that."

"I don't know exactly what that woman said to you, but that was more than five years ago."

"It doesn't matter, Bradford, we're not getting back—"

"There's something you should know about your precious friend," he said, interrupting.

"Who? Veronique?"

"Yes."

"What about her?"

"I don't know what kind of garbage she's been filling your head with, but she's the one who set this whole thing up."

"What thing?"

Bradford sighed impatiently. "Veronique was the person I was waiting for when we ran into each other at the Hilton. I suspect that she knew you would be there. She wanted me to catch you."

45

BARBARA LAUGHED. "OH, no. You don't expect me to believe that."

"Fine." Bradford picked up the phone on his desk and
held it toward her. "Call and ask her. I haven't been able to reach
her, but I'd put my money on it."

Barbara sank down into the chair in front of his desk, and Bradford replaced the phone in the cradle.

"She called me late that afternoon. She said she had just had lunch
with you at the Ritz and she wanted to talk to me about something
important concerning you. She wouldn't say what. She just asked
me to meet her in the lobby of the Hilton that night. I cancelled all
my business meetings and drove over there. I had been waiting almost an hour when I ran into you. Veronique never showed up, and
I haven't been able to contact her since."

Barbara shook her head to clear it. As ridiculous as what Bradford was telling her seemed to be, it sounded like the truth. He wouldn't have encouraged her to call Veronique if he was lying. And she had thought it was strange that Bradford had shown up at the Hilton the one night she was there. It was such an out-of-the-way place, and Veronique was the only one other than Noah who had known she would be there.

Barbara looked at Bradford, her eyes wide with horror. "But why? Why would she do that?"

"It's a long story, Barbara. I think she blames me for her ex-husband's bad business dealings."

"She mentioned something about him losing his company. But why would she blame you for that?"

"I loaned her husband some money, and when he couldn't pay it back I took over his software company. The board eventually forced him out. It was tough, but it was business."

Barbara closed her eyes and sighed. She knew that Bradford could be tough when it came to business. But she had always believed that was why he was so successful, and as she had with his mistresses, she had learned to look the other way whenever she heard that he had dealt harshly with a business adversary.

She still couldn't understand why Veronique would feel the need to deceive her over some bad business dealings with Bradford that had happened more than five years ago. She thought they were friends.

"And Barbara, there's more."

She opened her eyes and glanced at him sharply. She didn't think she could take more.

"You have to consider the possibility that Noah was in on it."

She shot up out of her seat. "No, no, no. He would never do anything like that."

Bradford lifted his arms. "Do you know him well enough to be sure he wouldn't?"

"But why? What would be his reason?"

"Money. What else? He needs it and she's got plenty of it."

Barbara thought back to the day Veronique had shown up at the Realtor's office when Noah was there. It seemed that things between her and Noah had heated up quickly after that, with Veronique's encouragement all along the way. And it was Noah who had suggested they meet at the Hilton that fateful night when Bradford caught them. Had Veronique recruited Noah for her little scheme? That would go a long way toward explaining why such a young and attractive man would be interested in her.

The thought that Veronique and Noah had planned this together made Barbara's stomach turn. She held on to the edge of Bradford's desk to steady herself.

"Why are you telling me all this now, Bradford? Why didn't you tell me right after you saw me at the Hilton?"

"I was too angry to think straight. It took me a few days to put it all together. I became more suspicious when Veronique refused to take my calls after that night. And I couldn't reach you."

It was true. She had hung up on him twice when he had called her at Noah's house.

She nodded. "I . . . I don't know what to think about all of this. I need to talk to Veronique." And to Noah, she thought.

"Good luck reaching her. Barbara, listen to me."

He walked around his desk and took both of her hands in his. "You have no idea how much I miss you. I've had some time to think, and I'm willing to forgive and forget about this thing, this fling, between you and Noah. All I want now is for you to come home and give us a chance to work things out."

Barbara nodded in a daze. This was all so confusing. Her good friend Veronique had stabbed her in the back, and it looked like Noah was in on it. He had seduced her to help Veronique get revenge, all for money.

Even harder to believe was that Bradford was actually telling her that he missed her and wanted her to come home. He hadn't held her hand and expressed affection like that in probably twenty years. Barbara had always thought that even if she lived another fifty years, she would never hear words like that from him again.

She swallowed and looked at Bradford. If anything was more startling to her than all she had just learned, it was that she realized as she looked into Bradford's eyes that somewhere inside her was a deep desire to return to the safety of home.

BARBARA SAT IN her Benz in front of Bradford's office and stared ahead with tight lips as she flicked her cigarette ashes out the window. She normally never smoked in her car but these were not normal times.

She knew what she had to do. She had to confront Veronique. And Noah. As much as she hated to think that he was in on all of this with Veronique, the timing of the whole sordid affair was impossible to dismiss. It was mind-numbing to think that two people she had come to trust and care for had deceived her like this.

She stubbed her cigarette out in the ashtray and stuck another between her lips. When she lifted her gold lighter, she noticed that her hand was trembling. She was a wreck.

She started the car and pointed it toward the beltway. The numbness she had felt ever since Bradford pointed out Noah's probable involvement began to thaw, and she was left with outright anger. Tears welled up in her eyes. How could he have done this to her?

Maybe she deserved all of this for leaving her husband and moving in with Noah. Now she realized how little she really knew the man she had taken up with. An old saying came to mind: The devil you know is better than the one you don't. How true that felt now. Bradford might be a jerk at times but at least she knew what to expect from him.

By the time Barbara pulled up in front of Noah's house, her pack of cigarettes was empty. She crumbled the wrapper and threw it on the floor in front of the passenger seat then glanced at her watch. It was five o'clock, and Noah would normally be home from his teaching job, unless he went straight to the real estate office. Barbara dreaded the possibility of facing Noah. If she never saw him again it would be fine with her. But she wanted to clear out her things and the sooner she got it over with the better.

She let herself into the house and went straight back to the bedroom. Thank God there was no sign of him, she thought as she hastily gathered her things from the closet and tossed them into her two Louis Vuitton suitcases. When she was done, she picked up both bags and carried them to the front door. She took her keys out of her shoulder bag, removed the one to Noah's house from the key-chain, and placed it on the coffee table.

She glanced again at her watch. If Noah wasn't back by now, chances were he had gone to the Realtor's office and wouldn't get home until late. She walked back to Noah's bedroom and searched the drawers in his desk for a blank sheet of paper. She sat down, fully intending to be brief and to the point about why she was leaving him. But she soon found herself pouring out feelings of hurt, betrayal, and anger at him for what he had done. She ended the note by asking him not to try and contact her.

She stood up, inhaled deeply, then walked back into the living room. She placed the note on the coffee table next to the key then picked up her bags, left the house, and walked briskly to the curb. She tossed the bags into the trunk, slammed it shut, and climbed in.

Now to deal with Veronique.

46

RUSH-HOUR TRAFFIC WAS horrible, and it was a full hour after leaving Noah's place before Barbara pulled up in front of Veronique's mansion. The butler opened the front door, took Barbara's fox coat, then escorted her to a sitting room that Barbara had never been in before. As with all the other rooms in Veronique's home, this one was beautifully decorated with European antiques.

Barbara paced up and down the antique carpet in her Gucci boots and jeans as she waited for the baroness. In her mind she went over and over what she would say. Why had Veronique done this to her? Weren't they friends?

All the questions flew out of her mind the minute she heard the door open.

"Barbara, how nice to see you," Veronique said. She was wearing a stunning red silk suit and her face was all smiles, as if nothing had changed between them.

Barbara took a step toward her, and the baroness froze.

"What's wrong, Barbara?" Veronique asked as she shut the door behind her.

"Bradford told me everything."

Veronique raised a brow. "What exactly did he tell you?"

"He told me that you asked him to meet you at the Hilton that night when you knew I would be there with Noah."

Veronique squared her shoulders, and her warm eyes hardened like steel.

"How could you, Veronique?" Barbara said. "I don't understand. Bradford doesn't either, really."

"Hmm. I'm surprised Bradford didn't figure it all out, as smart as he is."

"He thinks you're getting revenge for his calling in a loan he made to your husband five years ago."

"I see." Veronique gestured toward a chair in the salon. "Sit down, Barbara. There's more to what happened back then than Bradford is admitting."

As uneasy feeling came over Barbara, but she sat down in an armchair anyway as the baroness sat on a couch across from her.

Veronique smiled thinly. "I suspect that Bradford left out a few important details about that whole sorry episode."

Barbara said nothing. She had a feeling she wasn't going to like what was coming.

Veronique let out a deep breath. "Where should I begin? Bradford loaned Guy a large sum of money to expand his business, and we used the software company as collateral. Then the bottom fell out of the technology sector. When Guy realized that he wouldn't be able to pay it back on time, he went to Bradford and asked for more time, not much, a few months if I remember correctly. But Bradford insisted that he be paid promptly."

"He told me that."

"Just a minute," Veronique said firmly. "I'm sure he didn't tell you *this*, nor did he expect that I would tell you, probably. There was a time when I was too ashamed to talk about it to anyone, and he knows that. But my bitterness over the years has slowly replaced my shame."

Barbara squirmed.

"When it began to look like we were going to lose the company to Bradford, I went to his hotel suite and begged him to reconsider. I offered to do anything if he would give us just a little more time. Bradford had always flirted with me but nothing more than that, until that day."

Veronique paused and Barbara caught her breath. Oh, God. She knew where this was going and she didn't like it. She stood abruptly.

Veronique jumped up and glared at Barbara. "Wait," she shouted. "Don't you want to hear the rest? We made love right there in his room. Bradford got what he wanted all along—me."

Veronique paused to regain control of her voice. It was the first time Barbara had ever heard her raise it.

"And then . . . then he double-crossed me," Veronique said, her hands clenched into fists at her side. "He still insisted that we pay the loan back on time. I begged, Barbara, but he wouldn't listen. He practically threw me out of his room. When Guy found out what I had done—"

"How did Guy find out?" Barbara asked, interrupting.

"To this day I don't know. I certainly didn't tell him. But it was the end of our marriage, and I blame Bradford for that. I'll never forget that as long as I live."

Barbara backed away at the venom she heard in Veronique's tone. If this was true, Bradford had behaved horribly. Barbara knew Bradford, and it probably was true. A part of her wanted to apologize to Veronique, but another part of her blamed the baroness. It was a stupid thing she had done.

"So to pay Bradford back, you decided to try to ruin our marriage. You had this planned from the beginning, didn't you? That's why you moved to Silver Lake."

Veronique shook her head. "Not exactly. I'll admit that one of the reasons I came back to the States and moved here was to see what had happened to Bradford. But I had no idea you had this huge crush on Noah when I arrived. I just waited and watched and seized the opportunity when it came along. You have no idea how good I felt as I watched the drama unfold between you and Bradford at the Hilton that night."

"You saw it? Where were you?"

"In a rented sedan parked across the street. You looked right through the window when you drove by, but I managed to duck before you saw me."

Barbara swallowed. "How did . . . ?" She paused. "How did you get Noah involved?"

Veronique frowned deeply. "What do you mean? Noah wasn't involved."

Barbara stared at Veronique with wide eyes. "You mean Noah had no idea you were there that night or that . . ." Barbara paused to catch her breath.

"No, he had nothing to do with it."

Barbara closed her eyes. Thank God, she had been totally wrong about that. She opened them again. "I still don't understand you, though, Veronique. You have everything. Money, palatial houses, jewels, and a new husband who you say loves you dearly. All that couldn't make you forget something that happened years ago?"

"Those things are nice, no question. But they don't make up for losing your dignity."

WHEN NOAH ANSWERED his door late that evening, he was holding Barbara's note in his hand. He stepped aside quietly to let her pass. She entered and turned to face him as he shut the door behind her.

262 • CONNIE BRISCOE

"I'm sorry," she said, speaking barely above a whisper. "I . . . I acted rashly. I—"

"What the hell does all this mean?" he asked, his voice filled with bitterness as he interrupted her. He held the note up and began to read from it. " 'You have really hurt me with what you've done. I thought I could trust you. I thought you cared about me. Now I'm not so sure.' "

Noah looked up at her, his brown face filled with pain and confusion and more than a little anger.

Barbara glanced away and swallowed hard. "This morning I learned that Veronique set us up at the Hilton. She told Bradford we would be there and that was why he showed up. I thought you were involved. I'm sorry. I was wrong."

A deep frown spread across Noah's face. "Jesus. Why would Veronique do that?"

"It's a long story. She was getting revenge for something Bradford did years ago."

"And you thought I was in on it with her? I can't believe you thought I'd do something as despicable as that. Isn't it obvious how I feel about you?"

Barbara touched her forehead. "I thought so, but this is all so confusing. I didn't know what to think until Veronique told me you had nothing to do with it."

He shook his head sadly. "I thought you trusted me."

"I do, but . . ."

"No, obviously you don't."

Barbara sighed deeply. "That's more a reflection of me than you. I have a hard time trusting men. I'm sorry I doubted you."

"Don't keep apologizing."

"OK, OK. I should go. I just wanted to stop by and clear things up about the note."

"You also took your things."

"I need some time to think, Noah."

"I thought we had something special." He shook his head. "How wrong I was."

"It *was* special, Noah. But right now, I'm confused."

"Are you going back to him?"

"I don't know. All I know is that we moved so fast, you and I. Too fast for me."

"Given how little trust you have in me, I can't argue with that."

Barbara placed her hand on the doorknob and looked back at him. "You meant a lot to me, Noah. You still do. You helped me regain confidence in myself as a woman." She touched his arm. "I'll never forget that."

He smiled weakly and gently brushed her cheek. "Whatever it is you're looking for, Barbara, I hope you find it. I mean that."

Barbara left the house and walked slowly to her Benz. What *was* she looking for? she wondered as she climbed into the driver's seat. Bradford showered her with expensive gifts. They lived in a beautiful home with every creature comfort imaginable. They were admired and respected in the community, largely because of Bradford. He was unable or unwilling to fulfill her needs emotionally, but for the longest time, Barbara had let herself believe that what she had with Bradford was all she needed.

Then she met Noah, and he had made her feel loved and desired. In a way, Noah reminded Barbara of Bradford when they were first married, before all of his success went to his head. Now she realized that all the things she had with Bradford simply weren't enough.

JOLENE PACED THE floor of her lawyer's office and listened to the end of the tape recording of her last conversation with Brian Watson.

"If you had followed my instructions instead of doing it yourself and screwing up, we wouldn't be in this jam. But someone might have seen you, and it's too risky for us to have contact now. Maybe in a few more months if nothing—"

"A few more months shit. And fuck your fucking instructions. It got done, didn't it? Pay me now or I'm calling the cops on your ass."

"Well, that would be pretty damn smart, since you're the one who broke in and and tried to rob Pearl's place."

"Rob? It wasn't no robbery and you know it. You asked me to bust it up and I did. Now I want my money or I'm going to the cops."

"Go ahead then, stupid asshole. I'll tell them I had nothing to do with

it. It was a botched robbery for all I know. Who do you think they're going to believe? An ex-con or me?"

Slam!

Brian was obviously not as dumb as he looked. Jolene couldn't believe he had recorded their last phone conversations and that when the police closed in and arrested him he had handed over the tape.

"Bastard," she muttered under her breath.

"Excuse me?" her lawyer said as he shut off the recorder.

Jolene stopped pacing and cleared her throat. "What does all of this mean, Monte?"

He cleared his throat and ran his hands through his gray hair. "It means they've got a pretty strong case against you, Jolene—what with this tape, the fact that Pearl Jackson is involved with Patrick, and that Brian once worked in your office. Not to mention that several people saw Brian run away from the salon and drive off."

Jolene sighed and sat down in front of Monte. "Let me make sure I understand this. You want me to accept a plea bargain?" Jolene didn't like the idea of admitting she was guilty. But the tapes were devastating. There was no way she could explain them away. "What will that mean in terms of a sentence? Will I have to go to jail?"

He shook his head. "Since this is your first offense, they're offering a PBJ with restitution and—"

"What the hell is that, Monte?"

"Probation with payment of Pearl Jackson's business losses. About three-quarters of a million."

Jolene shot back up out of her seat. "That's not acceptable. I am not giving that woman one dime of my money. I just won it! I would have to go back to work. Hell, no. You're going to have to come up with something better than that."

"Didn't you win five million in the lottery last spring?"

"I had to pay taxes. And bills. I only have about a million and a half left."

Monte's eyes widened. "So you spent, like, a million dollars in less than a year?"

"It's my damn money. I'll do whatever the hell I want with it."

He held his hands out. "All right, calm down, Jolene. Considering the evidence, I'd advise you to take the deal. This case is not winnable and you could end up doing time in jail. With the plea bargain, you'll only have to do a hundred hours of community service, and maybe find a job after you pay Pearl."

Jolene stared at him. "You've got to be kidding."

"I'm afraid this is the best I can do, Jolene. The evidence against you is—"

"Don't keep saying that! What the hell am I paying you for?"

"I'm an attorney, Jolene, not a miracle worker."

Jolene touched her forehead. "What are the charges again?"

"Destruction of property, vandalism, conspiracy, and accessory to a crime."

Dammit. As horrible as this stinking plea bargain sounded, a trial could be a hundred times worse. It would drag things out and she might even be sentenced to prison. How would she ever face Juliette or her mother or anyone else for that matter? She slumped down. "I'll take the plea bargain."

P EARL PUT DOWN the *Washington Post*. The article about Jolene Brown's involvement in the break-in was unbelievable. She would never have thought that Jolene would do something so vicious.

She looked across the table at Patrick as he sipped his morning coffee. He seemed to be taking this harder than she was. His ex-wife, the mother of his daughter, had ordered the vandalism of Pearl's salon. Patrick looked lost.

She reached across the table, took his hand and squeezed.

"What will I tell Juliette?" he said, his voice cracking.

Pearl shook her head. "I honestly don't know what to tell you."

He stood and shoved his hands into his jeans pockets. Juliette had been living with Patrick ever since Jolene was taken to police headquarters for questioning a month earlier. Patrick and Jolene had agreed that would be best while Jolene was going through all of this.

But Jolene had insisted that she was innocent and that she was being framed by Brian in an act of revenge. As soon as she was cleared of the charges, she said she wanted Juliette back home with her. Patrick had wanted desperately to believe Jolene, but yesterday they learned that she had accepted a plea bargain and now it was in the newspaper.

"I have to tell Juliette the truth," he said sadly. "With it in the papers, she's going to hear about it from somewhere. I'd rather she get it from me."

"I think that's a good idea," Pearl said.

Patrick banged his fist on the countertop. "Dammit! What is wrong with that woman? I knew she was jealous of you, but this? What the hell was she thinking?"

"I don't get it," Pearl said incredulously. "She won the lottery and even before that she had more than I ever did."

"If you're talking about material things, yes. But not when it comes to character. She's not getting Juliette back. I don't want that woman raising my daughter. If she fights me on it, I'll take her to court and sue for custody."

Pearl nodded in agreement. She had no doubt that Jolene would fight to get her daughter back, and going up against her was obviously not something to be taken lightly. But Patrick was right. He had to do what was best for Juliette.

Pearl stood up, walked to the cabinets, removed a frying pan, and placed it on the stove. "The girls will be up soon. I'm going to fix us all a big breakfast—bacon and sausage, eggs, pancakes." Food always soothed the soul, and they could all use a little comfort now.

Patrick came up behind her and turned her to face him. He pulled her into his arms and hugged her tightly. She rested her head on his shoulder and they stood there silently for a moment.

"I can't tell you how sorry I am about your salon," he said. "Somehow I feel responsible now."

She looked up at him. "Don't be silly. I'm sorry that it turned out to be Jolene who hired that thug to break into my salon, but now that we know who did it, I feel at ease. Not knowing was the worst. A huge weight has been lifted off my shoulders. Does that seem weird?"

"Not at all." He chuckled and released her.

"What's so funny?" she asked.

"I was just tying to imagine Jolene doing community service."

Pearl had to smile at that thought, too. "It'll be good for her."

"Yeah, if she doesn't get out of it."

"Do you think she'll try?"

"I know she will."

"I'll be hoping she can't. Well, let me start on breakfast. Why don't you get the girls up?" She turned him around and shooed him out of the kitchen, then she went to the refrigerator, removed a half dozen eggs, and began to crack them open into a bowl.

Pearl's lawyer had informed her yesterday that the judge had ordered Jolene to pay her a large sum of money. Pearl hated the idea of taking money from Jolene but she needed it desperately. Insurance wouldn't cover all the costs to fix the salon exactly the way she wanted it, and she needed income until she could get back to work.

Pearl shook her head as she whipped the eggs. Jolene Brown jealous of *her*? Jolene had won five million dollars in the lottery, she lived in a house that was probably five times the size of Pearl's town house, she drove a nice car, and she had a beautiful daughter.

It just went to show that some people were never satisfied.

49

THE MORNING SUN streaked through the drapes in Jolene's bedroom, and she yanked the sheet up over her head. She hadn't been able to get a wink of sleep all night. Reporters from the *Washington Post* and *Baltimore Sun* had called repeatedly the previous afternoon. They had said that articles about the break-in at Pearl's salon were going to run the following morning and they wanted to ask her some questions. Jolene slammed the phone down on both reporters.

The last thing she needed were articles in the *Post* and the *Sun* about all of this crap. She had already been humiliated enough. Patrick was furious about how it would affect their daughter. Her parents weren't speaking to her. Her neighbors, including Veronique, all looked at her as if she was from another planet. And her party plans had been shattered.

Her alarm clock went off.

"Shit!" she screamed aloud as she sat up and shut it off. It was seven-thirty on a Saturday morning and she had to get up and drive all the way into D.C. to a women's homeless shelter to start her hundred hours of community service.

She moaned, fell back down on the bed, and pulled the covers over her head. She hated getting up early on Saturday mornings for any reason, and she damn sure didn't want to get up early for this. But the worst of it was that she would have to give part of her lottery winnings to that bitch Pearl. What a nightmare. She had been on top of the world and look at her now. Her only consolation was that Brian was back in prison, right where his ass belonged.

The thought of having to spend thirty days or more in jail popped into Jolene's thoughts—it was a very real possibility if she failed to show up at the shelter, as her lawyer had reminded her when she asked him how she could get out of performing community service. She threw the covers off.

God, was she sorry she had done this. It had been monumentally stupid. If she could go back in time to before the break-in and that first conversation with Brian Watson at the Holiday Inn she would. She grimaced. She should never have trusted that idiot to pull off the job. If she ever did something like this again, she would make sure she found someone with the smarts to do it right.

But what was done was done. Right now, she had to get this community service behind her. Then she was going to have to figure out how she would support herself. After paying Pearl, she would have several hundred thousand left in the bank, but the way she lived that wouldn't last much more than a year or two.

She got up, strolled into her walk-in closet, and picked out an off-white St. John pantsuit. Even if she was going to a homeless shelter, Jolene Brown intended to look her best.

50

BARBARA CLIMBED OUT of her Benz and carried her two Louis Vuitton suitcases to the front of the house in Silver Lake. She unlocked the double doors and stepped in.

Everything was just as it had been when she left five weeks earlier. The marble floor and crystal chandelier in the foyer looked as if they had just been polished, and fresh flowers sat in a crystal vase on the small round table in the center of the foyer. To her left was Bradford's study and its mahogany bookshelves, to her right, the music room with the handcrafted baby grand piano that no one had ever learned to play. Straight ahead a carpeted staircase led to the balcony on the second floor. All of it was spotlessly clean.

Phyllis appeared from around a corner, and they hugged warmly.

"It's good to have you back, Mrs. Bentley. How was your stay at the Ritz?" Phyllis sounded as lighthearted as she would have if Barbara had just come back from visiting a spa. The truth was a lot more complicated. After a week of living with Noah, Barbara had spent a few weeks at a local hotel because she needed time to think about whether she wanted to return to her husband. Barbara was certain that Phyllis knew better.

"Thank you, Phyllis. Is Bradford here?"

"Yes, ma'am. He's waiting for you in the library."

Barbara nodded as Phyllis reached for the suitcases and walked toward the kitchen and the back stairs to the second floor. She removed her fox coat, draped it over her arm, and headed for Bradford's study.

She opened the door and looked around. She didn't see Bradford, but a large elegantly wrapped package with her name on it sat in the center of his desk. She folded her coat across the back of a chair and tore the wrapper off to reveal a box from Bergdorf Goodman. She flipped the top open and looked down to see a dark brown, full-length sable coat.

She lifted the sable coat out of the box and draped it around her shoulders. As she ran her hands across the luxuriously soft fur, she heard a sound in the doorway. She turned to see Bradford standing there looking handsome as always in slacks and a beautiful gray shirt, holding two champagne flutes filled with sparkling water.

She caught her breath at the sight of him. It was amazing that he could still do that to her at times, even after all these years. Of all her possessions, many of them given to her by Bradford, none mattered more to her than the man standing before her. She still loved him dearly. That was why she was back at home.

But if their relationship was to work, things were going to have to change, as she had explained to him when they talked by phone over the past few days during her stay at the Ritz. He was going to have to be mindful of her needs, and they would both have to be open and honest in their dealings with each other. No more lunches with ex-lovers, no more long trips out of town without each other. No more lies, no more secrets. He might wheel and deal in his business but he was going to have to respect his wife at home.

She had also insisted on opening a bank account in her name only and that he keep it generously funded. The first check she wrote was to Noah, giving him the money to make a down payment on his house. Noah would never have accepted a handout directly from Barbara, so she had a cashier's check hand-delivered to him. When Noah called to ask if she had sent the check, Barbara denied it. Noah still suspected that it was from her, but the anonymity had allowed him to tell himself that it wasn't and to keep the money.

She hadn't told Bradford about the check yet. He still blew up whenever she mentioned Noah's name, and Barbara thought it would be best to give it a few weeks before telling him.

She smiled as Bradford handed her one of the glasses. "The coat is beautiful."

"And so are you. It's so good to have you home." He leaned down to kiss her, but she gently put her hand on his chest and held him back.

"It's good to be here," she said, "but I meant all of those things I said about us being honest with each other from now on. The furs and jewels are nice, Bradford. But what I want more than anything is attention from you. And no other women."

"I understand that, Barbara. I really do. And I've changed. Sabrina and I had lunch, nothing more."

"That may be true. But do you understand why I had such a hard time believing it?"

He nodded. "I haven't been the most faithful husband in the past. I have a lot of making up to do. From now on, I won't be having lunch with Sabrina or any other woman unless it's strictly business. I don't want you doubting me ever again. Or running off with other men because you do. You mean the world to me, and I don't want to lose you. I'm going to start doing a better job of showing you that."

Barbara nodded. She didn't know if Bradford could live up to all of his promises, but they both knew that she now had the strength to leave him if he couldn't.

She smiled. "That's what I wanted to hear. You should say things like that to me more often."

"To us," he said, lifting his glass.

"And new beginnings," she added.

They clinked their glasses and sipped. He took her glass and placed both flutes on his desk. Then he gently slipped the sable coat from around Barbara's shoulders and took her into his arms.

READER'S GROUP GUIDE

1. Author Connie Briscoe creates a distinct community with PG County and its inhabitants. How does Prince George's County reflect the current aspirations of African Americans? How does it not?

2. Economics are often pitched against the moral and ethical values of those living in Silver Lake. How does the importance of money and material things influence Barbara, Jolene, Countess Veronique, and Pearl? Are the moral and ethical cores of these women representative of people we know in our everyday lives? How so? How not?

3. What is the beating heart of Barbara and Bradford Bentley's marriage and Pearl Jackson and Patrick Brown's relationship? How do these relationships stand up in comparison to each other? Looking beyond the book's ending, can either relationship be declared a success or failure? Why?

4. What are your views of Barbara moving in with Noah? Was that a true show of strength to break away from an unhappy marriage or a ploy to get attention from Bradford? What would have happened had she stayed with Noah? Do you think they could have been happy together?

5. Even though Jolene has just about everything, how does her demand for more (money, men, recognition) prove to be her downfall? If you were a good friend of hers what advice would you have given her about her pursuit of Patrick and her hatred of Pearl? Do you think if she were open-minded, that perhaps her relationship with Brian would be different?

6. Do you find Countess Veronique's brand of revenge on Bradford satisfying? How would you have handled her situation to save her ex-husband's business?

7. Although women are the main characters of the book, what are the strengths and weaknesses of their male counterparts? What distinguishes Bradford from Noah, Patrick from Bradford, and Brian from the other three men? Can any of them be viewed truly and clearly as a hero, zero, or everyday man? How and why?

8. With his history as a womanizer, why do you think Bradford wanted Barbara back? Are Bradford and Barbara two sides of the same coin?

9. Do you believe Noah could have had a long-term relationship with Barbara? What compromises would they have had to make for a lasting relationship?

10. With *Can't Get Enough* do you think Briscoe has tapped into modern relationships between Black men and women? What elements has she incorporated that ring true? Are there any elements that you feel could be explored further or added?

CONNIE BRISCOE is the author of the *New York Times* best-seller *Big Girls Don't Cry,* as well as *A Long Way from Home, Sisters & Lovers,* a Blackboard bestseller, and *P.G. County.* She lives in Ellicott City, Maryland.